Ambrosia

Nectar Trilogy, Volume 2

DD Prince

Published by DD Prince, 2018.

Ambrosia

This book is NOT standalone. You need to read Nectar first.

~ Prologue ~

Tristan

I CAN'T FEEL HER.

Part of me knows she was right to run, and if she hadn't, I'd have to wonder if she was still the girl I'd fallen for or if maybe I'd ruined her. Who, in their right mind, wouldn't have run?

But the other part of me, that part that knows she's mine and that believes that because she's mine and because we feel one another so deep... that part wants her to refuse to exist without me.

That part of me is so filled with black boiling rage that I could rip myself to shreds because she left me and because I don't have a fuckin' clue whether she's still in one piece or not. I'm still groggy, but I ache. I ache because I can't feel her. She's been sunshine in the dark for me and I can't go back to the black, can't go back to the emptiness I felt; not after feeling her.

No.

I don't know if I can't feel her because she's sleeping or unconscious, if the tranquilizers aren't completely out of my system yet or are blocking her, or if maybe our connection is broken because she's dead.

I can only speculate on what happened after I cold-clocked and shot Sam. I only know I'm on the floor in this cage and the cage door and panic room doors are open. Sam is face first on the carpet by the bed and I'm lying beside a big crescent-shaped blood stain.

It's slick around my mouth from the blood -—her blood. Before dipping my tongue to the corner of my mouth I already know what it will taste like and I want more.

So
Much
More.

Despite being groggy and feeling as if there's a black abyss where my heart is supposed to be, something else is brewing in me. I can't put a name to it yet because I can't figure out whether it's evil or not and other than blood, I don't know what it wants.

That small part of me that knows she was right to run is relieved I can't feel her because I'm not ready to find her. I'm not ready, because I'm afraid of what I could be capable of when I do. Afraid of what I might be capable of if someone has her or if she's dead. I need to make myself wait...wait until she's stopped bleeding and then find her and fix this.

I just need to fucking find her before The Mangler, does. If he hasn't, already. He knows all about Kyla's blood, he knows she's mine, and he wants everything that is mine.

1

Victoria, British Columbia

REMINDER: THIS BOOK is NOT standalone. You need to read Nectar first.

Kyla woke up to birds singing and, after her morning rituals, was relieved to finally have stopped bleeding.

Finally!

That period, the period that would change the way she'd view her period for the rest of her days? It went on and on (and on!) at a very heavy flow for almost 12 full days and she'd started to wonder if it would ever stop.

Now that she'd had no bleeding for 12 hours, her stress levels were down to DEFCON 3 from DEFCON 1.

She stepped outside and looked out at the water. It sure was beautiful here, just like she knew it would be. Layers of scent filled her nose. Flowers, the water, and coffee. She was staying in a rented waterfront RV in a park on the outskirts of the city of Victoria, on Vancouver Island. It was about 4,400 km or nearly 3000 miles away from Tristan.

It felt today, so far, like the withdrawals had subsided a little, too.

When she'd left him, she'd planned to drive to the airport, but made a snap decision to take a scenic route that would be a little less obvious.

She found herself at the city's small island airport instead of the international airport. She'd parked his SUV (with the keys in the glovebox) at the train station near the ferry, carrying the bag. She had walked to the docks and then taken a ferry the short ride to the small

4

island airport and a flight, in a small plane, to Ottawa. It was weird being there, so close to her past, but she'd never ventured outside of the airport.

She took an empty leg seat on a small charter to Calgary. She stayed in a crappy motel overnight there, not sleeping, and then took a dawn-departing Greyhound bus to Vancouver.

She may have slept on the bus a little, she wasn't even sure. If so, it was a succession of nods rather than a deep sleep. She'd been on high alert the whole time, watching to see if anyone was following her and watching to see if anyone around her suddenly had the colour drain from their face. She was also in and out of the tiny bus bathroom repeatedly, bleeding so heavily she wondered how her body held so much blood.

After getting to Vancouver, she'd taken a ferry over to Vancouver Island. Maybe it was overkill to travel that way since she could've flown from Toronto's international airport directly to the city of Victoria but Kyla had been thinking at DEFCON 1.

She wanted far away and fast but knew a direct flight would make it beyond easy to be found. She didn't know if her multi-stopover, multi-mode plane, bus, boat trip would stop him from finding her or if he had the resources to find her easily despite her efforts and she didn't know how long she could safely stay put where she was now but she was exhausted, emotionally shattered, and a few days by the water in an RV that was relatively off the radar sounded like as ideal place as could be to get some distance, space, and to figure out what to do next.

How to go on without him...

By the time she arrived in Victoria and found the waterfront RV park to rent the park model trailer in, she was exhausted and numb. She slept for 14 hours straight. And when she'd woken up she was in full-on withdrawal or detox mode, or that's what she figured it *must* be.

She could barely breathe. She could barely think. She craved him like never before. She craved his touch, his scent, his voice, his teeth, their connection.

She'd shivered under the covers, unable to get warm, in a state of agony that could best be described as a pinching sensation inside every inch of every vein in her body.

Alternating hot flashes and cold sweats punished her for hours and hours with pinching inside and itching outside. It must have been because she'd finally stopped to rest. She'd been in full-on survival mode all the way there. When she stopped, finally, it was evidently time for withdrawals.

She chewed a pillow to muffle her cries because she was in an RV park that had trailers and motorhomes sardined together with only a few feet between each so didn't want anyone calling the police at what would've sounded like a woman being tortured. And it *was* like torture, like the worst stomach bug she'd ever remembered, but way worse. This was nothing like the feeling she'd had when withdrawals kicked in after being chained to his bed for days. Probably because he wasn't on the other side of the door. And, she supposed, because she'd evidently become more addicted to their connection in the days that had followed that incarceration. This was multiple times worse than that and it went on for days.

He'd said that he got stronger after each feeding and evidently, she also got more addicted after each feeding, too.

Mutual addiction.

At one point she'd dashed to the bathroom looking for a razor, thinking if she'd nicked herself and let out a little bit of blood it'd provide some relief. There were none there. She found herself at the kitchen drawer with a butcher's knife and she'd poked her arm with the tip of the blade. When she saw the red dot emerge she closed her eyes and tried to imagine his mouth on her, but it did nothing.

Kyla regained rational thought before opening her skin further and then rational thought disintegrated as she got paranoid about others smelling her blood and felt frantic, trying to cover it up and stop the bleeding with pressure. Finally, she collapsed back into bed and cried herself to sleep.

"Oh Tristan, what have you done to me?" She whispered this at least at one point but maybe she'd said it a hundred more times, too.

After a few days of feeling like she was at death's door, subsisting on meal replacement shakes and, at one stage, forcing herself into what felt like a death-warmed-over state to go to a nearby convenience store to buy more maxi pads, she felt slightly more human. Afterwards, while digging through the duffle bag for a change of clothes, (she'd bought a few things on the way and had added them to the bag, which still had everything in it that Tristan had packed) she heard something hit the floor.

It was Tristan's passport and it was wide open. Her heart thudded wildly as she lifted it and looked at his photograph. Her heart sank as her thumb skimmed over his two-dimensional, handsome face. The pain of seeing his face hit her in the gut like an iron fist.

She'd given her passport a few fleeting thoughts, including thinking that she might go down to the U.S. from there and if his passport wasn't at home it'd at least slow down his ability to get across the border.

Sure, he probably had a connection to get himself another one quickly, but she wanted every possible advantage. She'd probably stay there in Victoria for a little while, as if he was looking for her, he'd probably be watching the borders right now. It hurt so bad to think of him as the enemy, as the one to run from, but wasn't that how she had to think right now?

She couldn't let herself think too hard or it'd just hurt too much. Imagining him angry or hateful was something she didn't even want to fathom. All she could do was try to put one foot in front of the other, pull up one more breath and one more after that.

She put her head back down in the bed and put the passport on the pillow beside her and stared at his picture for a long time.

"Can you still feel me?" she asked the picture, "I miss you, but I had to..." Her voice broke. She tried to send love and apologies out into the universe through her mind. Who knew if it'd work and even if it did, what would it change? Nothing, probably. A dull snaking ache slowly worked its way through her veins.

She snapped the paper booklet shut and slid it under the pillow her head was on. She drifted off to sleep for another half a day, her hand on top of the passport.

After waking, she got dressed and decided to try to push the despair she felt away for now and head out and take a walk and buy some groceries and Advil to combat the never-ending headache, and hopefully the ache in her veins. She'd hardly eaten since leaving him and caffeine and meal replacement shakes just weren't cutting it any longer.

Tristan's bug-out bag had a combined total of $50K in it. She felt awful about having his money and had spent only around $3K Canadian so far, and most of it was on travelling expenses. She didn't like carrying that much cash with her, but she didn't know where she was going, so where would she keep it? She had her own bank card in her purse and had thought about withdrawing the $4,317 she'd saved up toward school, but hadn't thought about that until she'd gotten out of the province. Now it seemed dangerous to use it as it'd be a potential breadcrumb.

Some of her RV'ing neighbours were trying to engage her in conversation as she strolled out to catch the bus, but she gave quick answers and avoided long conversations, declining two offers: one from a retired couple on one side who'd asked her to come for a barbeque and the other from a young couple with a little baby who invited her to a campfire and for a few glasses of wine. Both were on vacation and looking to be friendly, but she felt like she had to emit a hermit demeanour. She was polite but not overly friendly and said she was just seeing the country and staying for a few days, but that she was unavailable that night.

She didn't need to draw any unnecessary attention. Anyone could be a vampire. She knew that sounded like a crazy, paranoid way to think, but that was the way she *had* to think right now. Maybe she should rent a remote cabin on the other side of the island and get away from people altogether for a little while.

Now that she wasn't bleeding, maybe there was less risk. She didn't know if there would be less risk around him or if what had happened had changed the dynamic of their connection forever.

Her scent clearly had an effect on Sam, too, which was odd, since she'd been having her period monthly since she was 12 years old and had obviously been in crowded places where someone could've been a vampire. She didn't want to panic but wondered if now she'd have to sequester herself now for each and every *Shark Week*.

Had the genesis of her connection to Tristan made the "nectar" instantly discoverable to other vampires? That had plagued her all the way here, through flights, bus rides, and boat rides.

She had been able to leave him, despite the bond. She figured that was a sign that she still had at least some of her own mind, which was a relief in one sense because it meant she hadn't totally lost it, but then in another sense it made things hurt even more because she knew her feelings for him must be real because she was able to walk away and yet distance hadn't changed how she felt.

Clearly, by the detox side-effects she had, there were residual addiction issues but regardless of the cause it didn't matter because whatever caused the feelings and attraction and addiction, it *fucking* hurt. It hurt deep. Deeper than cravings and deeper than the pain in her veins.

Whether it started because of his vampire charms and his looks and his talents in bed or not, and even if that bond cemented only because of the chemical reaction between them, she missed him right now and knew she would never ever feel what she'd felt with him with any other man. Ever. It just wasn't possible for her to have that depth of emotion for another individual, human or otherwise, real or brainwashed. The feelings he'd brought out in her had somehow given her hope about her prince, her ability to embrace emotion, hope for a *happily ever after.*

This was so depressing. It made her feel like she'd been gutted. She was mourning emotion that she knew she'd never had before and would never have for anyone else again. Ever. She'd never have a normal relationship. Falling in love again this deep wouldn't ever happen.

Happily never after.

Any emotion she'd ever feel for another man would pale if compared to the emotions Tristan had churned up in her. And that sucked.

VICTORIA WAS A COLOURFUL city nestled on a beautiful island that had a great vibe. She absorbed the atmosphere of shops and restaurants and flowers and people laughing and smiling. She could smell the water and see beautiful boats. This was a place she'd longed to live in before Tristan. Post-Tristan, she couldn't help but wonder what it'd be like to walk hand in hand with *him* on the waterfront? What would it be like to see the wind in his hair out on a sailboat together? How amazing would it be to sit at a little café staring at the water, drinking coffee together and staring into one another's eyes?

Those eyes...

It had been less than two weeks since she'd left him, but it didn't feel like this feeling of loss, this agony, would *ever* go away.

Kyla purchased a few staple items and went back to the RV. She sat outside on a lawn chair staring at the water for what might've been hours, lost in thought, until finally going to bed early.

She had a dreamless sleep but woke up at least ten times craving him. It was reminiscent of when he'd chained her to his bed for almost a week, only this time he wasn't punishing her; she was punishing herself.

She'd left. She could go back. She could call. She could suggest a test to see if he was still affected by her blood in that negative way. Yeah, and it could all go so horribly wrong, too, like it did last time, couldn't it? Only this time maybe she wouldn't be able to get away.

She still had no idea if she was able to break through to him with her words and her love vibes or if it'd just been that he'd been hit with enough tranquilizers to take down two elephants that had saved her life.

SHE WOKE UP EARLY THE morning after, relieved that her period was still gone. The pinching sensation was still there, but was a dull ache instead of piercing pain.

She decided to spend the day exploring the city. She bought a camera and snapped copious amounts of touristy pictures -—countless pictures of the skyline, the water, the flowers. She wandered through the streets and the Butchart gardens, where she admired lush flowers and plants. She loved how walkable the city was, that if she stayed she wouldn't need a car, how friendly it was, but she hated how miserable she'd felt, how empty she was.

Then she wandered into a public library and found herself at a computer, Googling Kovac Capital.

Don't, Kyla. Don't look back. Look forward! Survive!
She felt a nagging feeling as she did it but couldn't stop herself.
Could not.

She found a short press release on a business website dated 3
weeks back naming Tristan Walker as the new company president. It
said he'd been with the company ten years and was taking over for
Claudio D'Alonzo, who was the new CEO. No mention of a previ-
ous CEO. She Googled "Tristan Walker+Kovac" and found several
press images of him on Google Images. There was a photo of him in
a suit, shaking hands with an older-looking man in a suit and holding a large cheque between them for a children's hospital charity. She
found his corporate headshot with the Kovac logo on the bottom.
But that was all she found. He was fairly under the radar. Kovac's on-
line company activities looked underwhelming. They had a very basic one-page website, listing a downtown Toronto address and listing
a Montreal address as their headquarters. There were some blanket
statements about the company investing in a variety of business ven-
tures and that was pretty much it. There was virtually no social media presence.

There were way too many *T Walker* phone listings to go through
in order to find him, *if* that's what she wanted to do.

Nothing came up that matched the condo address and she hadn't
a clue what the address to the villa was. She didn't want the number
for his office but asked herself why she wanted his home number.
Was she going to call and tell him she was just making sure he was
okay and to say that she was sorry, but then plead with him not to
look for her? Did she just want to save the number and have it on her,
just in case she needed it? She was about to Google Claudio D'Alonzo, but decided she needed to let this all go.

I need to move forward!

She wandered out of the library and stopped in front of a bakery
window a few blocks down. The Kyla of a few weeks ago would've

gone in and bought a box of pastries. Kyla of a few weeks ago would've enjoyed indulging as part of an adventure in a new place. When she'd moved into Daisy's apartment the first thing she'd done was scope out the closest bakery.

But Kyla of today felt sadness at just the idea of even the aroma of dessert. She stared at the storefront with a faraway look in her green eyes for a few minutes, and then someone walked out with a bakery box and the aroma from the shop wafted under her nose and she had to swallow past a lump in her throat.

She felt bone tired, soul tired, so took a bus back to the RV park. En route, it passed a long and winding trail littered with dog walkers, runners, and cyclists, but while she stared longingly at the path, she didn't even feel like running.

Back at the little one-bedroom trailer she made a grilled cheese sandwich, ate just half of it, and went to bed early, still feeling out of sorts. Would she ever feel normal again?

IN A DREAM SHE SAW his face and heard his voice,

> *"You can't run away. I'm inside of you. You're inside of me. If you try to run and actually succeed at escaping for a little while, you'd be miserable. And it'd only be for a little while because I'd find you and bring you back and I'd be angry. Angry Tristan is, I think we've established, someone you'd rather not deal with, right? And I'll be hurt, too. Do you want to keep hurting me?*
>
> *You're hurting me, Princess.*

His face materialized in her dream. Black eyes, gray face, blood. So much blood.

She jackknifed upright from what felt like a dead sleep. The sheets were drenched with sweat. The RV was air conditioned so, why was she so hot? She glanced at the digital alarm clock beside her. 12:04 AM. She groggily staggered out to the little kitchenette, opened the fridge, and got out a bottle of water and downed it. She realized that she didn't feel any pinching in her veins, but the moment that thought fluttered by suddenly there was a funny throbbing in her throat; it was thrumming, pulsing.

She got into the shower and although her body felt hot and sweaty, her teeth began to chatter. Were the withdrawals back again? She was parched. She decided to get out and get another water. Before she opened it, she stretched her neck left and then right, thinking she needed to work out a kink. Then the same throbbing was in her wrist, but it felt stronger. She turned the light on and inspected her wrist, flexing her fingers and rotating it. She could still see a faint pink mark where Tristan had bitten her the night of the banquet. The throbbing was just below the surface in that same spot.

The throbbing got stronger both in her throat and in her wrist. Then she felt it on her hip, down low on her calf. On her shoulder. In her lower back. On her backside. Then her inner thigh. All these spots were all thrumming with the same sensation. Then her whole body started to pulse to a rhythm much like a heartbeat, especially strong in her inner thigh. *It was like it was his heartbeat.* Every time she'd listened to their heartbeats beating in time together it'd sounded just like this, it felt... personal.

She grabbed her inner thigh. "He's tracking me."

She said this aloud and dropped the water bottle and froze, horror-stricken. The sound of the bottle rolling across the floor a loud and hollow noise, almost like it was the only noise in the universe. Then after a beat, she shook the trance off and she started to pace.

This sensation? She'd felt it twice before. Once, in the woods outside his house, the night she'd run. Then he'd found her. The second time she'd felt it was right after her period started and he couldn't find her because she was in the panic room. She gulped and heard his voice in her mind, the night she'd run out of the house and he'd caught her.

"Tonight when you ran, I figured out I can track you."

Was he tracking her from 3000 miles away? Would she feel that all the way here? It wasn't as if she'd forgotten he'd said that, but she hadn't allowed herself to acknowledge that possibility until now. She bolted into the bedroom, flicked the lamp on, and sat on the bed, her palm over her mouth, her mind racing.

What do I do, what do I do, what do I do, what do I do?

Hope sprang forth for a nanosecond as she imagined the sensation of Tristan...what it'd feel like to touch him, to smell him, to be held captive by those eyes. Her head rolled back, imagining what it'd feel like to be touched *by* him.

No.

Bad, bad bad idea.

Red flags were flying up all over the place in her head and she couldn't sit still and wait and wonder. She jumped up and started stuffing her belongings into the duffle bag. She gathered up the toiletries that she'd bought and tossed them in, threw the dirty clothes in a grocery bag and stuffed it in her bag, then stuffed in the rest of her clean clothes. She tied her still wet hair up in a ponytail and put on some yoga capris and a clean t-shirt and then zipped up the bag and grabbed her purse.

His face flashed in her mind and she halted and took a deep breath and her neck went lax as her head rolled back.

His eyes. His gorgeous mouth. Those dimples.

In her mind she saw the two of them tangled together, felt heat rise in her, felt moisture down in her panties.

But then panic rose. She shook it off, pushed her emotions out of the way and pushed forward. The thrumming continued while her veins felt like they were thickening, her blood warming. It was such an odd sensation.

She didn't know where she was going to go next and didn't know if he was tracking her from 3000 miles away or 5 minutes away, but she was petrified out of her mind. She couldn't just sit here and wait for him to find her and wait to find out if he would have no choice but to kill her because the gray hulky beast inside him was either still there or would emerge as soon as he found her.

Maybe Tristan already knew the answer, though. Maybe he had found a way for them to be okay.

Or maybe he still wasn't Tristan. Maybe he was in that black-eyed gray-skinned monster form and hell-bent on finding her and finishing the job he'd started.

Where am I even going right now?

She had no bloody clue. She just felt the urge to move, to get out of this tiny box.

Once she got everything together she pulled her pink Taser out of her purse and held it in her hand, ready to use it. She then burst out of the trailer. She got halfway down the steps and then felt something catch her wrist. The second she did her nose caught a familiar sugary aroma and the throbbing in her body screeched to an audible halt.

"Going somewhere?" His tone was totally... utterly... flat.

It felt staticky around her wrist, where he touched her. When her eyes scanned his face, she thought for sure the wooden deck and the earth beneath it were going to fall away into nothingness. His strong warm hand was on her. Right then nothing existed other than those blue gemstones in front of her. Blue.

Blue.

She paled, and her knees started to buckle. She was about to go down. He caught her by the waist.

"Whoa," he said and gently backed her up and leaned her against the side of the trailer for support. She looked down at his big, strong, perfect hands on her hips and then her eyes travelled up his face, saw scruff on his dimpled chin, his defined jaw, his beautiful full lips, straight nose, sculpted cheekbones, then his eyes -—those eyes. The universe stood still for a moment as their eyes locked and the blue penetrated her soul.

The tension, the heat, the intensity were all palpable. He let one hand go and flattened it above her head on the building for support, clearly affected as much as she was.

He was breathing heavily, looking down into her eyes and then he began exuding something frighteningly intense that she didn't dare try to name.

"Inside," he bit off, grabbing the screen door handle and pulling so hard it came off hinges. He tossed it and it hit the deck with a clatter. Kyla was frozen in place, her mouth agape.

Tristan shackled her wrist again with his fingers, pulling her into the trailer with him. Then he let go, locked the inside door and leaned against it, arms folded across his chest, the expression in his eyes hard and on her. He glanced at the Taser in her hand and notched an eyebrow as if to say, "You think that's gonna do anything?"

Kyla dropped her bag and the Taser on the floor and then her palms clasped her face. She started to back away from him. Not thinking, she backed into the tiny bedroom. He followed, stalking like a predator, but staring coldly at her.

She whimpered when she realized she was backed into a corner, literally, and he was two inches away from her. The backs of her knees touched the bed. She sat. He towered over her, so close that she could actually feel his body heat.

"Well?" he asked expectantly, brows up. He put both of his palms above his head on a cupboard that hung over the bed.

A thousand scattered thoughts flitted through her mind. His presence was overpowering. His scent. His eyes. Her fear. Her pain. His mouth. Her love. His heat. She wanted to be invisible, get away, and lunge into his arms and directly into his skin at the exact same time.

"I..." she didn't finish.

He waited. He looked angry. No, furious. He looked absolutely beautiful. He wore a pair of faded black button fly jeans, a cyan blue soft over-washed t-shirt that was very close to the shade of his eyes, and a black leather jacket with a pair of Chuck Taylors on his feet. He had what looked like more than a few days' worth of stubble on his face. He looked tired, pissed off, dangerous. And sexy.

"Do you have any idea?" he spat, keeping his voice low, "of the hell that has been my existence since you left?"

Her mouth opened, but nothing came out. She began hyperventilating. His icy cold glare scanned up and down her body, then he repeated, "You. Left."

"You..." She huffed and then struggled for breath.

He looked expectantly at her.

"Almost killed me," she whispered, finally.

He looked off to the side, flashed a look of disgust, and then swallowed hard. His gaze returned to her, "Yeah. That's what the evidence suggested."

The look of disgust, that wasn't directed at Kyla, it was obvious it was directed at himself. A spark of hope lit but it quickly burnt out.

He scanned her face. "You had to know I'd find you. Thousands of miles away, hundreds of thousands of miles away, even. I *would* find you."

She closed her eyes.

"Did you think I wouldn't?"

She shook her head slowly, eyes downcast.

"Did you want me to find you?" His tone was gentler.

Tears started to roll down her cheeks.

"Answer me!" he demanded through gritted teeth.

She shook her head, trying not to look at him but catching a glimpse of a sour look on his face.

"Lie!" he hissed, "Don't lie to me and do *not* lie to yourself. I've been out of my mind not knowing if you were alive or dead. Do you know what that's been like? Look at me."

She squeezed her eyes shut tight.

"Look at me right fucking now, Kyla." His voice was low, menacing.

She opened her eyes and lifted her chin. Fury emanated from him. Despair lanced through her.

"Do you know what it's like for *me*?" she choked out, hoarsely, "to know that, yeah..." she swallowed hard, "you'd probably find me, but to not know who you'd be when you did? You could be any of three people and there's only one of them I'd wanna cross paths with. If only you were just him..." She wanted to collapse.

He thrust his fingers through his hair and then folded his arms across his chest.

"You can't... feel me?" she asked.

He let out a huff, "I can now. But I couldn't. Not until today. How did you turn it off?" His mouth was a tight line.

Her voice shrank even smaller, "I-I don't know. Then how did you find me?"

He let out a sigh and his posture relaxed a little. He pinched the bridge of his nose, "I didn't start tracking you until today when I got to the island. Couldn't feel you until I got here. I looked for you the old-fashioned way until today, bringing me to Vancouver yesterday. Tonight, I checked email and saw the ping in Victoria from the Kovac website when you landed there at that library. We track anyone who hits our site to determine why they're pokin' around. My people tracked the IP to a library in Victoria and reported it to me. From what I'd already found out about the path you took I knew it had to be you. I felt you the second I got off the boat."

The library? What a bonehead move. But now what? He was clearly pissed. But, his eyes were still blue so that was something.

Wasn't it?

"Damn it, Kyla."

She stared at the dingy-looking tiled ceiling and shook her head slowly.

"Talk to me," he demanded.

"Are you here just to talk?"

"No."

"What, then?"

He huffed impatiently, "Talk and then leave."

"You're leaving?"

"We're leaving. Don't play games with me."

"We? What'll *we* do? Wait for you to board the black-eyed crazy train again and really kill me this time? If that's what you want, fine, whatever. Take me back. Chain me to your bed." She shrugged.

"Kyla..." he warned.

A long moment passed.

"Tristan, I..."

His name coming off her lips must've been his breaking point. Before she got another word out, before she could say *I'm scared* or say *I'm sorry*, or before she even totally knew what she wanted to say, he surged forward and was on top of her, pinning her arms on pillows above her head. His mouth was a centimetre from hers.

"You. Left. Me." Accusation shot out of his eyes.

She was breathless, heaving. His proximity, his smell, the electricity coming off him...it was revving up every nerve in her body. Her blood felt hot inside her veins, but her skin felt cold on the outside. She was practically salivating to have him inside of her every way he could be. She wanted inside of *him* the only way she could be, through connecting via his teeth.

"You almost murdered me." She took a deep breath, "do you have any idea how frightening you were? My body was full of bruises. My arms, legs, my throat, my... soul." She choked up. "And Sam? How was I supposed to stay? He wanted me for breakfast as soon as I stepped into that, that *fucking* dog run. And you, you finally went down and not a moment too soon because I could've died, and he was down and I... I did the only thing that made any sense in this totally nonsensical situation. I ran."

Despite those being her words coming out of her mouth inside her head she was practically screaming *I'm sorry*.

He let go of her wrists and leaned back, still on top of her. One hand landed on the wall and the other on his forehead. His eyes were closed, his face full of pain.

"I waited," he said softly, not opening his eyes. "I made myself wait. And you don't know how hard it was. You can't begin to fathom how torn up I was not feeling you. You should've fucking called me. I could've got and kept you safe instead of wondering if you were taken or dead."

"And say what? I'm fine but don't come look for me because I'm afraid you'll kill me? I only stopped bleeding a few days ago. Did you know that? I thought it would never stop. If you found me when I was still bleeding? What? What the fuck? And what about when it starts again?"

His proximity was making her tingle. His thighs holding her down, his warm sweet breath so close to her face.

"So you had to run to the other side of the country? Could you not have gone somewhere and called me? I could've left the apartment, kept you there safe. I could've done something other than want to claw my heart out because it almost killed me to worry about you non-stop for all that time! I was in hell. And these will make sure it doesn't come back." He pulled an unmarked amber prescription bottle of pills out of his jacket pocket and slammed it on the small table beside the bed.

She shook her head, "You can guarantee that, can you?"

"No, but it's all I have at this fucking second."

"What about everything else? The danger? The missing blood? The addiction? Your rage? How was I to know if you'd ever be you again? I can't, Tristan; I love you but..."

He gasped, his lips crashed into hers and his warm hands were on her face. His breathing was ragged, and she tasted peaches, and grapes, and pineapple, oranges, cherries, marshmallows, and cream. His lips possessed hers, his tongue stroked hers. He held her possessively and it was heaven.

Ambrosia fruit salad...

She moaned into his mouth. Her body was like jelly. She hadn't meant to blurt that, hadn't even thought about it. It just happened.

"Say that again," he demanded softly.

"Say what? Ahh!" she gasped as he tugged on her earlobe with his teeth.

"You know what," he growled, rolled so she was on top of him, and caught her face in his hands. The anger melted away from his expression as his eyes scanned her face.

"That's not the first time I said that to you." Her lower lip trembled. She balanced on her palms, hovering over him, looking down at his gorgeous face, feeling tingles all over.

"I know," he whispered and sucked her bottom lip into his mouth and moaned, the vibration of his moan sending a wave of euphoria through every inch of her.

Her world stopped. "You know? You heard me?"

He nodded slowly, his eyes softening, warming. His fingers massaged her scalp. "I wasn't sure if I dreamt it. You just confirmed that I didn't."

A sob tore out of her mouth. She choked on it and then asked, "You really heard me?"

Did my love really break through and stop the monster? I broke through. I did.

"So, you love me, but you can't?" His eyes were filled with warmth and they pleaded with her.

She said nothing. She was sinking, getting lost in a sea of blue.

I could try.

He seemed to understand her unspoken thought and touched his lips to her nose, "Say it again," he said softly.

"I love you," she blurted, feeling all the air leave her lungs.

"With my name," he whispered.

"I love you, Tristan."

He gave her a brief squeeze and then abruptly flipped her onto her back, let go, and got up to his feet.

Huh?

Kyla was flabbergasted. Where was he going?

"I need to sleep," he muttered this and shook his jacket off, so it fell to the floor. Then he got his shirt, shoes, socks, and then jeans off.

Stripped to black boxer briefs, he climbed under the covers and plopped onto the pillow and threw his forearm over his eyes. She looked at him, accusingly, mouth hanging open.

After that declaration, he lets go and...and that's it?

Talk about feeling bereft.

She climbed under the covers and scooted over beside him. "Uh...Hello?"

"Hello."

"Uh..."

"I'm very mad at you." He muttered this, lifting his arm briefly and giving her a narrow-eyed look and as her heart started to sink she caught that he looked like he was trying to suppress a smile.

"Oh." She dug her elbow in the pillow adjacent to him and propped her cheek up on her palm.

"Yeah. So shhh, go to sleep. I'm tired. I'll deal with you later." Now he was definitely failing at trying to hide a smile.

"We're not going to talk?"

"Tomorrow. I haven't slept. I need to close my eyes for a little bit."

"You said you wanted to talk."

"Tomorrow."

She leaned over him and whispered in his ear, "You don't want to fuck me and drink some of my blood?" She used her phone sex operator voice, flicking his earlobe with the tip of her tongue and reaching between his legs, feeling smug about the fact that he was hard.

"Nope." He grabbed her hand and pulled it up to his chest and held onto it. She could see goose bumps on his forearm and was supremely pleased with that.

"You aren't going to tell me you love me, too?" Kyla asked, in a small voice, brushing her nose across the rough stubble on his jawline.

"M-A-D," he spelled out. His eyes were still covered, but now there was a goofy grin on his face.

"Oh," she pouted, "'kay, then."

He reached over and turned the lamp off, wrapped his arm around her, and pulled her close. She put her nose to his chest and inhaled him, threading her fingers into his hair. She listened to him breathing and to his heartbeat and felt like she was being softly lulled to sleep by all of it. His hand rested on the arch of her ear, his fingers tangled in her hair.

"But you're not *so* mad at me that you won't let me cuddle with you?"

"Nuh uh." He tugged on her ponytail.

"Good enough." she nuzzled in.

After a few minutes of nothing but crickets outside and the sound of his heart and his breathing soothing her, she felt him tense up.

Then he softly said, "Princess?"

"Hm?" Her soul wanted to sing at hearing the endearment.

"I will *not* let you go. Ever. You were meant for me. You were created to be mine. Somehow I still have remnants of a soul and I know this deep in there."

She choked on a sob. He wasn't done.

"I'm gonna make sure you don't ever have to run away from me again." His voice was soft, smooth, and she was overcome with the scent of warm caramel sauce. This was aromatherapy at its finest.

"'Kay."

"And I do love you, too," he whispered. "I love you more than breathing. More than blood, more than anything."

Wow.

Her throat was clogged. She let out a long stuttering breath.

"But I *am* mad at you. Don't ever fucking run from me like that again. We need a contingency plan for if things ever go wrong again. We'll make one. Okay?" He kissed her forehead.

"Okay," she said. She wanted him. She wanted him in the worst way. "and I'm *not* mad at *you*, Tristan. Even though you almost killed me."

He squeezed her and kissed her forehead again. "Thank you, baby," he murmured.

She wanted him to bite her. She wanted him inside her. But he just held her and stroked her hair until he fell asleep, which didn't take long. When his hand stopped moving, she wondered if he was showing her that he had self-control. Then she closed her eyes.

2

KYLA WOKE UP TO THE sound of a lawnmower and the scent of fresh cut grass. Tristan was still sound asleep beside her and for a split second all was right with the world.

All was not yet right with her world, of course, but here in his arms it felt like right was definitely possible and she wanted to enjoy the 'right now' while she could.

It was just a double bed, way smaller than the beds she'd been in with him so far, but this was good; she liked how close he was. She felt safe for the first time since she'd left him.

Safe was an odd feeling to have considering she'd run away to *be* safe but strangely, she did feel safe. It felt like she was almost whole. Almost. There was so much to figure out, yeah, but she felt like she might feel whole again when he drank from her.

She placed her palm on his cheek. The dark stubble had grown just past scratchy and was soft. He looked good enough to eat.

Isn't that ironic?

He also smelled amazing. She felt a burst of affection for him.

He opened his eyes and showed her the most beautiful shade of blue she'd ever laid eyes on. He smiled a little, flashing perfect white non-elongated teeth, "Good morning, sunshine." He turned toward and then kissed the palm of her hand.

"Brightest I've had in a while," she said shyly.

He pulled her onto his body and shivers ran up her spine. He rubbed his hands up and down her back and touched his lips to her temple.

"I can't believe you're here," she whispered and ran her hands up his arms.

She didn't know until he was back beside her just how much she'd missed this. She couldn't imagine never ever having this again.

But, was anything different? She knew there was a bottle of pills on the nightstand. Would they work? And beyond that what about everything else? What had changed? At this very moment all she really knew was that she was glad he was here, glad to feel him. It might be incredibly stupid, but because he was here the hollow and gaping hole of emptiness was gone.

"Okay, talk to me," she whispered.

"Not yet. Snuggle." He pulled her tighter against him.

"Can't breathe," she whispered.

He loosened his grip a little.

She nuzzled into his neck, reached down and ran her hand up the ridge of his erection, then squirmed against it, hoping he'd throw her down and take her.

"Mmmm," he murmured, the timbre of his voice making her body break out in goosebumps. He slid her yoga pants and panties down past her ass. *Yes!*

Then he threw his arms over his head and waited. "I was gonna make you wait," he breathed. "Punish you..."

"Oh yeah?" she whispered and started to tongue his earlobe.

"But, you may fuck me. Show me you're sorry."

"Oh, may I?" she giggled, feeling tingly in her nipples.

"You may," he said sheepishly, eyes closed. "I still might give you a spanking later; I haven't decided."

"Hm. Promise?" she teased and squirmed up against him.

He gave her a mischievous smirk. Kyla squirmed out of her pants and threw her top over her head and off to the side, then rolled his boxers down enough to get to his cock and squeezed it, watching him react. His eyes were still closed, but his mouth opened slightly and then he bit down on his bottom lip. She took no time guiding him inside of herself. She was ready -—more than ready. She leaned forward, putting her neck over his mouth, offering her throat to him.

He kissed it lightly, threaded fingers into her hair, and then pulled her head back by the length of her ponytail a little roughly to gain access to her mouth. She whimpered with need. He kissed her voraciously. She gyrated, she squeezed the muscles of her inner walls, absorbing the feel of every inch of him inside of her. He released her hair and grabbed her hips. His hands felt like they were on fire. He moved her the way he wanted, creating a fluid motion as he continued to kiss her hungrily.

She groaned into his mouth, loving the cinnamon toast taste of him while being full of him, but wanting his teeth on her. She needed his teeth on her. Bad.

She nuzzled her throat across his mouth, giving him access again. He grunted a frustrated sound and then flipped her over onto her back, then started to plunge deeper and harder into her, his eyes squeezed shut tight, an expression that looked like pain on his face.

"Baby," she begged, grabbing his jaw with both hands. She wanted his emotions inside of her, wanted that humming inside her veins.

"Can't," he whispered and opened his eyes. There was definitely pain there; he closed them again, tight.

He wouldn't look at her. He wouldn't bite her. He seemed, suddenly, like he was broken. Was he so mad at her for leaving? Did he really hold that against her? Or was he afraid the monster would wake up if he tasted her blood? Fear and pain pierced her soul. Her heart sank. He stopped moving. He was just there, inside of her, his face buried into the pillow she was lying on. He was breathing hard.

She pushed all of her fear and negative thoughts out, planted a kiss on his shoulder, and clamped her legs tight around his waist. She wanted to take him to a happy place in her mind as she visualized his face, his smile, his dimples, and felt joy well up in side of herself.

He let out a little grunt and balanced his hands on the mattress and looked down at her. His eyes blazed a brilliant blue. Something flashed, something darker but the blue burned through.

Two or three jerks of his hips and he pulled out. It was over, before she'd even gotten close, before he did. He didn't come, just pulled out and collapsed on top of her, burying his face in the pillow again.

Regardless, the proximity of him, the feeling of being under his body, it struck her as achingly beautiful. It was so nice to feel him inside of her, feel him so close to her. She didn't care about the sex right now, just wanted him close and it felt like this was the closest he could be without his teeth on her.

He stayed on top of her for a long time, just still, letting her hold him. She ran her fingers through his hair, ran her hands up and down his back, his rear end, feeling the smoothness of his skin, the strength of his muscles, planting soft kisses on his shoulder, and just enjoyed feeling his warmth, inhaling his scent. She closed her eyes and tried to focus on his breathing and his heartbeat, but then heard another power tool start up outside somewhere. He eased away from her. Then suddenly, he flipped her and was upright with her sprawled across his lap.

She gasped in surprise. He gave her bum a single hard slap. Her entire body tensed. She was shocked; it really stung! He moved her off his lap and got up out of bed. She was on her knees, afraid to sit down, the sting of his slap singeing her rear end.

"Pack up; we have a ferry to catch." He leaned over, touching his lips softly to her bottom right where it stung, and then he ruffled her hair as if she was a small child.

"Where?" She was probably as scarlet in the face as she was on the bottom.

"Arizona. First a ferry to Seattle."

"Adrian? That elder?"

"Yes."

Kyla got up and then headed for a shower. She rubbed her back-side as she walked away and shot him a dirty look over her shoulder. He lifted the Puma bag onto the bed and gave her a sexy wink.

SHE JUMPED IN THE SHOWER and while she was washing her hair, he stepped in. For a moment, she thought he wanted to continue what'd been started in bed but he was all about getting washed. She went to leave the shower, but he stopped her by grabbing her wrist and said, "Stay." So she washed his back while he washed the rest.

After the shower, she dressed in a pair of jean shorts and a button-up long sleeved white, thin, almost sheer, cotton hoodie with purple braided drawstrings. He got dressed in a fresh pair of dark button fly jeans and black t-shirt from the duffle bag. The fact that she hadn't ditched any of his clothes might've surprised him. She wasn't sure as he didn't say anything. She wasn't sure why she hadn't done it. She lifted the bottle of tiny pills from the table and put them in her purse, gathered everything else up and added it all to the bag and French braided her wet hair and secured the bottom with a ponytail holder.

"Uh..." He was leafing through the duffle bag, which was sitting on the coffee table in the sitting area of the trailer. He pulled out her passport and opened it and glanced inside the booklet.

"There's some more cash in my purse, too. And I can replace what I've spent with money from my own—-"

"No, I'm looking for my passport. Please tell me you didn't throw it away."

"Oh. No, it's, uh...it's under my pillow."

He quirked up an eyebrow at her.

She shrugged, cheeks flushed. He gave her a sweet smile and then he went into the bedroom. When he came out he was sliding both passport booklets into his back pocket, "Ready?" he asked, looking tense.

She nodded, feeling awkward and trying to gauge his mood. "I'll just drop this garbage bag in the bin and stop by the front office and drop off the keys. I'll be right back."

"I'll come," he said and slung the bag over his shoulder.

"I'm not running away from you," she defended.

Sheesh, watching me like a hawk, carrying my passport for me?

His eyes met hers, "Good to hear that. And I know. But I can't let you out of my sight right now."

"Because?"

"Because. It's dangerous." He strode past her, stone serious, out the door, grabbing the bag of garbage and the gym bag from her on the way. She followed behind him, frowning, and locked the door behind her.

"Why? What's going on?"

"Later."

Later?

This shit would have to stop *real* quick. She refused to be kept in the dark. But, she was going to give him some space for the moment because they'd been in one another's sights for less than 12 hours and her emotions were still all over the place. It was obvious his were, too.

KYLA LISTENED TO THE manager of the RV park grumble and huff about her checking out early. Kyla told the middle-aged woman with the wrinkles and colouring of someone who drank a few nights a week and smoked two packs a day, that she didn't need the deposit back, just wanted to hand back the keys. She knew that if the woman had gone down there she'd see the screen door was now gone and that'd forfeit the deposit, anyway.

Tristan hovered in the doorway of the office while she did everything and then when the manager muttered that she had to go investigate the condition of the trailer before finalizing the paperwork Tristan sauntered up to her, leaned over, put both palms on the desk, and then he looked her in the eye and calmly said, "You're going to sign off on that and give us the original file. You don't need a copy. Kyla Spencer was never here. You've never seen her or me in your life. Give her the deposit back."

The woman stood still while he spoke and then nodded at him after he stopped speaking and then dazedly handed Kyla the $500 cash that was held as a damage deposit.

"I should leave something for the screen door," Kyla mumbled to him.

"Fuck it, it'll take nothing for them to put it back on," he growled and then grabbed Kyla's hand and impatiently rushed to the parking lot. He clicked a keychain button and a black Impala chimed as the doors were unlocked and the engine started. He opened the passenger door for her. She got in, feeling astounded at how easy it was for him to get the grumbly cantankerous woman to just agree.

"Where's your phone?" he asked.

"I left it at your condo," she was a little taken aback.

"Not that one. Your original phone." he nodded toward her purse.

"I, uh.."

Tristan snapped his fingers in front of her face, impatiently, "Get with it, Kyla."

"I ditched it." She blinked hard at his callous demeanor.

"Ditched it where?"

"Back home."

"Good."

"Why? What's going on?"

"I'm just making sure you don't still have it."

"No, I don't. Why?"

"Tracking."

"Who would—-"

"Later." He backed out and they were on the road.

She looked out the window, feeling pissed about being dismissed so flippantly.

"Kyla, don't," he warned, "I need you to not."

"Not? Not what? Not wonder what's happening? That's like saying not to blink when someone is about to poke me in the eye. You can't *not* tell me what's going on and expect me to be a deer in the headlights. I'm not that woman back there. I'm not Julia."

"That's for sure!"

She huffed out a big breath.

He gritted his teeth. "I'm not in a good place right now."

"You think I am?"

"Kyla..."

"What?" she spat.

He took a deep breath. "I have a lot to say to you but I'm using every iota of self-control I have right now to make damn sure I don't grab you and drain you dead. Is it too much to ask that you just PLEASE give me a wide fucking berth?"

Kyla clamped her mouth shut and stared out the window, blowing out a long slow breath through her nose.

A few minutes later, they were pulling into a waterfront parking lot.

Tristan produced a cell phone from his jacket pocket and pushed a few buttons.

"This is Mr. James, I rented the Impala just as you were closing last night. Yeah, I'm parking it at Belleville Street. I'm catching The

Clipper here. In the glovebox, yeah. There's one arranged on the other side? Good. Thanks." He hung up.

"James?"

"So no one tracks me. Let's go get you some caffeine before we board. Lack of it is making you grouchy."

"Me? Yeah, and lack of blood's making you grouchier."

Who would be tracking them? Sam? Someone else?

He flashed her a dirty look, got out, slung the duffle bag over his shoulder, and grabbed her hand and they walked to a little coffee shop. Tristan fiddled with the phone, removed the battery, then dropped the pieces in the trash can on the way in.

Going to a waterfront café hand in hand... they were about to be on a boat together where she could smell the sea while looking into his eyes. Everything she'd dreamt of just yesterday and here they now were. But this wasn't a vacation. He wasn't a happy 'fantasy come true' moment. And she didn't know what was next.

When is he going to talk to me?

When he passed her a coffee he said, "Take a pill."

"Is it going to mess me up? I already had that shot and..."

"I don't know, but it's a must. Take it as soon as you wake up every day. You can't forget."

She made a *well duh* face and he shot her a dirty look.

She took the pill, and then she decided to focus her attention on nothing but the bliss inside that coffee cup for at least the next few minutes.

AN HOUR LATER ZERO more words had been exchanged between them and the boat was leaving the harbour.

They found a quiet place to sit on a bench outside on deck. He put his arm around her and she rested her head on his shoulder, inhaling the layers of Tristan and the sea in the air. It was a heady combination. Him reaching for her and then just sitting together in amicable silence as the boat pulled away from the harbour left her with a peaceful feeling for a moment. She let out a happy little sigh.

He squeezed. She looked up and saw dimples.

Dimples. Her eyes welled up.

He looked at her warily.

"Happy tears," she whispered.

"Really?"

"Really. You can't feel it?"

"Sometimes I need to hear it, too."

Damn, he was beautiful. He kissed a tear with his lips and then licked his lips. He flashed the dimples again. She touched his left dimple with her index finger and he caught her finger between his teeth and winked as her eyes widened.

She snatched her hand back and tsk tsk'd him,

"*So* very naughty, Mr. James."

He gave her a smile that melted her insides and said low, "You're the naughty one and I think you might be in need of another spanking."

Kyla flushed scarlet, "Hm, maybe."

She soaked in the feel of a gentle breeze, staring out at the water, watching Victoria harbour move away from them. People on deck moved toward the railing.

A few minutes later, he interrupted her thoughts by leaning in toward her ear, "Princess?" His voice was low.

"Hmm?" she answered dreamily.

"I know who the Toronto Mangler is."

It might as well have been the sound of a needle screeching harshly across a vinyl album, the way it made her feel.

"It's Liam Donavan. He was at our table at the banquet. He knows about you, about your blood. And I haven't been able to find him."

Those words smashed her happy thought bubble, rendering it a thousand shards of glass lying right there on deck.

Her hand came up to cover her mouth.

"When I couldn't feel you all I could think to do track him down to make sure he didn't have you, but I couldn't find him. I couldn't find him, and I couldn't feel you. I was...." He took a breath and then continued, "Sam is holding the fort back home. Despite what happened, I'm working with Sam, from a distance."

She opened her mouth to speak, but he continued.

"He says that as long as he doesn't get within 100 feet of you he'll be fine, and he's worked hard to convince me he has no ulterior motives. I believe him. It was just the heat of the moment, the scent of your blood unleashed something instinctual in him. He says Adrian has an experimental drug that can block him from reacting. We can test it to see if he can be around you after having smelled your nectar."

"I *really* don't think you should trust Sam." She played with her braid.

"Well, that remains to be seen. But, that's another new strength that's intensified: my ability to read truths and lies in people. There's something Sam isn't telling me but I'm reading that he has good intentions. I'm proceeding with caution with him. So, uh, you should also know that Joe's gone," he said, then waited a beat before continuing, "After the banquet I saw him, and I was able to read him clearer than ever. That first taste of nectar intensified my strength and I had new telepathic abilities, especially with younger vamps. After you left I went back and I got him to admit things; he admitted he'd told Liam about you. I knew my instinct was right. They'd been planning to nab you from the event when it was planned at the house. Joe was a pawn, didn't know Liam's full intent. Liam wasn't a supporter of my promotion, so was probably looking for dirt on me. Joe probably told him enough that Liam put two and two together about you, but I'm sure he had a backup plan for the hotel. If we hadn't left early... I did some digging and it all points to the Toronto Mangler."

She swallowed hard and touched her temples with her fingertips. "So Joe's gone. Gone where?"

"Gone, gone. Ended."

She held her breath for a minute. Tristan had killed him? The man she loved was capable of violence, she certainly knew that, but murder was a hard pill to swallow.

"Liam Donavan wants my position and your blood. He won't get either," Tristan said, his steely gaze was aimed at the horizon. His eyes didn't look light blue right now; they were more of a stormy gray. She swallowed hard.

"Now you know why I'm being so cautious."

She exhaled and nodded, feeling numb.

For the next while, they were both quiet. She watched the water, lost in thoughts, brooding over their circumstances. He still had his arm around her. He shifted, finally, stood up and walked over to the railing. She followed.

She stayed quiet for a while, then broke the silence, "Are you still mad at me?"

"It took my anger down a few notches when I finally felt you, felt your regret, that you were missing me. A few more when you said you love me."

"What did you feel?"

She could see he was sort of chewing his cheek. He shook his head and leaned farther over the railing.

He eyed her darkly, "Let's not. I can't be alone with you here and if I start talking I won't care who's around. My self-control is questionable at the moment."

Her belly dipped.

She sighed, "I have to pee. How's that for breaking the spell? Be right back." She turned on her heel to walk away, thinking that if he bit her she wouldn't have to ask about how he felt. She'd *feel* how he felt.

He caught her hand, tension in his eyes, "I'm coming."

"We're on a boat. I'm not going anywhere."

"Still coming."

"Fine, whatever," she shrugged. He followed her to a restroom and made her wait outside while he checked it.

"Clear," he said and motioned for her to go in.

Was that really necessary? Could there really be someone waiting in the bathroom to 'get' her?

She shook her head. She had to think the same way he was. Normalcy bias was a dangerous thing. Her gut instinct of rolling her eyes at anal over-cautious behaviour had to end. Now. Otherwise, she'd become one of those distressed damsels in the movies who were too stupid to live because she'd walk into a dark room even when she knew there was a killer loose.

When she came out he said, "Let's go to the cafeteria and get you something to eat. I'm not afraid you're going for a swim, Kyla, I just need to make sure you're safe, that we aren't being followed." He took her hand.

"I know. Sorry. When did you last... uh...feed?"

Maybe withdrawals were adding to his paranoia, making it worse.

"Yesterday."

"Yesterday?" That came out as an accusation.

He squeezed her hand reassuringly, "Blood drive in Vancouver before I came to the island. No human contact. I wouldn't come to you on empty. It took the edge off, at least."

"Oh."

"A little," he added.

Kyla winced.

"I'll wait until we get to Adrian's before I feed from you. Don't offer me your throat again. We'll take blood from you carefully and I'll take it from a test tube while you're safely tucked away. Then we'll see what happens."

"You know this Adrian?"

"No. But my Grandfather trusted him. He has an excellent reputation. He's a doctor. He's an elder."

"You trust your grandfather?" As soon as she said it she tensed, thinking it might be a mistake to say such a thing.

"Good question. Just another thing on my growing list of things to figure out."

She was relieved that he understood her concern. She could tell he felt her same concerns by his reaction. He'd never met his grandfather but yet lived in his grandfather's world, trying to walk in the footsteps of a man that lived a lifestyle that Tristan now questioned. It was perplexing; perplexing indeed.

"Do you have other family?" she asked.

"My mother," he answered, looking uncomfortable.

"Where—-" she started to get ready to ask questions, but he cut her off.

"Not now, okay? Not now."

She met his gaze and his eyes had pain in them. He shook his head slowly, looking at her like he was imploring her to drop it.

She dropped it.

THEY ATE A LIGHT BREAKFAST of fruit cups and bagels in the cafeteria side by side and then she curled her feet under herself and put her head on his shoulder and yawned.

"Close your eyes for a bit, baby," he said, and she nuzzled in and closed her eyes, absorbing the mingled smell of his leather jacket and the smell of him.

"You smell so delicious," she whispered.

"Not as delicious as you," he whispered back and kissed her forehead.

She drifted off, wishing that this was the start of a great adventure, not a quest to find a way for them to be together without him killing her, without someone else killing her. The way he'd blurted all that information on deck was abrupt and startling, to say the least. How much worse could it get? She knew that was a very dangerous question.

WHEN SHE WOKE UP HE was staring out the window, looking deep in thought. He had his arm protectively around her. She reached up and started rubbing his chin.

He flashed a smile at her, "I need to shave," he scratched at his cheek. "It's driving me crazy."

"You look so rugged and sexy."

"Oh yeah?" He raised an eyebrow.

"Yeah. Mm. Yummy." She curled in closer and wrapped her arms around his middle and gave him a squeeze, "How far?"

He kissed the top of her head, "We're pretty much there. Look."

Kyla sat up and stretched, "I slept for a while, I guess." She looked out the window and could see that land was close.

"Yeah, you did." He looked at her warmly.

"I could be insulted that you're so happy to have not had my company or my brain bothering you for the last few hours. But I'll let you off the hook. This time."

He smirked.

"What's the plan?" She rested her head against his chest again and circled his chin cleft with her index finger.

"The plan is we grab a rental car and zig zag down towards Phoenix. Then, I tuck you away someplace safe while I meet with Adrian privately. Then we go from there."

3

BY THE TIME THEY GOT through customs and to the parking lot, a silver Mercedes E550 convertible Cabriolet was waiting for them. It had the top down and it sparkled in the sun, looking very inviting.

"*This* is a sexy car," Kyla said as she caressed the door.

The rental company rep smiled at her and got into a car with his co-worker and drove away. Tristan smiled while closing the trunk with their bag in it.

"It is. Hop in."

He reached into the glove box and pulled out a map. He examined it for a few minutes while she put on her seatbelt and got situated. She put her purse on the floor between her feet and reached over and turned the radio on.

A Def Leppard song, Love Bites, rang through the speakers. The singer sang about not wanting to touch her because making love to her would drive him crazy and then when the chorus started singing about how love bites and bleeds she flicked the volume off. A shudder worked its way up her spine.

Tristan let out a heavy sigh, "It's what I need."

"What is?"

"That's the next line of the song."

"Oh. Oh ya."

"Rather fitting, huh?"

"Mm hm."

Oh God, I love him. Please let us figure this out.

THEY WERE SOON ON THE road, the top down, and the sun was shining.

"How long to get there?" Kyla asked.

"A few days if I do all the driving and we stop at night," Tristan answered. "I'm not taking the most direct route, in case anyone finds out we landed here. Four or five days. Maybe we'll take six."

"Okay, good, you're doing it. I hate driving."

"Hate?"

"Hate. I have my license and I can do it if I have to but I hate it. I get aggressive and have terrible road rage. People shit themselves when I'm driving."

Tristan burst out laughing.

"And that's funny because?"

"You think I'm going to shit my pants out of fear because of your driving?"

She giggled, "I wasn't talking about you, Mr. Big Bad Scary Vampire. However, maybe we *should* put me in the driver's seat next time the gray monster rears his head, huh?"

Tristan shook his head, "Bad joke."

"I know, right? Maybe not," Kyla mused, "But it might be a good sign if we can start to laugh about it."

"Not ready to laugh about it," he said, stone-faced.

"Yeah, I guess me either. Or at least I shouldn't be. Then again, my emotions are a mystery to me these days." She shrugged.

Kyla pushed the negativity that threatened to creep in away and stretched, soaking in the sunshine. It would be nice to be alone together for that amount of time.

But then she felt her heart sink again, thinking that a lot of that time would probably be spent obsessing about what'd happen when they got to Arizona. She didn't want to obsess. She just wanted to enjoy a few days with him, try to make this road trip less than ominous. A few days alone with Tristan could be nice -—so nice.

She fiddled with the radio tuner and stopped at the Hinder song from her ringtone. She stopped and leaned back and smiled, eyes closed, listening. She reclined the seat a little bit. His right hand covered her left one and he squeezed.

"You know this song is actually about a guy thinking about cheating on his girlfriend with his ex, right?" she asked him.

"Have no fear of that. It was just that one line that really got me."

She let out a hearty belly laugh.

"You have a great laugh, Kyla," he said. "I want to hear more of it."

He let go of her hand and caressed her cheek.

"Thanks," she smiled at him. "There are other sounds I make that you seem to like, too."

He chuckled and squeezed her thigh. Then his face changed, and he looked like he had the weight of the world on his shoulders. Kyla tried to ignore it, not wanting her own angst levels to multiply his.

Amicable silence followed for the next few hours as they listened to music and watched the scenery.

THEY STOPPED AT A MOTEL once it started to get dark. They chose a motel with a neighbouring Cracker Barrel restaurant. Down the street was a Walmart so Kyla suggested they go for some extra supplies after eating.

"I'm starved. Let's hurry." She pulled his hand toward the restaurant.

"Then you want me to shop with you... at Walmart?" He looked mortified.

"I know it's not your usual speed, Mr. Giorgio Vamp-mani, but we can get you a razor for that three hundred o'clock shadow and some sunglasses for driving and a few other things, including snacks for the road tomorrow. Everything we need. One place. And it's cheap."

"Alright...well, let's get you fed and then check in to our luxurious suite at the Econo El Cheapo motor inn and then we'll go to... Waaaalmart?" He put on a southern drawl and drew out the Walmart word as he put the convertible top up and Kyla stretched in the parking lot.

"Hey! Walmart is frickin' awesome. Okay?"

He shook his head at her and wrinkled his nose. "You're crazy."

"Don't be such an elitist!" she teased.

"I'm trying," he replied with sincerity.

She gave him a shy smile. "You're doing good."

"OUR FIRST DATE, KINDA," Kyla said, smiling as they sat. The scent of cinnamon in the attached country store was inviting, but it wasn't anywhere near as good as the cinnamon toast taste of him in bed that morning. She was suddenly anxious to get back to the motel and get to bed. Her face flushed.

He smirked and when she caught his expression, she flushed brighter. He seemed to be fully aware of what she was thinking about.

"Hey," she said sultrily, "What are you in the mood for?"

He lifted the menu and gave her a sexy look right back, then said, "I'm thinking ham and mac & cheese with some cheese grits and corn bread."

So not sexy but still sexy, strangely.

She wiggled her brows. "Very southern of you. I think I'm having the country fried steak."

"What about dessert?" He arched a brow at her, and now there was an innuendo on the table.

She moistened her lips and used her phone sex voice, "I'd like to binge on dessert. I haven't binge indulged in dessert in too long. Way. Too. Long."

Tristan chewed his cheek and Kyla felt heat prickle along her spine as his heated gaze moved from her eyes, down to her chest, and back up. Then he swallowed hard and looked down, his expression dropping. Kyla frowned.

Was he afraid of being intimate with her? Was he afraid he wouldn't have self-control?

She reached across the table and wiggled her fingers, motioning for him to give her his hand. He did. She squeezed it and tried to give him a reassuring look. This guy was always trying to be so strong for her and she could see underneath the mask of confidence was a man who was a mess. He was obviously afraid of what he was capable of as well as afraid of outside sources that could harm both of them and through all that he had to search for her, knowing that she was hiding from him and afraid of him.

She wanted to burst into tears. She didn't. She held it together. He was smiling all of a sudden.

"What?" she asked.

He shook his head, "I love you." He squeezed her hand tighter and then leaned forward and touched his lips to hers.

"I love you, too." It was getting easier to say. She added, "So much, Tristan."

He closed his eyes and he let out a slow breath, appearing to savour her words.

Dinner was pretty good, and they talked like a couple getting to know one another. Kyla loved how normal it felt. He was more than a pretty face, too; he was smart, well-read, they had similar political views, and she could see how he'd make a good choice to run a company -—even if that company wasn't exactly mainstream. The conversation was easy, normal, fun.

She knew it wasn't a normal date, of course; they were on a mission, a potentially life-altering one, and he was a vampire and she had coveted weird blood, but it felt almost normal tonight. Two people enjoying a hearty meal in public and being happy for a moment. She knew Tristan was hyperaware of their surroundings. He could see the entrance and looked narrow-eyed at everyone who entered the restaurant, but he seemed to be enjoying their time together, too.

When the server offered dessert menus, they both stared at one another as if they shared a private joke. Kyla chewed her lip, thinking about tasting him, about having him taste her.

His gaze heated under her stare and the waitress finally cleared her throat, obviously uncomfortable at being smack dab in the middle of what must've looked like imminent intercourse. Tristan thanked her, but declined dessert and then dropped money on the table. They then walked hand in back hand to the motel where he checked them in.

The room was a standard motor inn type place with two queen sized beds, a TV, dresser, and a bathroom. It was pretty unremarkable, but it was clean and definitely a step up from that RV Kyla had slept in back on Vancouver Island.

He dropped the duffle bag on a bed. "Shall we go on a shopping spree?" He quirked up an eyebrow at her.

WALKING THROUGH A DISCOUNT department store with him was so far-fetched she found it comical. He eyed large skid loads of household items with the curiosity of a tourist at a museum. Kyla chuckled at the scene, thinking that the whole package that was Tristan Walker did *not* say discount department store; that was for sure.

She was more than certain she didn't look out of place in her jean shorts and summer hoodie with her messy braid and sneakers. He wasn't dressed up and just in jeans and a t-shirt but still, every inch of him screamed hot sex and money in the sort of way that just didn't say shopping at your local discount department store.

Almost every woman in the restaurant and now in the store seemed to look twice at him. Some were slack jawed and some flushed red, probably from the instant carnal thoughts that invaded their minds. She knew how drop-dead gorgeous he was. He had magnetism. She was under no illusions about the fact that she probably looked like a total Plain Jane in stark contrast. Tristan belonged in a corner office of a high-rise office building or on a red carpet with supermodel arm candy. Not in a discount department store in some suburb somewhere in Oregon with the likes of *her*.

She stopped in the accessories section, picked up a pair of sunglasses, and popped them onto his face. She screwed up her face and took them off and then popped on another.

"Having fun?" he asked, looking mildly amused.

"Yes. So much. Here, let's try these." She found another pair. "Perfect."

He shook his head, "You're crazy."

She found him a nice pair of cargo shorts, "Try these on?" she asked.

He glanced at the size, "They'll fit." He looked at the tag again. "Bum? Seriously?"

Kyla gave him a loud kiss, cracked the gum in her mouth, popped the shorts into the basket he was carrying, and pulled him along.

"We need a cart."

By the time they left, they each had extra clothes and toiletries, sunglasses, plus flip flops, there were drinks and snacks for the motel room and the road, and they hadn't even spent $200.

"Wow. Who knew? I've been missin' out!" Tristan looked at the receipt. "Walmart *is* frickin' awesome."

"*You're* crazy," she said and bumped him with her hip. Then she climbed into the basket of the cart with their bags and ordered, "Push!"

He pushed the cart fast, jogging through the half empty parking lot. She felt light and airy. She pushed away that nagging feeling that told her it wasn't going to last.

WHEN THEY GOT BACK to the motel, as Tristan was putting the key card into the slot on the door, she felt a whoosh of anticipation in her belly and knew her panties were damp with arousal. She stood behind him and saw his tight buns and goosed him. He was startled and looked over his shoulder, shocked. She winked, feeling totally brazen.

His expression dropped as he opened the door. "Someone's been in here."

She followed him in.

"Put your back against that wall." He pointed to the wall.

She felt her heart drop as she backed up into the wall just inside the door.

He looked under the beds and then in the bathroom.

"It's clear," he mumbled. A quick inspection of the Puma bag and he seemed satisfied.

"Maybe it was just a maid."

"Must've been," he said. "It was a woman. Not a vampire."

"Wow. You can tell."

"Lingering scent. All of my senses are stronger than ever, especially since..." he stopped. "It's useful, my ability to scent is sharper than ever."

She nodded. They hadn't yet talked much about what happened. She had a feeling the changes after that event were pretty poignant. She just wanted him right now, not baggage, not fear, not knowledge, just him. Hot sex after a fun date. Was that so much to ask for?

They stared at one another; Kyla against the wall, Tristan standing right in front of her.

"I want you," she whispered and stepped forward, closer to him.

"I need to hold back," he pushed her gently back against the wall pinning her by the shoulders warily. His eyes scanned up and down her body and she could see he was fighting his urges.

She whispered, "Just let me. I'll do it all." She dropped to her knees and started to undo his jean buttons, realizing she hadn't given him the pleasure of her mouth on his cock yet.

He took a step back. "No. I can't right now. I'm too..too..." He stopped talking and took a deep breath.

"But this morning you just let me..."

"Can't do that again. It took every ounce of my control to hold it back and we both know how disappointing that was. If I let go, this thing in me, it could get out; I feel like I have to hold it back. I don't know it well enough yet. I've got Jekyl *and* Hyde in me and Hyde's a stranger. I don't trust him."

She swallowed hard and got to her feet, furrowing her brows.

He continued, "It doesn't feel like I have to get pissed off to lose it. It doesn't feel like I have to taste or smell blood, even, for this Hyde to get out. It feels like it's just below the surface, *just*. My physical strength has almost doubled in intensity and there are new ones. And it, whatever monster you woke up, is very close to the surface right now, always, but especially right now, like I'm sharing my body with someone else, someone who wants to take over." He swallowed hard. "We have to get to Adrian's, figure out what I'm really dealing with here. Then we can go from there."

"You're going to spend the next few days with me, not drinking my blood, not having sex at all?"

He shook his head, "I almost lost it this morning. More than once. I can't."

"Tristan, maybe I should just hide. I'll stay here. You go. Go to Arizona. Then come get me when it's all figured out. I just don't know if it's a good idea for us to be in close proximity if, if..."

If I don't even know if you're about to lose control!

"I'm not leaving you." He folded his arms across his chest.

"I won't take off. I promise."

"I know that. It's not that. I won't leave you unprotected."

"Then let's fly. We'll be there in a few hours."

"No, no paper trail. It's bad enough someone can find out I crossed the border from the ferry manifest. I didn't have time to get us new identities."

"But what if you can't hold it in?" She flopped onto the bed and stared at the ceiling. He flopped beside her.

Something rose in her, "Maybe I can help you control it," she said.

He was about to speak, and he didn't look happy.

"Hear me out." She put her index finger over his lips and started to speak quickly, "I think I talked you down last time. It might've been the tranquilizers, but it might've been me. You remembered what I said and as soon as I said it, you were becoming you again. Maybe if you..." she shrugged. "I could—-" He grabbed her wrist and flipped so that he was pinning her on a bed.

His eyes darkened, "You think *you* can control this? I'm not sure how much longer *I* can fucking control this!"

He stared at her for a beat and then blew his hair out of his eyes, rolled off her and got to the floor and started to do push-ups.

What's wrong with me?

Kyla knew she sounded ridiculous, asking him to put her at risk like this. She sounded like a junkie begging for a hit. She decided to just shut up. She stared at his muscular back for a second. His muscles flexed as he went up and down and up and down. She imagined being underneath him as he did that. She shook herself back to reality when she heard him growl her name.

"Get out of my head," she told him, covering her eyes.

"If I knew how." He mumbled and started doing the push-ups faster.

"Would you? If you knew how?"

"No."

"I didn't think so."

There was a pregnant pause. She got to her feet, "I'm going for a bath."

She figured it'd be a good idea to leave him alone for a few minutes.

"Wait. That scent is nagging at me. I need to know what it's from. I need to make sure. Follow me."

"Huh?"

"Now," he growled and grabbed her hand and the room key card and then they headed to the front office. Tristan got right in the space of the desk clerk, a young guy, maybe 25, who looked like he desperately needed a shower.

"Who was in our room?"

The clerk went into what Kyla could see was an instant trance.

"Marabelle. Maid."

"Where is she?" Tristan demanded.

The clerk pointed to a hallway adjacent to the front desk.

Tristan moved in that direction, taking Kyla with him. Down the long hall were a few closed doors and one was slightly open. They stepped into a utility room with motel supplies and a washer and dryer. A woman in a maid's uniform put towels into a washing machine. She turned around and her expression on Tristan was instantly carnal.

She had short dark hair cut in a pixie style and big hazel eyes. Tristan let Kyla's hand go and got instantly in her space. He sniffed close to her hair and Kyla felt every hair on her body rise.

The woman's eyes went hooded and her lips parted. She looked like she was ready to be kissed.

"You were in our room. Why?" Tristan demanded.

Kyla felt prickling at the back of her neck at how close Tristan was to the maid.

"I was just ensuring you had everything," she replied and looked at Tristan like she wanted to eat him for breakfast.

"What did you touch? Have you told anyone about us?"

The carnal look dimmed. "I've told no one. I checked your towels and toiletries. I accidentally skipped your room on my rounds this morning earlier and saw you leave so I made sure everything was in order. I didn't want to give you any reason to complain. I need this job."

Tristan stared at her for a beat and Kyla felt anger rise.

"Get away from her!" Kyla shrieked.

Tristan glanced over his shoulder at Kyla, looking both surprised and bewildered.

"What?"

"Get. The. Fuck. Away. From her. Move back!"

The maid didn't even look in Kyla's direction. Her gaze was fixed on Tristan.

"Kyla?"

Kyla's chest was heaving up and down. She was wide-eyed and frantic.

"Forget we spoke," Tristan said to the maid and the maid nodded.

Tristan grabbed Kyla's hand and marched back to their room.

"Did you really think I was gonna hurt her?" Tristan was incredulous as he shut the door.

Kyla was backing up, fingers on her temples, trembling.

"I wouldn't have hurt her, baby. She wasn't an enemy. I just needed to get a read on her to make sure of it, that's all. Make sure she wasn't mesmerized by someone else... to get information, to plant anything in our room."

"I didn't think you were gonna hurt her," Kyla said.

"Then what was that about?" Tristan looked baffled.

"I just got this overwhelming... I don't know ... jealousy. I thought you were gonna bite her and then the way she was looking at you and with the way she looked... I know I shouldn't think that, but it was like..."

He shook his head. "Primal instinct?"

"If you didn't get away from her when you did I think I might've actually gone after her. Because her eyes are sorta like mine."

He snickered.

"It's not funny."

Horror started to sink in. Kyla felt murderous in that room, like she wanted to gouge that pixie maid's eyes out so that they wouldn't be greenish.

"It's kinda funny," he said and folded his arms across his chest. He had a big smile on his face.

She let out a grunt of frustration. "I'm going for a bath."

She grabbed both the Puma bag and a bag with some toiletries they'd bought at Walmart and went into the bathroom.

She turned the water on, plunked the plug in, and got in and lathered up her legs with shaving cream and pulled the cover off a disposable razor.

She chided herself for being jealous like that when he'd done nothing to make her think he'd ever cross that line with another woman. She also chided herself for her behavior before then, when she was clearly thinking like a guy, with her vajayjay, instead of her brain.

She didn't know if Tristan had been stopped back at the condo because of her declaration and her feelings or if it *was* because he'd been shot by enough tranquilizer to take down a few elephants, and here she was, trying tempt him into something that might go badly.

What was this bond they had doing to her?

She didn't like how clouded her judgement felt. She'd run away from him out of self-preservation and yet here she was offering to do experiments with no controls and no help in place. *And* wanting to gouge the eyes out of any dark-haired green eyed woman who looked his way.

She was craving him, and that morning had done nothing but rev her cravings up a notch. There was no climax for her and he hadn't bit her. She couldn't believe her train of thought. She didn't know how to get sensible Kyla back. And the idea of him with anyone else?

"Ah!" *Oh fuck.* She'd nicked her ankle with the razor and it was stinging.

A little red line trickled down her foot. Her eyes widened. She shoved the foot under the still running water.

Fuck, fuck, fuck! How could I be so stupid?

She stared at the bathroom door, feeling her heart pump loudly. On the other side of the door he was trying to control himself and she'd just split her fucking ankle open while shaving because she wasn't paying attention!

She kept the leg under the running water, praying the bleeding would stop fast and taking slow and deep breaths to try to settle herself down.

The bathroom door flew wide open, crashing loudly into the wall. Tristan's eyes were huge. They were still blue, but his mouth was

open. He looked absolutely livid. He obviously smelled it from outside the door!

Blue. Don't turn black, don't turn black!

She winced and applied pressure with a washcloth, dropping the
razor onto the floor, staring up at him horror-struck. His eyes landed
on the razor and then followed up to her face, almost in slow motion.

She raised her palm at him to halt him, "Sorry! It was an accident. Go, go, go! Hurry, get out. I'll get it to stop."

He fell to his knees beside the tub and put his head in his hands.

"Tristan," she whimpered, starting to tremble hard. "Go out. I'll
make it stop. Please."

He was shaking his head and taking slow and deep breaths.

Oh no.

Shaving your legs near a vampire was beyond dumb, of course it
was, but never in her life had she cut her legs shaving before.

I'm so fuckin' stupid. Don't turn gray, don't turn gray!

She shakily applied pressure tight to her ankle with a wet washcloth and prayed for the bleeding to stop. It was like time stood still.
Then he looked up at her. His face looked normal. His eyes looked
normal. She didn't know what to do so she just sat, wide-eyed. The
water was still running and the tub was only minutes away from over-
flowing. She held the washcloth tighter.

He leaned over and turned the taps off. She swallowed hard.

"Lift the cloth."

She didn't move. It was like she was paralyzed. Tristan huffed
in a, 'I'll do it myself' manner and leaned over and lifted her ankle
slightly and took the cloth from her hand. For a split second it
looked okay. Relief washed over her.

Then she saw the red dot spring forward again. She choked on
a sob, feeling fear grip her heart as it grew in diameter. She gripped
the side of the tub and braced the other hand against the tiled wall

to steady herself. Tristan leaned over and put the tip of his tongue to the spot. Kyla's eyes very nearly bulged from her head.

'Ahhh," he groaned loud as her blood touched his tongue and he leaned back for a second and exhaled in slow and staggered breaths. It seemed like that moment was suspended in time. Would he lunge and kill her? Would he be okay? He let go of her ankle and rose from a squat, up straight.

"Bed. Now," he commanded.

Huh?

He arched a brow at her, looking so unbelievably sexy she thought she might spontaneously combust. She felt a mixture of fear and desire surge through her at the exact same time. She was immobile.

"What part of *now* don't you understand?" He flashed a grin.

She gulped, got up, and not-so-steadily reached for the towel but he scooped her out of the tub before she got to it and in a nanosecond, she was on her back on the bed and his shirt was up and over his head. He spread her legs wide and first licked the ankle wound that was now punctuated by a fat droplet of blood and then his tongue traveled up her leg past her knee, up her inner thigh, and landed directly on her more-than-ready wet, hot, and very much wanting girlie parts.

She almost detonated on the spot. His mouth on her, down there, his eyes, filled with passion, looking very much like a man on a mission. Brilliant blazing blue and hungry, he didn't have black eyes. He didn't have gray skin. He seemed okay.

"Oh yeah, babe," she moaned. *Oh yes, yes, yes!*

"Let it go and come hard, baby. This is gonna be fast. I'm gonna bite as soon as you hit it."

She never would've guessed that a few words would take her over the edge like that but those, along with his tongue, and along with his unshaven jaw causing friction on her inner thighs did. They *so* did. His voice and his tongue lifted her to a celestial place and she free-fell into a gust of sensation that spurted everywhere. At what would've been the tail end of her climax he extended it by connecting with his teeth, right on that spot on her inner thigh where he'd bit her the very first time.

She felt the hum, a blooming, and then a tidal wave surged through her. At first it was painful, then sweet, and then confused, then dark and angry, and then soft and sweet again.

It was like an orchestra was in her veins and there were different instruments playing at varying tempos. Sweet and melodic harps, angry dueling violins; it alternated from pain to sweet pain to amazing. It was different. It was scary. It was exciting. She felt dizzy. She was spinning and spinning and her body started to tremble as she hit yet another peak and her mouth opened.

Sensation swirled as she looked down at the man she loved, loving every hair on his head, every tooth in his mouth, and every emotion he was nourishing her with. She had a moment of clarity.

He helps me feel; helps me want to feel.

She heard his zipper and then he grunted her name as he was about to thrust his cock into her.

"Wait," she breathed and flipped, pushed him onto his back, crawling backwards down his body, and took the tip of him into her mouth. She twirled her tongue around and then wrapped her lips tight and applied suction.

He let out a sexy groan and gently gripped the back of her head. Kyla couldn't take all of him in but used her hands to compensate for the areas that couldn't fit into her mouth. He seemed to be enjoying every minute of it but abruptly pulled back.

"Mm, Tristan..." she pouted; wanting him to finish that way -—wanting him to come apart under her.

"I need to be inside you. Now." He flipped her and then in an instant thrust deep into her, eased out, and then began a rhythm of depth and gyration. He slammed repeatedly into her, holding her face and staring into her eyes. She touched his face and then realized his eyes were turning black.

She gasped, "Oh, Tristan. Don't. Please, baby." She felt like the bottom was dropping out on her. *Oh fuck. Not now.*

"No, s'okay. I'm fine," he breathed reassuringly, and then his eyes were bluish and she felt anchored again. "I'm better than fine. Tell me you love me."

"I do. I love you."

"Tell me you're mine."

"I'm yours." Relief washed over her.

"Tell me you want me."

"I want you so much."

"Never leave me again."

"Okay, babe."

His voice went hoarse and his eyes went black again, "Never."

"Never."

"Tell me no one will ever fucking touch you but me. Ever!"

She gasped, fear spiking at his intensity, at how his eyes were gray. Dark gray.

"Tell me!" he demanded.

"Never. No one."

"No fucking one! You love me?" His voice softened. The look in his eyes was so soft.

"Yes."

"Say it again, baby."

"I love you." She caressed his face and his eyes were blue again.

"Again," it was a plea.

"I love you. I love you."

"Even though this is fucked up and I'm dangerous and I'm damned to hell?"

Her heart sank. "You're changing. It's not too late. You're not damned."

"I wish you were right. Dig your nails into my back. I'm going for your throat. Hang on tight."

"Are you sure?"

Would he be able to stop?

"Now, Kyla."

She grabbed his shoulders and held on tight. When he bit in, the same war flew through her veins, but even more powerfully. Possession, protectiveness, love, bliss, hunger. It was dizzying. She started to weep. She could taste rocky road ice cream. She could smell sugary marshmallows mixed with fire. Her veins and her core ebbed and flowed with pleasure and pain. He pounded and pounded and drank and drank, fingers digging into her hips. It felt so good. It felt so right. It felt like it was what she was made for. She was nothing but sensation, nothing but his.

"I really, *really* love you," she wept, and the orgasm gripped hard. He let go of her throat and arched his back as her nails dug in. His mouth was open, his face was ecstasy-filled, and his eyes were now blue flame-colored. He shuddered as he found his release.

"You're mine and I'm yours," he said tenderly and feathered kisses all over her face. "We're forever, princess."

She brushed her hair out of her eyes and wrapped her body around his, feeling light and airy, feeling whole.

"That was..." she started, but couldn't finish. *Fucking amazing!*

She looked at his face. His eyes were closed, but he had a little smile on his lips. She touched the cleft on his chin and planted a kiss on his full soft lips.

"Your eyes kept changing colour. They were like disco lights," she whispered.

His eyes opened. They were his usual blue. He frowned.

"We made it," she whispered, "We survived."

His expression relaxed, and he let out a sigh. "We did."

He pulled her closer. "A million tonnes just lifted off my shoulders," he said.

If only that was the whole war.

"Talk to me. Tell me what was going on inside of you. Tell me what else I need to know."

"Want a drink?" He went to get up.

"I'll get it. Gotta wash up, anyway. You? Water, Coke, grape?"

"Water."

She pulled away and then spotted blood on her nails. She gasped and looked at them.

"Tristan!" she exclaimed, "Turn over."

His back was scratched and bleeding in a few places, only lightly, but there *were* distinct nail marks.

"You're bleeding!" *Oh shit!*

"Shhh, it's okay. Let's go wash your hands." He jumped up and guided her to the bathroom. He turned the taps on and soaped her hands up, rubbing them gently, rinsing them under the water.

"Tigress," he purred in her ear. She felt the heat rise in her cheeks.

"Keep rinsing," he told her, kissed her temple, ran his tongue from her clavicle up to her earlobe, and then he disappeared back into the bedroom.

She let the hot water run over her hands for a good 2-3 more minutes, scrubbing her hands and using her nails to scrape under her other nails.

Tristan's blood? Wow, scary.

She went to her purse and pulled out a small bottle of hand sanitizer she'd always carried and saturated her fingertips with it, then went back to the washroom and got cleaned up, then got drinks from their bags and put extras into the mini fridge and then passed him a bottle and opened a can of grape soda pop for herself. After she guzzled half of it, she threw herself back on the bed, feeling exhausted.

She examined her nails again, "You okay?"

"So much more than okay." His voice was husky. He leaned over and let out a little growl into her ear.

She smirked and lifted her leg up in the air and then examined the ankle.

"I only shaved a quarter of a leg. Either I need to finish or not wear shorts tomorrow."

He touched the tiny, now lightly scabbed-over, razor wound.

"It was the perfect amount. I smelled it and rushed in here before I could stop myself and then I felt something in me, something lifting my confidence. I tasted it and it was a tiny amount, but I felt stronger, yet I was in control and knew I could handle a real feed. I thought it'd push it back by drinking, that maybe that's why it was so close to the surface, because I hadn't fed from you. But, I'm different. It's all different. It's not two personalities, I'm one. But, I'm different. I have to get to know myself again. I can't explain, but I need to know my limits; right now I feel like a stranger to myself. Stronger but a stranger. Does that make sense? I don't know what'd happen if you got your period ,but I'm closer to being in control now than I was."

She ran her fingers through his hair and nuzzled in. "At least we have time. Thank God. We're going to figure this out, Tristan."

"We are." He kissed her forehead.

"Let's run, Kyla. Let's go out for a run. Now."

"Really? I'm shattered."

"I feel like a billion bucks. A hundred billion bucks."

"I won't be able to keep up. My body feels like spaghetti. That was a seriously intense session there, Mr. Vampire."

"Follow me in the car."

"Seriously?"

"Seriously. I need to run and can't leave you alone. Follow me in the car, okay?"

AN HOUR LATER THEY were back at the motel. Tristan didn't feel the need to sweep the room before relaxing, saying he smelled nothing new, and Kyla was relieved. She was spent. She collapsed onto the bed.

They'd driven to a highway back road and then he'd gotten out and jogged while she drove slowly behind him, with the blinkers on as he ran, praying no police would spot them. It was uneventful, thankfully.

"I'm gettin' a shower," he said, "Leaving the door open. Don't go to sleep yet. If anyone knocks or anything odd happens, you come into the bathroom immediately, okay? Anything odd at all. I'll be fast."

"Okay," she mumbled and yawned.

He leaned over and grabbed her chin, "Okay?" his eyes were dead serious.

"I said okay," she was irritated.

"You don't seem to understand the gravity here," he growled.

"No, Tristan, gravity understood; I get it. Just leave the door open."

She did not like his tone, nor the aggressive intensity coming off him. She grabbed his wrist and pried him away from her chin with a pointed stare and very pointed thoughts about being manhandled.

He took a breath, "You don't know how dangerous it'd be if he got to you."

"Uh, yeah, I can imagine. Do you want me freaking out while you're in there? How's that going to make you feel? Want me to come sit in the bathroom while you shower?"

"Yeah, I do. Shower with me."

"Too tired. Just be fast."

She curled under the blanket and flicked the TV on. She heard the shower turn on. He left the door open and the shower curtain open, so he could see her.

"You're drenching the floor," she called, yawning, staring at his naked body.

Yum.

She fought sleep, watching his strong corded arms and large strong hands move up and down his sudsy body, but even his personification of male beauty wasn't enough to keep her awake after those earth-shattering orgasms and the fact that she'd had to drive behind him running for all that time.

By the time he got into bed a few minutes later, she'd been dozing. He got in bed beside her, smelling like soap and shampoo and toothpaste, and feeling all warm and hard. He cupped her between the legs and slid one, then two fingers inside as he tongued her earlobe.

He was being more possessive than ever. She imagined it must be because someone was after them and out to take her from him. Maybe it was the beast inside of him, too, the addiction to the nectar. She moaned, feeling so tired, but not able to resist. She arched back into him and parted her legs wider.

After a quick romp and a spectacular climax where he did all the work, she went to get up to go wash up.

"Need to pee?" He asked.

She shook her head. "No, just need to clean-up."

"No," he murmured, "Don't wash me away."

"Mmm-kay."

She sighed happily and nuzzled in and drifted off to sleep wrapped tight in his embrace. As they fell asleep, her thoughts drifted back to when he first started to explain what he knew of their bond. He'd said a woman with enchanted blood bonded to a vampire would fight to the death before letting another vampire feed from her.

After what happened tonight, after the idea of another woman with him and how it made her feel, what it made her want to do...would that turn Kyla into some sort of warrior if Liam Donavan *did* find them? She didn't want to think on that now.

She was so relieved that they'd gotten the awkwardness out of the way --—feeding and making love. And that it hadn't gone horribly wrong after all. It had been more than frightening when his eyes kept changing, like he was teetering between personalities. But, it had gone okay. She fell into slumber with a small hope that maybe things would be okay after all.

4

"WE MAKE ONE ANOTHER feel," she whispered to him, rubbing her thumb pad up and down the cleft on his chin. They were in bed, lying on their sides and facing one another.

The sun was starting to rise, and she'd woken up to him watching her sleep. She'd nuzzled into his chest, then looked up into his eyes and they'd stared at one another for a long time before they started to talk.

"I'm not whole if I'm not with you," he answered, "I feel so much now."

"Me either. And me, too. I used to bury my feelings, ignore them, run from them, do whatever I had to do to not stop and feel them. Not now," she said, knowing that her emotions didn't just impact her; they impacted him, too.

"Good. I feel your feelings. They're amazing. You should feel them, too. What I like best about feeling your feelings is how you feel when you feel *my* feelings. Now, *that's* incredible." He traced her ear with the ridge of his thumb, "It's like mirroring."

"Mirroring?"

"Ever put a mirror in front of another mirror and it just reflects endlessly?"

"Yeah," she smiled. She knew just what he meant.

"That's what it feels like when you feel what I feel."

"Some of them, my feelings, they aren't fun, though." She winced. "I've gone from pushing emotion away to obsessing about everything. I'm driving myself cuckoo."

"It'll get better. I promise to do my best to keep the seesaw leaning in the fun direction, as much as possible, okay?"

"'Kay. What's the plan today?"

"We get as much road behind us as possible. Tomorrow night, we'll be in Southern Nevada. We'll stop there and stay the night."

"Vegas?" Her eyes lit up and she sat up. Las Vegas had been something she'd always wanted to do. She loved the idea that many hotels had different themes, so it was like you were in Paris, then in New York City, and then in Rio, and then in Egypt, and then medieval times and all in the same day if you wanted. Shows, slot machines, doing the touristy thing. It sounded fun. Sounded normal.

"If you want. Some fun?"

"Uh, hello? Yes!" Kyla was excited.

"Alright. Then we'll hang out there for the night and then get back on the road the next day."

"Or maybe a day or three or three hundred after that?" Kyla raised her eyebrows.

Tristan pulled her on top of him and kissed her forehead. "Maybe we should just get the whole Adrian thing over with. And besides, he's waiting. Let's not prolong the inevitable. We can go back to Vegas afterwards. Maybe find a little Elvis chapel?" He raised his eyebrows.

What the fuck?

Kyla's heart skipped a beat. She chose to ignore that comment, unsure if it was a joke or what and definitely not ready to even think along those lines at this moment.

"Or..." Kyla pulled away and sat back up, "We avoid going to Adrian's for as long as possible in case it goes horribly wrong."

"Not very pragmatic to procrastinate, sweetheart."

"I'm not CEO material like you, I guess. I'm totally fine with prolonging and procrastination where *this* situation is concerned."

He laughed. He was trying to keep it light; so was she. The Elvis wedding chapel thing must've been a joke.

Must have.

But, there was an undercurrent in the air trying to grab her and drag her back down due to her fear of the unknown.

She leaned over and started scrubbing his cheek with her nails. "When are you gonna shave this off, anyway? You're quickly going from rugged and sexy to not too far off mountain man territory and I gotta say: not feeling it."

She stood up, about to go to the washroom, but he reached over, hooked his arm around her waist, and hauled her back onto the bed and pinned her.

In truth, he was totally sexy and highly fuckable with his unshaven face. Maybe even more so.

"Yeah, well you're one to talk with your partly shaved leg, mountain woman! Maybe we should both just head for the hills and live in the backwoods with our hairy selves, huh?"

He planted a big wet raspberry on her belly. She squealed and tried to get away. He started to tickle her.

She squealed again, "No, no, no, don't! I can't, I can't handle tickling, I can't, I..."

He stopped for a second, "Oh...have I found another one of your weaknesses, maybe?"

"Eek!" She dashed off the bed, but he caught her and pinned her on the adjacent bed.

"No tickling, please. I can't breathe when I'm tickled, I—-"

Something flashed in her memory, ugly scenes from a foster home. She pushed it back. Tristan must've felt it because he stopped instantly.

"You okay?" He was suddenly serious.

She nodded and tried not to give that ugliness any further thought.

"Tickling is not my weakness." She poked at his chest, backing off that bed and then backed up toward the bathroom.

"Oh no?"

He was smiling, but she could feel that he was holding back, unsure about her reaction to the tickling. He stalked toward her.

"Dimples..." She poked at his naked chest again, accusingly, "Now *those* are my kryptonite. Show me those and you can have anything you want. Any. Thing."

"Anything?"

He gave her a glowing gorgeous smile, dimples on display, then caged her against the wall beside the bathroom door and ravished her mouth with his. She raked her fingers through his hair and linked her leg around the back of his knee, grinding into him.

"You are insatiable!" He hoisted her over his shoulder and whacked her rear end before putting her back on the bed and hovering over her. His smile was so bright he lit up the room.

She fingered a dimple, "I'm sorry that I made you worry about me when I left. If it helps, I was a mess the whole time we were apart."

"That helps," he said sheepishly. "We need to talk about everything that happened."

He laid down on the bed beside her and spooned her close.

"You've got stuff to tell me, too."

"I will. You first." He touched the back of her neck with his lips.

"Will you?" she asked, dubious.

"I will," he answered softly.

"Sam reacted first. He turned gray and shot you as soon as I stepped into that cage. Why didn't that ever happen before in public? Is that something I'll have to worry about from now on?"

"Dunno yet. I'm guessing something happened after you bonded with me. Even before then. After the first time I fed, I think. But, especially after the nectar."

"So... nothing will ever be the same."

He shook his head, "Not likely."

"I can't ever have my period again. I need a hysterectomy to keep myself alive. I'll never have babies. I mean, I never knew if I wanted kids, but to know that I'll never..." she choked up. Then she realized she'd said all that out loud instead of just in her head.

"Shh, one day at a time. It doesn't make sense to just jump to conclusions." He put his palm to her face.

Yeah, he might not want me to get a hysterectomy. If I stop my periods, the nectar stops.

She stared off into space for a minute.

He shook his head, "Don't start that. If I haven't proven to you by now that I love you..."

"Get outta my head."

"Kyla. Baby. I hear you louder and clearer than ever. I can't help that. And it's not just in your head, it's written all over your face, too."

"I have to pee."

She got up.

He gave her a skeptical look.

"I do! I was on my way there a minute ago. I guess you can't read my bladder yet? Sucks to be you."

He sighed and pinched the bridge of his nose, so she huffed as she marched past him to the bathroom.

When she climbed back into the bed he was on the bed, eyes on her.

"So, Sam?" He urged her to continue.

"He shot you. Before you did anything. The second he saw me his fangs shot out and his face turned gray and he attacked you first, before lunging at me, even. He saw you as a threat. I felt a gush of bleeding and then you reacted. But first he shot you and then you shot and hit him, and he went down. Then you, you like...lunged for me. I tried to get away, but I couldn't. And then it got sexual."

She took a big gulp of water, "Ugh. I need coffee. Badly. I won't even try this in-room coffee. Can we?"

WHEN THEY GOT BACK with coffee and pastries she took her period prevention pill and he urged her to continue.

She sat on the bed and he pulled her down against him. She put her cheek on his chest.

"It was sexual for me because of what you were doing but for you, it seemed like it was just about the blood. I'm sure I was about to die. You were going down on me while choking me and drinking and then you let me go and you made this roaring sound and then grabbed me and I could swear you were going to end my life, but I told you I loved you and your eyes changed and your temperature began to rise, but I didn't know if it was the tranquilizer. You passed out.

You passed out and I didn't know what to do, but I looked at Sam and thought, 'I can't make *him* not kill me with nice words and nice thoughts', so I ran. I ran because I was afraid of him and afraid of you because I didn't know what stopped you. I know I wanted to be what stopped you, but I didn't know if that was naïve of me to think that way, so I just left. I didn't know what I'd do, how I'd get over you, how I'd even survive without you, and with the possibility of getting killed by another vampire, and I've been in the pits of despair and with serious withdrawals or something, but that's—-"

He cut her off by tipping her chin up for a soft kiss, then said, "I heard you, heard your voice from far away. I must've been unconscious, but you said you loved me in my dreams. You had this bright aura and I could feel your emotions stronger than ever, but I thought I was dreaming and then it all went black. I woke up and you were gone, and I had all kinds of blood on me. I couldn't feel you.

There was gnawing inside me, this overpowering urge to inflict pain because I couldn't find you or feel you. Sam almost took the brunt of it, but he talked me down. I knew he went off. He and I talked it out. He said as soon as you stepped out of the panic room the aroma was like meat cooking to a half-starved half-crazed man.

His instinct kicked in and I was the threat he had to remove to get to
you.

Just like I reacted reflexively to the barrier between you and me,
the locks. He talked me down... I came close to ripping his throat
out, but he convinced me he could help, that he wouldn't come near
you until he could get some of that tonic from Adrian and test it.
I can read intentions, I can taste lies, even more now than before. I
didn't taste any lies with him. I'm still being cautious, but I believe
him.

And anyway, I don't think you just walked out, Kyla, the more I
think about it, I think you shut down. I should've been able to feel
you. You were still in the city when I woke up, I checked everything
out when I started to look at you and timing-wise, you weren't that
far. You were in the city for a few hours after I woke up before you
caught that flight. If you weren't sleeping I'm pretty sure you found a
way to turn it off. Or maybe my body turned you off. I don't know."

"I didn't sleep. Not for two days. And I *was* numb, Tristan.
Scared and numb."

He cuddled her close, "Okay. We're gonna figure this out. I will.
I will stop at nothing."

Their eyes locked.

"Nothing," he repeated and ran his thumb across her cheekbone.

They stared at one another for a beat and then he said, "Let's get
going."

They passed the maid as they left. She was pushing her cleaning
cart toward them and when she saw Tristan her mouth dropped. She
looked at him with sexual hunger, but it was as if she'd never seen
him in her life. Kyla felt anger rise in her. Tristan threw an arm over
her shoulder and hauled her closer.

"Easy, princess; keep those claws sheathed."

Kyla made a "grr" sound as they passed the woman on the way to
the front office to check out.

He chuckled.

"TELL ME ABOUT KOVAC Capital," Kyla suggested. They'd been on the road for a few hours and she figured it was a good time to learn more about him, about his life, more about the obstacles they were facing.

Tristan was driving, looking handsome as always, with his strong hands on the wheel, hair blowing in the breeze, his eyes hidden behind sunglasses. He was wearing cargo jean shorts, sandals, and a black t-shirt. Kyla wore a racerback apple green A-line sun dress. It was hot out. Her curly hair was up in a messy bun and she had flip flops on her feet.

"It's a company. It makes money. I've got a pretty traditional-looking executive position." He shrugged.

"Traditional-looking, *looking* being the operative phrase? You said you also work to keep vampires secret. I'm sure you have stories you could tell. Close calls?"

He nodded. "I keep money flowing in and I work to stop threats, keep our secrets safe. I'm on a few councils."

"Is the money made honestly?"

"We do use our influence in some areas," he admitted.

"You're not giving much away..."

"This stuff is irrelevant." He shrugged.

"What happens when you get the next promotion?" she asked.

He shook his head, "More autonomy. I report to Claudio now and wouldn't. I'd have more direct contact with other leaders. Some larger scale decisions." He shrugged again and then turned up the radio. His jaw was tight. Kyla's spidey senses were tweaked.

"You don't wanna talk about this?" She turned the radio back down.

She saw a muscle flexing in his jaw. He didn't answer.

"You keep trying to keep me in the dark, Tristan. That shit won't fly with me."

His mouth tightened.

"Seriously," she muttered.

"The last thing I need is to worry about how you'll deal with shit. It's shit that's irrelevant. I'm president of a company. I'm in a high-ranking position on a council that runs the company and that works with others to protect vampires from being discovered. My council works with other councils as a collective, to protect our secrets. End of."

"It's *that* bad? The stuff you keep from me?"

He shook his head. "We know how well it went when you knew I had to deal with that vamp with a taste for kids. You really want more of that?"

"Is there a lot that's *that* bad?"

"There's a lot of a variety of things and some of it you don't want to know, believe me. And it's stuff that just doesn't factor right now. There's no need to add more stress on top of everything else."

"You've been treating me like a mushroom, Tristan."

He didn't reply, and she guessed by his expression that under his sunglasses he'd likely rolled his eyes.

"Keeping me in the dark, feeding me shit..." she added.

He shook his head. "Baby, listen..." he started but then he didn't finish.

"I'm on a need-to-know basis with you. I have been since we met. I understand that there's stuff that's irrelevant, but you need to *get* that I'm not okay with being the 'little lady' that you keep in the dark."

He roughly ripped his sunglasses off and glared at her, "And with everything we're dealing with, Kyla, I *need you* to *know* that you can trust me. There's shit you *don't* need to know, stuff that doesn't factor for you and me. Trust that I am doing everything I can for us. It's all for us."

He made a sudden lane change and laid on the horn for a sec, frustrated at something on the road that Kyla hadn't even noticed. She suspected it was more about him being frustrated with her than with other motorists.

"Who you are, what you do, who we're dealing with in terms of your colleagues slash compadres, or whatever... it factors."

"Yeah? You find out shit you don't like; you don't get to leave. Then you have to deal with shit you won't want to deal with and it puts distance between us. Why would I do that to you, to us?"

"I don't get to leave," she said with a sneer, "*Nice*."

He got louder, his driving got more erratic. "No matter what you find out about me, you don't get to leave me, you know this. You're mine and I am not ever letting go of that. So, princess, I get to make the fuckin' choice about whether or not I want you burying bitterness about the things I've done, the things I did before I knew you, the things I have to do to protect you, the people I have no choice but to deal with. I choose *no*."

"I'd rather deal than—-"

"No! Believe me, you wouldn't rather deal. And I'm not the same as I was before I met you, so giving you a bunch of ugly details doesn't give you an inkling of who I am now. I need you to trust that I'll keep you safe, that I'll share knowledge about Kovac and about my past if it helps us, but I will *not* burden you with shit that will do nothing but hurt you. There's nothing productive about you learning about any of that. Nothing but pain for you if you do."

Kyla folded her arms across her chest, which was burning with emotion. "Don't call me princess when you're yelling at me," she said, meaning to come across pissed-off but instead coming across hoarsely, her voice cracking.

The anger drained from his face. He reached across the centre console and took her hand. She yanked it away and re-folded her arms across her chest.

The next three hours were filled with loaded silence and if it was possible to shoot daggers at him with her brain, that's what she was doing the entire time, although she was doing it while also trying to stop herself from agreeing with him because he had a point.

Her stress would filter through to become his stress and they both had enough of that already. She hated it when her brain reasoned with her that he was right because she almost always came to that conclusion after a temper tantrum.

Arrival in their next motel room was punctuated by her slamming the bathroom door so she could take a long shower and get a minute to herself. The room was a lot like the last place. It was a typical single storey motor inn with drive up rooms that contained two beds, small sitting area, TV, and a bathroom.

This one had its décor done in dusty rose and forest green, it was very 1980's, but it had been the only motel for a long stretch of road and she was glad they'd finally stopped. She wished they could just get a plane to get there. But then again, that would bring reality to her sooner and that reality could be worse than anything they'd endured so far.

Approximately 45 seconds into her shower he stepped in with her. She huffed. He stepped close and put his hands on her soapy hips. She spun around so her back was to him and got her face under the shower stream. He gripped her hips more aggressively and spun her back around to face him. She looked down, meaning to aim her gaze on her feet but in front of her was his chest, abs, and his impressively erect penis so she instead aimed her gaze on the ceiling. He took her by the chin. She shrugged him off and tried to spin around again, but he pinned her against the wall, hips against her, hands on her shoulders.

"Princess," he said softly, pleadingly.

Kyla's heart sank.

"I need you, baby," he whispered against her temple and then his hands gripped her rear end. His lips found hers. She wanted to pull away. She almost pulled away. She was so *fuming* mad at him. But, he gave her a smile and showed dimples and so she glared at him.

"Pulling out the big guns? You play dirty," she grumbled, poking a dimple.

He laughed, then advanced and got her earlobe in his mouth and his fingers tightened on her ass. "I'll take every advantage I can get. And I'll show you a big gun. Let's play dirty. Together."

His hand slid down her ass and his fingers slipped between her cheeks and found her centre.

She whimpered. He looked supremely pleased.

Yeah, she wasn't happy about his secrecy, but she knew he needed her, needed to feed, and she also knew that she'd get a release, too, and she needed it right now, big time. With connecting with him and the subsequent orgasm, she'd get his emotions and she'd get to purge the tension for at least a little while.

"I need to be inside you," he said against her throat, kissing her on the collar bone. "Need you so bad."

A wave of arousal crashed over her. She hooked a leg around his hip and said, "I need to be inside you, too."

He took his cock into his hand and ran the tip over her clit and then slid it along her slit.

Then, suddenly, she lost sensation as he started to back away. She whimpered and thrust her hips forward, seeking maximum contact. She got it. He gave her a knowing smile as he got the tip inside her and backed her against the shower wall, moaning as he rolled his hips upward until he'd slid in, right to the final inch. He grabbed her hand and planted a kiss on her palm and then planted kisses in a line up from her wrist to her shoulder, then sank his teeth into her shoulder while rotating his hips, hard.

She grabbed handfuls of his hair with both hands and shuddered a stuttered breath, feeling him inside her physically as well as emotionally. Tristan drank for a beat and then kissed her shoulder, shut the water off, and hoisted her up so her legs were around his waist and he carried her out of the bathroom to the closest bed.

As her back touched down on the mattress he unfastened her legs from his waist and threw them up over his shoulders and stared into her eyes. She was on fire with desire, inside her head she was screaming MORE.

More fucking, more drinking. More closeness. More.

He ran his hand down her leg, ran his tongue across his full bottom lip, and she gave him a pleading look. He smiled and caressed her cheek.

"Tristan, please," she whined, knowing that begging and that saying his name would have an effect. A split second later he thrust his pelvis forward and slammed in, to the root. His eyes were blue, but he looked so intense, so determined, so pissed off. Kyla let out a shuddering moan and panic spiked.

"More begging," he demanded.

"Please, Tristan. Please fuck me. Please bite me. Now."

"Mm..." He sank his teeth sank into her calf and he moaned as the blood started to flow. She started to feel what he felt. He felt hunger, voracious hunger; hunger so intense it was like no emotion she'd ever felt from him before.

"More," she moaned.

Take it.

Take it all...

He ploughed into her harder and harder while drinking and rubbing her just where she needed it and after he shuddered out a "Baby...." he then kissed the bites.

When he finally came, he grunted so loud that it gave her goose-bumps all over.

Using all the strength she could muster, she crawled under the blankets, closed her eyes, and then slipped into a deep sleep with her body against his. It'd only been just getting dark when they checked in and although Tristan had fed from Kyla, Kyla hadn't had anything for dinner, but they slept straight through until morning.

She woke up to blissful sensations. Tristan was feasting on her throat, rubbing her clit with his fingertips. Around and around his fingers went and she could hear him swallowing.

"Take it, baby. It's all yours," she whispered and caressed his cheek.

They hadn't talked further, hadn't worked anything out, but she knew she had to give a little on the issue of him guarding truths from her.

For now.

Regardless of the fact that it went against her grain to simply let someone else call the shots, she had to think smart here.

He could feel what she felt, meaning her stress would multiply whatever stress he was already feeling. Plus, he was right, she hadn't reacted very well when he ordered that *Frankie the vampire* be 'ended'.

Tristan was the man she loved, a man who'd travelled 3000 miles to get to her and he was the one trying to keep her safe. She would just have to take things a day at a time and hope that he'd feel safe enough with her to open up to her in time. Maybe she didn't need to know all the bad stuff he'd done in the past, but she felt like she *did* need more info than what she had gotten so far.

Maybe she didn't need more confirmation that vampires were more dangerous, deadly, calculating, and callous, especially after seeing Sam steal Julia from her life, after seeing Sam shoot Tristan with a tranquilizer gun without a second thought, after knowing Rebecca had snapped Julia's neck out of sheer jealousy, and after coming to terms with being Tristan's prisoner, after his employees had stolen her from her life in order to be food and a warm body for him that night.

She was on the verge of another climax. He was hungry. So hungry.

"Love me?" she heard him ask but he sounded far away.

She felt spinny. "Yeah."

"You gonna come for me, baby?"

Sensation took over and her orgasm was explosive, so explosive it hurt. As she was coming back down to earth she looked into his beautiful love-filled eyes and then Tristan started to go fuzzy.

SHE WAS BEING SHAKEN gently but his voice was filled with urgency, "Kyla!"

Tristan was holding her up and tipping orange juice into her mouth, "Drink baby, drink."

She drank a little.

"What's wrong with me?" she mumbled. She felt so weak. She felt lightheaded and her body was numb. Her insides felt hollow.

"I took too much. Drink more juice. Fuck, I'm so sorry. I'm gonna run and get you something to eat from across the street. I'll be as fast as I can."

Kyla took a few mouthfuls and then Tristan put the orange juice bottle beside her and dashed out the door. She closed her eyes and then what seemed like an instant later, she felt the sensation of being lifted.

"Baby," Tristan was holding her in his arms and he sounded panicked, "please wake up."

She opened her eyes. They felt so heavy. She blinked a few times. Her mouth was so dry.

"Princess?"

"Heyyy. My Prince," she smiled.

She felt a little bit like she was drunk.

"Thank fuck."

"My beautiful vampire-prince boyfriend."

"Baby, drink."

"Hm?"

"Drink this."

"You're beautiful, Tristan. I can't believe you love me."

"Shh, drink. Tell me after you're better how much you love me."

He put a water bottle to her mouth. After a few sips, he went fuzzy.

Then later, she didn't know how much later, she felt something else against her lips.

It tasted like chocolate milk but there was a weird taste in it. It was a meal replacement shake. She'd drank enough of these while she was apart from him that she never wanted to drink them again.

"Yuck."

"Keep drinking, princess. You need nutrients."

As soon as she swallowed it down it came right back up and she projectile vomited on both the bedspread and the rug.

Tristan carried her to the adjacent bed and got her a cool cloth for her face.

"Stay sitting up. Don't go back to sleep, Kyla."

She watched him stripping the other bed and then he started going fuzzy again.

"Baby, please try to stay awake for me?"

"Fuzzy..." She passed out.

Later, she didn't know how much later, she heard him on the phone,

"No. She skipped dinner.

A few times. Some big feeds. She's been coming in and out. A bit delirious. Puking.

Fuck. I know.

Okay, alright.

You don't have to fucking tell me that, alright?

I'll call you back.

No. Fuck.

Whatever.

Bye."

She was on her side. He was beside her, sitting, his hand on her back, rubbing sweetly. She drifted back under.

Then she woke again, and he was talking to a woman in a maid's outfit. She was handing him a paper bag. A phone rang. She started to wade in to sharper consciousness slowly.

She heard him say, "Right, we'll be there in a few hours."

"Where?" she asked softly.

He lifted her hair off her face gently.

"Hey, how're you feeling?" He looked so relieved.

"Hey. Really tired. Thirsty. I have to pee."

"I've packed up. I'm gonna carry you to the car."

"Why? What's going on?" she felt so groggy.

"I've chartered a plane to get us the rest of the way. It's risky but this is the best way for us to get to Adrian's quickly after what's happened."

"What's happened?"

"Fuck, baby..."

"What?" She tried to sit up. She felt so weak. Her head was pounding.

Tristan looked tormented.

"It was an accident. You didn't eat, didn't replenish your strength and I fed too much. Your emotions kept urging me to take more and I..." he shook his head, "I had trouble stopping."

Kyla felt spinny. Tristan passed her a bottle of water.

"Just a few sips. Go slow," he said. "Take this." He passed her three different pills with a bottle of Gatorade.

"What are they?"

"B vitamin. Multivitamin. Gravol, to help you keep it down."

It seemed, after a few sips and a few breaths, that it would stay down so she got up to go to the washroom, feeling really weak.

She caught a glimpse of herself in the mirror. Yuck. The horror! Her hair was a rat's nest. Her skin was ghostly white.

"You put clothes on me?" she called out.

"Twice. You've been burning up, cold sweats. It was bad. You were out over 24 hours, close to a day and a half."

She poked her head out from the bathroom and gave him a small smile. He didn't return it. He looked stressed.

"Can I get a shower before we go? My hair is like a rat's nest."

"Yeah, we have a few minutes if you're quick. I'll join you. I don't want you alone in case you faint again."

The shower was all business. Tristan was attentive, though, washing her back, scrubbing her hair while she leaned, sometimes against him, sometimes against the wall, still feeling weak.

She got out and then he did his own washing while she dried off, sitting on the toilet lid. After she got dressed in black short cargo shorts and a new red tank top with a crocheted light cardigan hoodie, he loaded the rental car with their bags and she told him she was fine to walk, so he held her hand as she followed him to the front desk to check out.

Half an hour later, they were at an airport and then not long after that they were on a small plane with a dozen seats, just the two of them with the pilot and co-pilot.

He was quiet, staring out into the abyss outside the small window, still holding her hand. He hadn't let go. He hadn't cracked a smile. He was so tense that she felt herself cowering at the overpowering tension emanating off him.

"Hey?" she asked after a long while.

He looked at her. His face was filled with pain.

"You okay?" she asked.

"Yeah. How you feelin'?" He straightened, and his expression relaxed a little.

"Okay. Like I have a hangover a little. But okay."

He nodded but flexed his jaw a few times.

"What's happening, anyway?"

He shrugged, "Just wanna get you there and figure out what's what. I don't like what happened. I... got carried away. You hardly ate anything that day. You were pissed off at me in the car, so you barely ate anything, the way you tend to do when you're pissed, and even though you skipped dinner I took a big feed and then again in the morning, and ..." He shook his head, looked supremely pissed. "Your body wanted it, wanted me to keep going and I listened so I lost control. I can't let that happen again, no matter what emotions you give off. You need to look after yourself and I need to look after you. I need to check my fuckin' self."

He ran his hand through his hair. "I was so fucking scared," he said in barely a whisper, "This last day has been one of the longest in my life. Called Adrian. He recommended I rush you there. That's what we're doing. I don't like the breadcrumb trail with Liam on the loose and I sure as fuck don't like Adrian getting any sort of upper hand before I can truly suss things out, but fuck. I've tried to cover my tracks. Hopefully, it worked."

She winced.

"I'm so fucking sorry, princess. So sorry."

He put his head down in a defeated posture.

She snuggled into him. "I'm okay."

"Barely."

She put a hand on his neck and tried to give him a little massage. The tension didn't leave his body. At all.

"I've gotta stretch my legs and powder my nose. Is that the bathroom over there?"

Tristan waved in the direction of the washroom. She kissed him on the cheek and whispered, "I'm okay, babe. I am."

He nodded but didn't smile. She gave his bicep a squeeze and made her way to the bathroom.

After doing her business as the toilet flushed she glanced in the direction of the bowl, and at that glimpse she flinched. Was that a reddish streak on the disappearing toilet tissue? She did a double take, but it was too late. The toilet had emptied.

"Oh my god!" she gasped and yanked her clothes back down and got a wad of toilet paper and dabbed and then looked. Nothing.

Was that her mind playing tricks or was her period back? She stood there, heart thudding hard against her chest wall, freaking right out.

She wiped again trying to dip in a little. Nothing on the toilet paper.

She righted her clothes, zipped up and stood still, looking in the mirror, handfuls of her hair in her hands, having a total freak out.

There was a knock at the door and then she heard Tristan's voice, "What's wrong?"

He obviously felt her fear.

She was afraid to open the door. What if she set him off, what if she was about to get her period? He handled feeding, but what'd happen if he was faced with her menstrual blood again?

If that was the start, then within a very short time she'd be gushing again. He'd said she'd been out for over a day. Did she miss the dose of the period prevention pill? How the heck would she survive on a tiny plane up in the air if Tristan transformed to black-eyed gray hulky vamp? She'd be dead, the pilot and co-pilots would probably be killed, and then the plane would go down and kill Tristan, too.

Fuck!

"Kyla!"

The lock thunked open.

Shit!

"Tristan, wait!" she shouted, pointing at the door stupidly, as if he could see her pointy finger, "Stay there. I'm okay, just wait a second."

She leaned against the door, unzipped, got more toilet paper and checked again.

Nothing.

"I need to know what the fuck is happening!"

She opened the door but just peeked out.

"I thought I saw blood in the toilet. I don't know, though. It was as it was disappearing down the drain. I'm not sure."

His eyes went round, but remained blue. His skin tone was normal. Nothing was changing with him other than him appearing concerned. Very concerned.

She watched him a beat. "Did I miss a dose of that pill to stop my period?"

He shook his head, "No. I got it into you and you didn't throw up that time. You haven't thrown up since."

She winced. "Barely even been a week since it stopped? I thought we'd have a month..."

"You don't know for sure if it was blood?"

She shook her head, "No. I thought it might be, but the toilet was flushing when I saw what might've been blood, but I don't know for sure. I'm not sure. A plane'll be a very very bad place to be if this is what it is, and it sets you off again!"

"Fuck." He squeezed his eyes shut tight

After a beat he shook it off, "Okay, we land soon. Come sit down and let me think for a minute."

She hesitated, "Let me check one more time. Get me my purse? I've got tampons in there. I'll put one in, just in case. Maybe it'd stop it from coming out, stop you from scenting? I dunno. It's worth a try."

He nodded, "Good idea."

She shut the door.

When he returned with her purse she checked again and nothing. She put a tampon in. She walked back to him and cautiously sat.

Kyla's heart was racing. She hoped and prayed that she was mistaken with what she thought she saw, that the nectar was not about to make another entrance. She hadn't been crampy, no zits or anything like that that often accompanied a period. Maybe she hadn't seen what she thought she'd seen.

Tristan fidgeted until they were told that they had to buckle up for landing.

When they got out into the airport he said, "I'm putting you in a hotel room while I figure out whether or not Adrian's is safe. I'll get us disposable phones. If you start bleeding, you call me, and we'll go from there."

He hailed a cab and got her to a ritzy hotel. He checked in under an alias and then left to get a rental car and head to Adrian's. He did this with focus, despite Kyla feeling like the world crumbling around her was imminent. When she was finally alone with her bags, with the rest of Tristan's bug out bag money, just in case (he'd insisted), with two large boxes of super tampons that the concierge had delivered, and with a disposable phone that had been programmed with Tristan's disposable phone's number and thankfully, no sign of bleeding, she collapsed onto the king-sized bed and took slow breath after slow breath.

He'd kissed her sweet and long, running fingers through her hair and holding her close before he left, "I'll see you soon, okay? As soon as I can."

She'd nodded, feeling emotional.

"Order room service. Eat. Don't leave the room. Take the vitamins. If I'm not back by morning, take the hormone pill, too. I'll talk to the concierge and make sure they know to get you whatever you need."

"Be safe," she'd pleaded, worrying, hoping, praying he wasn't walking into some sort of a trap.

He'd kissed her again, "I love you."

"I love you, too."

And then he was gone.

She was alone.

Wow.

Alone.

Weird.

He trusted her. He wasn't afraid she'd run. Or, maybe he was scared to death she would but had no choice. She was very apprehensive about what might be next. She had a bad feeling, but she was trying to shake it off.

When she undressed to take a bath, she noticed a red thread on her stomach, and another one fell onto the floor when she was changing. The new tank top? Could a red piece of thread have been what went down the toilet bowl in the plane? Maybe all this panic was for nothing. She was still planning on watching vigilantly to be sure.

She took a long bath and then ordered a pizza and some grape Crush, which wasn't Fanta as they didn't have any, but it was still grape pop so would do the job. She watched a sugary sweet, totally predictable romantic comedy, and then fell asleep after two episodes during a True Blood marathon on HBO. She woke up to the disposable cell phone ringing.

"Hello?"

"Hey."

His voice made her heart want to sing.

"Heyyyy..." She sat up and turned the TV down.

"Hey," it sounded like he was smiling.

"Hey," she repeated and giggled a little.

"God, I miss you," he said. "What's happening?"

"Nothing. Phew. I had pizza, watched a chick flick, some vampire porn, and snoozed."

"Yeah, I thought it was kinda quiet in my head. Wait, vampire porn?"

"True Blood. TV show. Vamps, werewolves, shape shifters, lots and lots of the sex."

"The sex?"

She laughed, "Mm. Hm. Hope you enjoyed the break from my brain. What's happening with you?"

"Well...let's just say it's been enlightening. Very enlightening. Can't elaborate over the phone, baby, but I'll be a few more hours. I'll call first, make sure you aren't bleeding before I come. I've hired a security agency to watch the room until I get there. They will be there in about 2 hours, max. Hotel security has been keeping an eye up until now. I'll text you when they're there, so you know you're good."

"Enlightening, huh? Colour *me* curious. And I feel fine. No cramping, no sign of Aunt Flo. It might have been a total false alarm. I had red thread on me when I changed. From my top. Maybe that's all it was in the toilet. Call me or text me and keep me posted?"

He breathed a sigh of relief, "You bought that red top at Walmart?"

"Yeah,"

"Wouldn't have happened with Armani..."

She laughed.

"I'm just sayin'..."

"Loose threads can happen to anything. Don't you dis my Walmart, y'hear?"

He chuckled.

"God we're weird. Listen to us being silly when all this shit is happening."

"Sometimes levity is the best medicine, princess."

"Yeah."

"Okay. Well, I'm gonna run. Love you. Go back to sleep and have sweet dreams, sweet girl. Miss you. Stay in the room."

"Miss you too. I will. Be safe, okay?"

"Don't worry. Later." He hung up.

She kept waking up throughout the night. She tried not to torment herself wondering what was happening, what'd happen next, but she couldn't help but wonder what Tristan was dealing with.

She was woken up at 7:30 in the morning with a text.

"Good morning, sunshine. Take your pills and vitamins, ok? Order breakfast for both of us? I'll be there in a half an hour if you're good? Let me know asap."

She got up, peed, changed the tampon and saw that there was still no period, and replied,

"I'm good. See you soon. xo."

5

THIRTY MINUTES (ON the dot) later there was a knock on the door. Kyla excitedly dashed to open it. She threw it wide, a beaming smile on her face. But standing in front of her wasn't Tristan. It also wasn't room service, bringing up the crepes stuffed with scrambled eggs and topped with hollandaise sauce that she'd ordered.

It was a tall good-looking guy in a light bomber jacket, jeans, and cowboy boots wearing sunglasses and a baseball hat. He had a grin on his face. His grin reminded her of a toothpaste commercial. He removed his hat and glasses as the *Oh Fuck* registered and the smile died on her face.

Liam Donavan. His long blond hair was tied back in a ponytail.

In an instant, before she had a chance to make a sound or for it to even fully register, he was pushing her back, shutting the door, grabbing her throat, and then his fangs appeared and instantly sunk in at the curve just above her collar bone. Just like that. There was the sickening sound of skin breaking and he was taking her blood. Taking what was supposed to only be Tristan's.

Intense cold, colder than she'd ever experienced, climbed up from her toes and shot out her fingers and, with strength she didn't know she had, she heaved him off. He landed on the rug on his backside.

His skin was greyish, his fangs were out. He, too, had blue eyes. Nothing like the beauty of Tristan's and they didn't appear to be changing colour. She was acutely aware of the open wound on her throat and her blood trickling out.

She was about to grab for the cell phone on the nightstand but before she got it he moved lightning fast, was back on her, pinning her to the bed and then he pierced her throat again in another spot near the first, the sickening sound of more of her skin breaking, and doing it loud. Way loud.

Where was security? Where was Tristan?

Brutally cold pain surged again like an electrical current, passing up through her and she dug her nails into his shoulders and shoved simultaneously, making him fly back as if he'd been thrown by a big gust of wind. The grey of his skin disappeared, and he look shocked for a moment but shook it off, smiled, and the fangs retracted but then came right back out.

She was upright, sitting in the bed, and his body had slammed into the dresser causing the mirror to fall over, smashing on him as he'd crumpled to the floor, but before she had a chance to move he lunged again and moved with superhuman speed, ripping his jacket off and tossing it, as he came at her. But she volleyed him back with both palms and he hit the dresser again. Hard.

He snarled and came at her again, this time ducking and grabbing her ankle so that she fell backwards in the bed and then he was on her. Right on top of her.

"No!" she screeched and that cold feeling surged but then ebbed half way up, leaving her feeling weak. So weak. Like she'd used up every ounce of strength she'd had. But it was as if he'd suddenly gained all the strength she'd lost.

Liam's teeth were on her throat again. He held her down; she couldn't get him away. His hand went up her jean skirt and roughly ripped her panties down her thighs. She screamed bloody murder, trying to squirm away but getting nowhere.

His fingertips touched between her legs and then she felt pressure as he yanked the tampon string, releasing her throat, glancing at it and then tossing it aside, and he pushed a finger in for a second, pulled it out and looked at it and then thrust a finger back in, painfully. He let go of her throat and looked to her eyes. "Be good."

He was trying to mesmerize her while violating her. He pushed his finger in harder.

She tried to squirm away, "Tristan's coming. Tristan'll be back any second and he'll rip your fuckin' head off."

She heard fabric ripping. It was the panties coming apart as he got them completely out of the way.

"Better get my fill then." He bit down on her throat again, she heard him swallow, then he let go, gasping, "You taste so fucking unbelievable. Your blood is so clean, so pure. Even better than hers."

"I'll rip your head off myself!" she cried and felt something rise in her, something that was fucking pissed.

She tried to kick, to thrash, to move, but he had her pinned to the point of being immobile. His finger was plunging in and out faster, harder. She was so bone dry it was agony. He started trying to circle her clit, "C'mon!" he ordered, staring into her eyes. It did nothing for her.

That hand left her skirt and he got his pants undone while he still pinned her with his other hand and most of his body weight. He got his dick out and it was against her opening. Pushing.

Oh God, no. Please no.

Absolute horror filled her as he pushed in a little, trying to get in despite the fact that Kyla didn't have a smidgeon of moisture down there, and his fanged mouth descended again toward her throat as he muttered, "Tristan isn't the only one who likes to fuck pets while he feeds and fuck have I ever got an overwhelming urge to get inside you. I need to fuck you almost as much as I need to drink from you..." His thumb hooked her bra aside, sliding over a nipple when the door crashed open.

It was Sam.

Liam flew off her of his own accord and rushed toward Sam while putting his dick away. Sam was stalking toward him with fangs out.

Oh no!

"Run!" Sam hissed at her, attempting to pin Liam to the wall. Sam had a small dagger with a glimmering green-jeweled handle in his hand and he held it up over Liam's head. Both of the men had fangs out.

Kyla scampered, adjusting her clothes as she ran as fast as her legs could carry her out the door, not looking back, running down the hall, past a tuxedo-wearing hotel employee who was just standing dumbfounded with a room service cart near the elevator, and she burst through the doors to the stairwell. There were two (presumably dead) men in dark uniforms tangled up together on the landing of the stairwell. They both had bloody, mangled throats. She couldn't stop to think, to even take in the grisly scene; she hopped over them and bolted down the stairs, two steps at a time, down several flights and then out into the lobby, out through the revolving door and then she was in the street -—a busy main street in downtown Phoenix with traffic and noise and people everywhere.

Fuck. Fuck. Fuck. Fuck. Where do I go?

God, Tristan, where are you?

She was dressed in her jean skirt, a tank top, and ballet flats. She had no phone, no purse, no money, no underwear. Her throat was bleeding in multiple places and she was trembling all over. There was pain between her legs where he'd tried to force his way in and something hideously filthy blooming inside of her right now. She pushed that emotion away and bolted for an alley and watched the front entrance of the hotel, partially hidden by a dumpster.

Minutes ticked by as she tried to catch her breath and then she saw Sam emerge from the hotel. He was wearing faded jeans, a black suit jacket, un-tucked grey button down, and he had dark glasses on. As he stepped out, he reached into his pocket and pulled out his cell phone, looking completely composed but then she saw Tristan emerge from a nearby car, tackle Sam, and roughly pin him against a wall.

Thank God!

She tried to send calming vibes to him, so he'd know she was okay, although she wasn't even a little bit okay. He must be out of his mind if he was feeling anything remotely close to the fear and other emotions she had to have been emanating.

Sam was explaining something to him with a lot of hand gestures that looked like an effort to calm Tristan down and then he flashed his blazer open, quickly showing Tristan the handle of that dagger, which was in an inside pocket. Tristan let go of him.

Tristan's palm flew to his forehead and he paled and then looked around the street and Kyla started to feel the thrumming of him tracking her. She leaned against the stone wall beside the dumpster and slid to the dirty ground, staring right at him, tears trailing down her cheeks.

Goosebumps prickled her skin. She wanted to call his name, but couldn't find it in her to even form a single word. It dawned then that this alley was so much like the stone tunnel of her nightmares. This was daylight and there were other things around but the stone? It looked the same. Where she'd touched it, she'd left blood.

Her blood? Liam's blood where she'd dug her nails into his shoulders? Maybe her own blood from the wounds on her throat? She didn't know.

She shuddered and frantically wiped her hands on the ground. As she looked up from the ground their eyes met. Tristan had seen her. He pointed at Sam and barked out something and Sam slipped back into the hotel as Tristan made his way across the street.

Then Tristan was there, squatting in front of her, his hands examining her throat. His irises were coal black.

"He will die the slowest most painful fucking death I can give him!" he snarled as he took his blue and grey striped button-down shirt off and put it on her. He lifted her into his arms but said nothing. The word *livid* didn't even begin to describe the vibe coming off him. He carried her to a black car and put her in the passenger seat and got in and looked at her throat. He ripped a piece of the shirt, tearing a strip off the bottom and then he used the fabric to dab at her throat.

"Fuck," he growled and then put his mouth to one wound, and then the other. The pain in her throat was instantly gone.

"I can fucking taste him. Fuck!" he roared, making Kyla's body jerk in response.

Tristan left the car, slamming the door and leaning against the door, effectively blocking her from Sam, who was back, standing there with the duffle bag, Kyla's purse, and the other bags from the room. He was talking to Tristan.

People passed by, oblivious, on their way to work, to wherever, with no idea they were watching two vampires talking to one another. Well, it was more like Tristan barking orders than talking.

Sam looked at Kyla through the window and for a second, he looked a little green around the gills. He took a step back and then another step and waved Tristan to follow him. Tristan spoke to him, pointing at him, looking very displeased.

He took the bags from Sam and then tossed them in the back seat behind Kyla and then without saying anything or even looking her in the face, he got into the front seat and slammed the door, turned the key, and squealed away from the curb.

She fastened her seatbelt, practically hyperventilating. As they sped away she saw Sam standing on the sidewalk, leaning over, hands on his denim-clad thighs, looking like he was trying to catch his breath.

"Fuck!" Tristan hollered, making her jump.

"Fuck!" he repeated and punched the dashboard beside the steering wheel, doing a significant amount of damage to it. He was driving like a madman on a racetrack. The anger on his face, the vibe in the car, it was like a raging angry life force.

Kyla let out a giant sob. He slammed on the brakes, making her body jerk forward hard against her seatbelt. They were on a quiet side street. He pulled up against the curb and got out of the car and then climbed in the back seat and leaned over, undid her seatbelt, pulled her limp body into his arms and held her tight against his bare chest, letting out a sound of absolute anguish. He was shaking. She was shaking. She was bawling.

She looked up at his face. His irises were still black. His fangs were out, and he was taking slow deep breaths as he stroked the back of her head and her back. He was completely pissed. He closed his eyes and took a deep breath. His fangs retracted. He took another big breath and blew it out slowly. He kept stroking her for a minute and then pulled the bag over that was beside them and got into her purse and pulled out the bottle of Purell disinfectant gel and liberally doused her throat with it and then did the same to her hands. He must've already closed the wounds on her throat with his mouth as they didn't sting. Then he grabbed a handful of tissues from a dispenser on the back of the driver's seat and started to wipe her throat. The tissues were now red.

Tristan's chest was heaving up and down and he looked about ready to explode. She grabbed more tissues and frantically wiped her hands, "His.... his bl-blood..." she stammered.

He grabbed her face in both hands, "Please forgive me. Please, princess, forgive me." His fangs were back out.

She shook her head, "It's not your fault."

His teeth retracted, "It fuckin' is. *I* let that happen. *I* was negligent. I can't believe I allowed that to fucking happen. I've failed you. Again. A-fucking-gain! I don't deserve you. I'm so goddamn sorry."

She burrowed deep into his arms. "Shut up and hold me."

She ugly cried into his chest for a little while and then he lifted her hair away from her face and tipped her chin up so their eyes met.

Tristan was hoarse when he then asked, "Sam said he was raping you. Was he? Was he raping you?"

Kyla nodded a little, "Sam burst in the room and they started to fight. I tried to fight him off. I couldn't... He only..."

Tristan let out a pained animal-like sound and squeezed her tighter.

He picked up the phone from the front seat and dialed, still holding her close, "Adrian. Sam Jasper just saved Kyla. Liam was feeding from and FUCKING RAPING HER!"

At the sound of those words, words that sounded like they were ripped from the bottom of Tristan's gut, Kyla's crying went uncontrollable. Big stuttering broken sobs. Tristan kissed her forehead but let go of her.

"No, we'll be there tomorrow. I need to take her somewhere for a while and ... and ...

No...he got away.

No, I'm cool. I said I'm fine, man. She's not okay but she will be 'cause I'm gonna fucking kill that motherfu—-

No... Sam's heading to you as soon as he finishes clean-up at the scene.

Two security guards. Ripped throats.

Yeah, Sam said it worked but it was wearing off a few minutes later when he got near her.

Whatever.

Can Liam track her now that he's fed? Anything else I need to know?

Fine. You check your end and make sure no one is fuckin' feeding him info.

Better not be!"

Tristan left the vehicle. Kyla was shivering. She spotted a bottle of water in the half-zipped duffle bag so grabbed it and started to drink it. She choked a little but then got some down. Then she opened the door and poured water on her still dirty hands and then wiped with the rest of the tissue from the car. Tristan was outside pacing back and forth on the sidewalk of the residential side street while talking on the phone. She couldn't hear him. She poured the last of the bottle of hand sanitizer on her hands. She wished she could bathe in it.

After a few minutes he got back in, grabbed a t-shirt out of the bag and put it on, then got out and into the front seat and started to drive. Kyla was still in back, shivering, hiccupping, eyes shut tight.

After a few minutes, they were at another hotel. It was another high-end swanky hotel, definitely too high-end for the fact that she was wearing a bloodstained jean skirt and a man's button-down shirt (that was torn) over a bloodstained tank top.

He opened the back door and took her hand and their bags and then they walked in and to the front desk. He checked them into a room under an alias, telling the desk clerk not to ask any questions and telling the clerk not to remember him but to contact him if anyone asked questions about him.

He waved off a bell boy who offered to take the bags, carrying them himself, and then they were in a second-floor hotel suite, the bellboy following.

It was big, luxurious. Tristan dropped the bags and then tipped the bell boy who'd opened the door. As he attempted to give them a tour of the room and explain their amenities Tristan said, "Get the fuck out. You'll have no memory of us," and then when the guy immediately obeyed, Tristan shut and locked the door.

She sat on a sofa, arms around herself. Tristan went to the bar and poured a big glass of something and downed it. Then he disappeared into the bathroom and she heard water running.

He was back. He picked up his phone and started to dial, "Go wash his stench off," he bit off.

Kyla jerked in surprise.

His eyes instantly went sorrowful, "I'm sorry. Sorry. Please, baby, go wash your hands really well and then take a bath. I have calls to make. I'll get food. Are you okay? Are you hurting? Need me to help?"

She shook her head, "I'm okay."

She wasn't. Not remotely.

She pulled the plug from the bath he'd started and instead showered. Robotically. She felt dirty. So dirty. So, no bath. No way did she want to sit in water that held any part of him.

Nothing had entered her veins while Liam drank, nothing like emotion. All she'd felt was cold. And with that cold had come immense strength to push him off. But then he'd caught her off guard and fed again and then he was stronger, so strong that she couldn't fight him off. She'd felt no further cold.

Any woman would find Liam Donavan attractive. Kyla, before falling for Tristan, would've thought so, too. But what'd happened was absolutely repulsive. If Sam hadn't come when he did, Liam probably would've drained her. Or, at the very least, he'd have stolen her away with plans to get the most out of her he could before he drained her bone dry out of greed.

What was Sam's story? And what was with that medieval-looking bejeweled dagger?

After getting as clean as she figured she could get, she found a hotel robe and wrapped it around herself and padded back out to the bed. Tristan was just ending a phone call. He was looking out the window, his back to her. He tossed the phone down and thrust his hands through his hair and let out a big breath.

"Hey," she whispered.

His shoulders slumped and then he turned around slowly and looked at her. He looked pained, hurt, sad. Really sad.

"Hey. Come here," he said but then he moved to close the distance and took her into his arms. He was smelling her. He sniffed her throat and then sniffed and examined her hands. He walked her to the bed and they got on it. He held her close. She put her face into his chest and inhaled his sweet scent and closed her eyes. She fell asleep in his arms, his palm on the back of her head and his other arm around her waist.

She woke up, still in his arms, her cheek and her fist on his chest. She looked up at his face. He was staring at the ceiling. His face was like stone. His eyes were still dark. Not black but not quite bright blue. His expression was so hard and so angry.

"I have things to tell you," he said.

She nodded and sat up.

"There are a lot of things you need to know all outside this Liam shit. And the Liam shit...it's too fucking much on its own."

He was quiet a minute, then said, "I have to kill him before he gets near you again. But right now, I need you to tell me what happened."

"He knocked when it was time for you to come and I didn't look out, I just...I opened it cuz I thought it was you or room service. I shouldn't have opened the door."

"Babe, he killed the security guards. Sam found them dead. Even if you hadn't opened it, he would've gotten in."

Kyla shivered, remembering the two men in the stairwell.

"What happened?"

"He bit me a bunch of times but didn't get much blood because I kept knocking him back. It was like I was stronger than me but not strong enough. He kept coming at me. I kept feeling these, these...cold surges in my body with this strength I didn't know I had but then it was gone. It was there but then it was gone."

"Fuck."

"Tristan, please feed." She threw her arms around his neck, "Feed from me and make love to me, make love to me gentle and sweet and cover what he did and do it until I'm exhausted, so I can sleep this off. I need to sleep some more. A lot more. I need to sleep this away."

He shook his head, "I can't fucking touch you that way."

She choked on a sob, thinking that he wouldn't touch her because he felt like she was still covered in his stench. Her heart plummeted to the bottom of her stomach.

"No, princess. It's not what you think," he whispered as she let out an audible sob.

"You're ovulating," he added.

"I'm what?"

"You're ovulating."

"I'm ovulating?"

"Yeah."

"Ovulating?"

"Yes. I knew it the second I got to you outside the hotel in that alley."

"How?"

"You just are. I can't tell yet if he... if he fertilized..." The sourness on his face felt like a kick in the teeth, "It'll take a few days for me to tell if—-"

"He...he was inside for a second, barely inside, not even all the way. I don't think he could've. As soon as he started to try to get in, Sam burst in."

Tristan breathed out slow and squeezed his eyes shut tight, looking so relieved. But it only lasted a split second and then his eyes went stone cold, "You're mine."

"I know."

"That motherfucker!" He flipped her and started scenting her all over. He inhaled at her stomach, put his nose between her legs, got back to her throat and inhaled.

He sat up and then let out a slow breath, "It's too soon to tell but I don't think he got you preg..." He didn't finish the word, "I need to go. Find him. Fuckin' kill him. How do I do that and keep you safe at the same time?"

"Honest, babe, he wasn't even all the way in. Mostly it was his hand down there and at my chest. He'd only started to try to get in, but he didn't get far. I was so ... so dry..."

He growled, looking like he wanted to smash something.

"Lure him to us," she said, "then get rid of him."

He nodded, "It might happen anyway. He wants more. I know he does. I don't know if he can track you or not now that he's fed multiple times. Adrian doesn't think so. But if I fail...he'd drain you. Or, he'd get you pregnant and then you'd probably die giving birth to his, his..."

"Tristan," she sighed, voice full of pain.

"Right now, all I want to do is get you pregnant. Then no one else can. I want to fuck you and feed from you so I'm sure to be strong enough to crush him and anyone else who comes after you. So you're strong enough, too. You gain strength every time I feed, too, baby. It's all I can do to stop myself. It's like I have this primal need that I have to fight off. That probably means he didn't get you and you're still ovulating and I want to fuck you until you can't walk, I want to plant my seed in you so fucking much. It's all innate. All of this is. But if I do it, giving birth will probably kill you. If I leave you to go off and try to catch him, I put you at risk of being caught and killed or getting pregnant and if he doesn't kill you, you probably die as you give birth to *his* baby."

"God..."

"If I lure him to us, you're not safe. If something went wrong... and there's so much you don't know. So many things I found out. Fuck. And you could've fought him off but you're still weak from my almost draining you before and then not feeding from you yet today and *I* put you at that disadvantage, so he fed and then he fed again, making him strong enough that you couldn't fight him off. If he feeds again...I'm a bad guy, princess. I'm not good. I'm not your prince charming. The only reason I didn't kill you out of hunger that first time is become of my bloodline and self-control. Vampires take. Kill. Deceive. It's what we are. We are entitled, we believe humans are made to serve us. *You* were made to serve me."

She shook her head.

"You were! Wait until you get the truth. Fuck. You'll understand then. You need to know that we do not hesitate to kill, lie, steal, cheat. If you can't serve us or feed us, we kill you. Unless we find a reason to turn you. Then you become what we are. If I didn't love you and that love didn't wake up some latent humanity in me, *I'd* kill you before sharing you with someone else.

And he's not super vampire or a royal. He'd absolutely kill you. He killed his enchanted blooded pet and that sent him on that killing spree. What kind of a threat will he be on *your* blood? He's out there now, processing it, getting stronger after feeding from you. And you're ovulating so it was innate for him to try to fuck you." His nostrils flared, "He probably waltzed in there with no intention of sex but then couldn't fucking help it. I've got to stop him."

"Okay, I have questions."

"I have so much to tell you. So much."

"Sam? Why was he there? How come he didn't attack me?"

"That's part of the problem. Sam. Fuck. If he wasn't there, Liam would've done more damage. He probably would've taken you and run. But the fact that he was there is not a good thing because it means I'm dealing with even more disloyalty. Sam found Liam but then followed him here; clearly he figured out which hotel I'd booked us into. Then Sam was hot on his heels. Sam is on that experimental drug Adrian wants to use on me. That's why he didn't attack you. But Sam should've warned me. He clearly has more loyalty to Adrian than me."

"Okay, listen to me for a sec." she said. "What if you make me what you are. Then Liam can't take me, kill me, or get me pregnant. Make me become a vampire and then it solves all our problems."

"No fucking way."

"But isn't that how this is destined to go?"

"What?"

"Standard vampire romance, right? The vampire falls for the human, the human falls for the vampire, and then she becomes a vampire and they live happily ever after. Isn't how this goes? That's how it always goes."

"No. Not even close."

"Why not? You were turned. What if I..."

"No. Most female vamps are even worse than males. They're diabolical. They're cold. If I'm rotten, a female vamp is festering and putrid. I refuse to make you into that. I'd give up your blood, never again have it or the nectar, I love you *that* much that I don't want you to be a vampire. You won't be you. And even more important, you won't wanna be you. There are things worse than death for you. And being a female vamp is worse than being dead. If I turned you, you'd hate me." He stopped and got a faraway look in his eyes, then softly added, "Just like Becky. Only with you, I wouldn't be able to bear it."

"Becky?"

"Rebecca is a walking, talking, blood-sucking piece of hatred. She hates me for turning her."

"Wait. What?"

"Andre loved her, and she was dying. She had a brain tumor the size of a grapefruit. He was keeping her, feeding from her, loving that she wasn't mesmerized. He fell for her and hard. She was the sweetest fucking thing, baby, the sweetest girl. So fuckin' full of life. She was on the verge of death and I was newly vamp and I was working for Andre. He's from a strong bloodline and he was teaching me the ropes, grooming me. And I saved her on her death bed by turning her. For Andre. For her. So she wouldn't have to die. He was losing her, and he was a mess and I told him to turn her but he said he couldn't, that she wouldn't be Becky anymore. She was wasting away, and I was so green, still so human-like that I didn't believe it could be *that* bad, so *I* turned her, thinking I'd help him keep her. But, it was a mistake. She wasn't the same. Rebecca became evil, hateful. Now they're in a prison together.

He won't give her up because of who she was and neither of them are happy because of who she now is. There's a very small piece of Becky left in that evil bitch vamp's body and that small remaining piece hates my guts for turning her into a monster. She kills for sport. And because she was turned with my blood she's a powerful fucking monster. She's a tortured soul who hates herself. She wishes she were dead because she can't help but be evil. Believe me, I don't ever want to say goodbye to you; I'd pick goodbye before turning you into that. Rebecca lives in a hell-on-earth because of what being a female vamp means. I thought vampire Rebecca was better than no Becky but I was wrong. If you had been there the night she ended Julia, you'd have been killed. Or, if she knew how much you mean to me, she would've turned you, to ruin you, to hurt me back."

Kyla was numb.

"I need to tell you more."

"I can hardly breathe. I want to puke."

"I'm sorry that this is your fate. I don't know what we'll do, but I will do everything I can do to save you from this."

"My fate?"

"The *more* part. There are other things I found out..."

"Give me a minute."

She felt the biggest sense of impending doom she'd ever felt. She had no idea what he was about to say but she had a horribly vivid sense of déjà vu. She knew it was big. She knew it was bad. She knew she needed a minute before she could hear it. She'd been harassing him to tell her shit but now she didn't wanna fucking know.

"I'll stop. You've had more than enough for one day. We'll go to Adrian's compound tomorrow morning. We'll talk more about it there."

He spent the next while pacing, fidgeting, looking out the window, stepping into the hall or the bathroom and making phone calls. Kyla didn't have it in her to harass him about the evident secrecy.

She curled up in the bed with the remote control and tried to get her head together. She felt gross. She couldn't let her brain think too hard on Liam being interrupted in the act of rape. She couldn't think too hard on what Tristan had said so far. Her mind was whirling. Hard. Fast. She wanted to vomit it all out, to rid her body of all of it.

Even though Liam didn't get all that far, she still felt invaded, so thoroughly invaded. He'd touched her, started to violate her sexually, and he'd taken her blood. And it didn't feel remotely like it did when Tristan had done the same thing.

But why?

Tristan had fucked her after she said No. Tristan drank from her regardless of whether she wanted it. But it was different. It sounded totally stupid but in her core, she knew it was different because she felt like she belonged to him. On some weird deep level, she felt like she'd always belonged to him.

Tristan ordered in some Chinese food delivery, but she only ate a little. He talked her into finishing soup and some stir-fried vegetables as she stared at the TV listlessly, trying to ignore his pacing and fidgeting.

When it finally got dark and she got under the covers to sleep, he climbed in with her and held her close.

"Maybe I should say I'm sorry you ever met me but not gonna lie," I could never be sorry we met. But I *am* sorry for what he did. I'm so fucking sorry I left you vulnerable. I should've prepared for that, wish I could've had a vampire army prepared to fend him off, but I didn't want *any* vampires near you. He must have had an army of people watching for me to find you that fast after we took that charter. Fuck. I bet you wish you'd never met me."

She wrapped her arms around him and said, "No. How could I wish you away? We met for a reason. I refuse to believe that it was so you could destroy me. You broke down my wall and gave me beautiful sensations and emotions. I refuse to believe that it's just so I can feel pain. I know there's more and I don't know what else there is, and I don't want to know tonight. I've waited this long, I can wait one more day. Tell me tomorrow. I *do* know that I feel something I never ever fathomed I could feel. We have to fight for our happily ever after, Tristan. I don't know what it looks like, but I believe it's worth fighting for."

"There *were* reasons we met, absolutely. But that's part of the problem. And it *is* worth it. I will do everything in my power to find a way," he said with conviction. "I'm sorry I made you vulnerable and I'm sorry that he did what he did to you. I want to undo it. Cover it. Make it a memory and then erase it. Right now I wish I could entrance you for just five minutes so that I could make you forget what he did. I know I can't but as soon as possible, I'll do everything I can to help you forget, help erase his mouth on your throat, his body touching you. I'll erase it because he won't exist any more. He doesn't exist for you now. Okay?"

"Tristan?"

"Yeah?"

"Instead of turning me, what if *you* get me pregnant," she whispered.

"Kyla..." His voice held not a shade of anything good.

"Hear me out. If I'm ovulating despite multiple types of birth control, then I will start bleeding again soon if I don't get pregnant. That's a given. Right?"

He sighed.

She continued, "It's obvious. These pills won't stop my period if that shot didn't stop me from ovulating. So that means in a few weeks I'm at risk of you killing me because I'll start bleeding and you'll turn into the gray monster. Get me pregnant and that'll erase at least one threat. Then we have nine months to figure out how to save me."

He tensed up.

"Your mother survive giving birth to you?"

"Yeah, but you don't get it."

"Maybe I'll survive too. There won't be any nectar for at least nine months, so we will have that time to figure out."

"Kyla..." his voice was pained. "There's shit you don't know..."

"And then I can give you a baby," she whispered, her voice sounding like it had never sounded.

She felt hope rise in her, "A baby, made from you and me. Imagine that?"

Emotion filled her.

A baby. Tristan's baby.

She felt warmth all over.

His eyes roved her face and then they went liquid. "We would make the most beautiful baby in the world."

His eyes were finally light blue again.

She nodded, tears filling up in her eyes. She'd always liked kids but hadn't spent much time around them. She'd never really given much thought to the notion of being a mother. But right now, the idea of having Tristan's baby?

God...

"But no. Because there's too good a chance you wouldn't meet him or her. There's too much risk that our child would never know your beauty. Your beautiful eyes, your beautiful touch. Your spunk, your sass, how crazy you can be, the sound of your laughter, how amazing you smell. He or she might never know it because you could die. Then I'd have no Kyla. If I don't have you? I won't risk it. I'd rather have nothing but you than everything in the world without you."

"So instead, you risk in a little while me bleeding out nectar and you maybe killing me. Or Liam getting me and *for sure* killing me. Or him raping me, getting me pregnant, and then I die anyway and leave *his* baby in the world."

"If he got you and got you pregnant, I'd get you back and then we would have it aborted," Tristan's expression was stone cold.

A shiver ran over her body.

She took a deep breath,

"If I get the chance to make a baby it can't be with him. No way. And how powerful will he be if my period starts and he gets me then and gets *that blood*?"

She felt his body tense even further.

"If you make a baby with me, I won't get my period. And if I'm pregnant, will it change the composition of my blood? Maybe it would. Maybe he wouldn't even want it... maybe..."

"Stop. You need the rest of the facts. Sleep. We'll talk later."

"I won't sleep. No way can I sleep. Just tell me the rest. I need it. Just spill it all."

"*I* need to sleep."

"Well I won't be able to."

"Try." He re-arranged the blankets over them and kissed her forehead.

"If I close my eyes, I'll keep seeing him, feeling his teeth on me, and feeling him trying to—-" she shuddered.

"I'll help you sleep," he said, and his fingers found their way into her panties. At first, she jerked in surprise and Liam's touch flashed in her mind.

"No. Don't let him do that to us," Tristan growled, "Don't let him take this from us. Let *me* touch you so that you'll only see me when you close your eyes."

Kyla took a breath, "Slow it down," she pleaded.

Tristan gently caressed her hips, her belly, her breasts, and he took his time caressing her and building the fire until finally, she wanted it. He picked up on her want and then his fingers found their way back into her panties and he rubbed her at her centre. She reached for his cock, but he stopped her

"I'm okay. Just you," he said, and she cuddled close and wove her fingers into his hair.

"Please, honey. This has been a shitty day. Let me help you go to sleep with something happy, too."

"Okay, princess."

She put her hand on him.

He continued until, after a really long time, she finally shuddered and moaned his name and then about thirty seconds later, he shuddered and moaned her name.

He stroked her hair and her back and kissed her forehead and eyelids and she cuddled up closer to him.

"Where's your Mother, Tristan?"

"Montreal."

"You see her?"

"Not much."

"No?"

"It's complicated."

"You have other family?"

"No."

"Why don't you see much of her? Does she know about ..."

"Kyla, let's sleep."

She sighed, "I'm tired. So, you get a reprieve."

He got out of the bed and went to the bathroom. A moment later he was back and she felt him relax.

"But I'll be asking more questions tomorrow," she added.

He kissed the top of her head. She nuzzled in and closed her eyes.

She didn't know that he stared at the ceiling, in agonizing pain, mulling over some gut-wrenching options and decisions until a few hours later when she started to thrash and cry in his arms in the throes of a nightmare. At that point he tried to settle her down but couldn't comfort her with soft words or with his strength.

He couldn't figure out how to help until she said, "I need to feel you." Then he knew he could settle her down with his teeth. So he bit her and he fed just a little bit. He bit at her throat over a spot where Liam Donavan had dared to take what was his and he didn't let his hunger take over. He didn't let her hunger for him fuel his appetite like it'd done when he'd nearly drained her a few days before. He didn't let her know how distraught he was. Instead, he let himself feel what he felt for this girl. He let himself feel the scope of emotion he felt for Kyla Spencer.

And she settled down and fell back to sleep on her back, his mouth found the crook of her neck. He kissed it gently. There was a peaceful little smile on her gorgeous face. He'd done that; he'd given that to her. He felt warmth settle in his bones, so he closed his eyes. But he wouldn't forget what that other vamp did. And that other vamp would pay.

6

SHE'D AGAIN DREAMT of being in that stone tunnel with a snake around her arm, squeezing, while blood ran down the walls, but this time her parents were there. She'd jolted awake and panic spread at seeing the empty space in bed beside her, but it only lasted an instant because then Tristan emerged from the bathroom, showered and dressed.

"Phew," she said aloud, and he gave her a half a smile.

"Mornin' baby. Get ready? We'll get breakfast on the road." He leaned over and kissed her forehead.

She nodded and sat up.

He started packing up the few things that were out of their bag and she headed for a shower.

En route to Adrian's, which was less than an hour away, he told her that there were others at the compound and that other than Sam, only Adrian knew about her, so she needed to act mesmerized in the presence of other vamps.

"I've told them back home that I'm here on business. A select few know about you."

"Who knows?"

"As far as I know, Adrian, Sam, and Claudio. Liam, obviously. But I don't think anyone else knows. Other than... well... I'll fill you in on that shortly."

The look on his face made her blood run cold.

"Other than who?"

"Baby, just a little longer. It's better I explain when we're there."

"Claudio? When did that happen?"

113

"Last night. After the Liam run-in. I called him. Well, I called him last night, but he already knew. He's known all along. I found out after my initial conversation with Adrian, but I needed time to chew on that before talking to him."

"All along?"

"Yeah. This was staged." His expression hardened.

"What was?"

"Us." He merged onto a highway.

"Us?"

"Sam guided Joe to that bar. Joe thought he scouted you for me but that wasn't the case. You were chosen for me. Sam made Joe think it was his idea."

"Uh, what?"

"It's better that we do this when I'm not driving. I think we'd better do this when we're stopped. There's good news, too. There's a way to keep you safe from me."

"Then stop so you can tell me."

"Kyla, let's just—-"

"Stop the car and fucking talk to me!" she demanded, "There," she pointed, "gas station."

He sighed and pulled in to a gas station and restaurant rest stop parking lot, through a drive-thru to order coffee and then he pulled over.

"We need to get you breakfast."

"Fuck breakfast. Talk."

"Not fuck breakfast, Kyla. You need your strength. You can't skip meals, or I have to skip meals. I don't like to fuckin' skip meals!"

She was staring, agape, "Are you fucking kidding me right now?"

He pinched the bridge of his nose, "It's gonna take time to catch you up. I'm sorry. That was callous."

"Catch me the fuck up then and, uh, now would be good."

She opened the tab on her coffee cup and took a small sip.

"Pill." He mumbled this and passed her the bottle from the duffle bag.

"This? This is useless."

"We don't know that. Take it. And while you're at it, put this on."

He passed her a silver choker necklace with a tiny circular loop.

She rolled her eyes, popped the pill in her mouth, and swallowed it down with a sip of coffee. The coffee was too hot. It took a minute to recover. She looked at the collar.

"That'll tell others who see you just how off limits you are. When we get there, put sunglasses on and act like you're entranced. I'll get you someplace safe and private. Then Adrian will sit down with us and go over things. He's in the know."

"In the know?"

"He's involved in all of this. Deeply."

"Deeply?"

"Yeah. He's the orchestrator. And he has something that can help."

"Care to elaborate?"

"Not until you're safely in there and past the other vamps. The less you know going in, the less chance of you wigging out. Remember when you and I are in there, anything we say could be being recorded, even when we think we're alone. Don't give anything away. I trust no one right now."

"Tristan, you are freaking me out."

"Drink your coffee; eat a muffin. We'll be there soon. Then we'll go from there."

She stared off into space.

"I love you. I love you so much. I'm gonna figure this out. Okay? Trust me?"

She nodded.

"You do?" he prodded.

She sighed.

"I do." She settled down.

She wanted to ask a million questions, but it'd wait. All the weeks of wondering the truth...

In a few short minutes it sounded like she'd get it. Finally, the truth. She put her hand on his thigh and he rested his hand on top of hers as they pulled back onto the highway.

"Eat the muffin," he reminded her and put the paper bag into her lap.

"I'm really not hungry."

"I need you strong so I can feed so I can ensure I'm strong enough to protect you and so you are strong. I can't afford to skip meals when someone wants you. If you weren't weakened because I'd almost drained you the day before and because I hadn't fed that day, it might've ended differently. If you were strong when Liam got to you then you might've been still fighting him off when Sam got there instead of being bloody and violated."

Well, that certainly didn't make her feel any hungrier, but she picked the muffin up and forced it down.

ADRIAN'S WAS, INDEED, a compound. As they approached a tall stone fence with black iron gates, she took in what looked like a resort with a large fieldstone mansion and a few smaller buildings.

Tristan explained that it was, in essence, the main hospital branch in North America for vampires. A vampire hospital, vampire rehab resort slash retreat, and a research facility where experts in vampire medicine resided, did surgeries, research, and helped vampires with medical problems.

Tristan told her this as they approached, saying that Adrian was a respected elder, a good friend of Tristan's grandfather, and a doctor, even back in his human life. He was just out of medical school when he was turned but then he used his medical background from when he was human to help vampires with medical issues. He'd honed those skills considerably after being turned.

He explained that yes, most vampires had healing abilities, but there were illnesses that were unique to them, illnesses that took longer to recover from, depending on the health and background of the vampire, as well as the need for counselling, addiction therapy, and help with other problems. Adrian's had a full staff with other vampire medical staff members with varying specialties, with everything from hypnotherapy to food poisoning when a vamp consumed from an unhealthy human. He said he also did research as well as offered solutions to many vamp problems. Sometimes herbal, sometimes other solutions, even surgery. Tristan didn't elaborate any further than that and Kyla was too overwhelmed to care all that much. There was so much on her mind as they approached the gates.

He told her he'd give her more information after they met with Adrian but reiterated that he might not be able to talk openly inside the compound buildings with her for a little while after meeting Adrian.

Once they were inside the gated compound, which was manned with two gate guards, they drove up to the front circular driveway of the large grey fieldstone mansion, and there was a man standing outside, dressed business casual in tan cargos and a khaki button-down shirt. Tristan passed her a pair of sunglasses and she put them on. The look he gave her was all business, reminding her how important it was to pretend. They certainly didn't need any more threats.

"Wait for me," he told her.

She braced herself as best as she could, hoping it would be enough, and he got out of the car, shook the man's hand, and then he rounded the car and opened Kyla's door, reaching for her hand. Another casually-dressed man took Tristan's keys and got into the car to drive it away.

Kyla met the gaze of the man, feeling like his eyes pierced hers straight through the sunglasses. He was very attractive. She quickly looked past him, straight ahead, unsure if anyone else was around, so trying to appear blank. Kyla thought he resembled James Franco a little, dark kind of curly hair, vividly bright green eyes. They were also like those Lite Brite or LED bulbs, like Tristan's but a sparkling emerald green rather than icy blue. He was tall and fit and looked to be in his mid to late thirties, maybe.

"Kyla," the man greeted softly, a magnetic smile on his face, "I'm Adrian."

"Hi Adrian," she answered, quietly.

"Tristan, let's get you and your lovely pet here inside. Follow me to my office." The vamp had a huge smile on his face.

The foyer had a large chandelier overhead, dripping with ruby-colored stones. There were orchids and roses in vases all around. The furnishings were sumptuous. Walls and floors were white marble, clean, palace-like. Tristan held her hand and they followed Adrian down a long hallway toward a set of large dark wooden double doors.

Just before they hit that set of doors another door opened in the hallway and two women stepped out in front of them.

"Trisssstan!" one of them cooed as she approached. She was a tall brunette with striking features. She was dressed in an ivory pantsuit, killer ivory high heels, and was dripping with diamonds at her ears, throat, fingers, and wrists. The woman beside her was a blonde bombshell dressed in black. She eyed Kyla up and down, with scrutiny, her eyes landing on the necklace Kyla wore.

Kyla felt like a hobo in contrast to how these women were dressed. Kyla was wearing skinny distressed boyfriend jeans, t-strap black sandals, and a white chiffon button down that had a big cut-out in the back, making it almost backless. She had her hair loose in curls down her back as well as a little bit of make-up but she looked casual, completely casual.

She was Walmart or Old Navy, or maybe H&M or The Gap on a good day and they were Nordstrom or Neiman Marcus or whatever. She didn't even know many of the expensive names and brands. Tristan was in jeans and a tee-shirt but he still looked like Armani. He didn't even look Walmart when he'd worn Walmart!

"Celia," Tristan nodded but didn't break stride.

"Catch up later?" The dark-haired beauty blatantly flirted, but glanced at their linked fingers. Kyla wanted to claw the woman's beautiful face but held her temper in check.

"Absolutely not," Tristan gave her a tight fake smile and the woman snickered. As they passed one another, he gave Kyla's hand a squeeze.

Adrian opened double doors and ushered them inside.

Kyla let out a breath. Tristan gave her hand another reassuring squeeze. Adrian motioned for them to sit down in front of the desk. It felt like a professor's office in an old-world style university. The wall behind his desk was lined with books and the desk was adorned with antique desk accessories.

Kyla removed her sunglasses as she sat. Adrian's gaze met hers and their gazes locked. He gave her a warm smile. Despite its warmth, her blood ran chilly for a second as some sort of awareness prickled along her spine. She tilted her head and regarded him carefully. She almost felt like they'd met before. Something about him was familiar and unsettling.

"Why is Celia here?" Tristan demanded, his voice harsh.

"I needed some of her skills for a project. Unrelated to yours, not to worry. She'll be busy." He waved his hand dismissively and then he leaned back in his chair and said to Tristan, but kept looking at Kyla, "How much does she know?"

"Not much," Tristan answered.

Kyla tore her gaze away from Adrian and looked to Tristan.

"Why don't you begin? I can fill in gaps where needed," Adrian said.

"Brace, baby," Tristan said, "there's a lot that's about to come at you."

She nodded. But there was no way to brace for what was coming.

Her world was about to be blown to smithereens.

"Adrian is your grandfather."

Kyla's body visibly jerked, "My what?"

"He's your mother's father. Your mother? She was half royal vampire. Your father had vampire DNA as well, though not quite as much as your mother and it was from a turned vamp. They both had rare blood types. Because of that and because you're not turned, this is what makes your blood what it is. Enchanted."

Kyla frowned.

Adrian spoke up, "I've devoted my life to science. Science that often helps our kind. Some that has even helped *your* kind. I've sired a number of vamps in my life but I've also fathered a number of children as part of my work, which has included many efforts in a various medical trials. Some children have survived. Some haven't. Some of the women survived birth, some haven't. Your grandmother survived giving birth to your mother. We've been interested in seeing how things would pan out with you, particularly since you'll be the first among some very specific experiments to reach the age of 25, next week, in fact. If you'd roll up your sleeve..." He stood and reached into a drawer and removed a syringe.

Kyla felt panic rise, "Um..."

And her birthday wasn't the following week. Her birthday wasn't for a few months.

"Roll up your sleeve, Kyla," Adrian repeated, staring right in her eyes.

She remained frozen but glanced at Tristan.

Tristan straightened up, "A minute, Adrian."

Adrian smiled and nodded and then left the room, closing the door behind himself.

"What the...?" Kyla whispered, wide-eyed.

He put a hand on her arm reassuringly, "Right, so I told you my visit was enlightening. Sam had the blood taken from the lab I was using. It was rerouted and sent here. Adrian examined it, but he wants to examine your blood now, after the bonding, as well as mine, after having had your blood for this amount of time as well as because of the nectar I consumed."

She gave her head a shake and thrust her fingers into her hair. "Excuse me, um, I'm a little...stunned over here. Do ya think just maybe... it might've been good to drop that, all that, in advance for me?"

"I've been weighing the right way to handle this, Kyla. I planned to talk to you yesterday but with what you went through I decided to wait until we got here. You can ask questions this way. Adrian watched your mother grow up from a distance and she didn't know she was half vamp until everything went down. Your parents, due to having specific highly coveted blood types, with vamp DNA, were matched to meet up. They were mesmerized into meeting and mating. They had you. You were taken. Adrian eventually found you and you've been watched ever since. As you were approaching your 25th birthday, they arranged for you to be delivered to me so that they could see if—-"

"Taken? Watched? Wait a minute. I'm an experiment? *We*, you and me... this relationship, it's an experiment!" Kyla jumped to her feet.

Tristan nodded and reached for her hand, "Sit."

"Our relationship is an experiment. You didn't know about this?"

"No."

"We can't trust him. Can we?"

Tristan gave her a look, "Of course we can."

But she read something else in his eyes. She was about to push it and Tristan gave her a look that froze her in her tracks. If Tristan didn't trust Adrian, he obviously didn't want Adrian to know and he had already warned they could be under surveillance. She took a big breath.

He squeezed her hand, shaking his head, "Let's give him a sample and then we've got more to talk about. Ask him questions, if you want."

She nodded slowly and sat back down. Her heart was beating so loud. She felt faint.

What on earth was going on here?

Tristan stepped out into the hall and then returned with Adrian.

Kyla slowly rolled up her sleeve and Adrian approached her.

Tristan stopped him, "I'll do it."

Adrian gave a knowing smile and passed the syringe.

"I understand. I'm the same. Very protective of my special pets."

Kyla looked up at him, this man who was a relative. How bizarre it was to stare up at a man who looked not much older than she was but who was her grandfather.

"Your eyes. I have your eyes," Kyla blurted as it dawned on her. Hers weren't luminescent but if they were, they'd be exactly the same. The same cat's eye shape, the same shade of green.

He smiled, "You do. Your mother does, as well. All females from my line do."

My line? Not my family. My line. Wow.

Adrian sat on the corner of his desk in front of Kyla, watching Tristan seal the spot with a kiss. Tristan licked his lips and then winked at her.

"Ask anything you'd like to ask," Adrian said to Kyla but was looking to Tristan, his eyes on Tristan as Tristan put the two vials of blood into his own pocket.

"I'll be supervising your testing," Tristan told him.

Adrian gave him a smile, but Kyla was fairly certain the smile was fake.

"Refreshments?" Adrian asked, standing up and rounding his desk.

"Kyla could use some food. She hasn't eaten much today."

"I've arranged to have lunch sent to your room shortly." He picked up his phone, "Fritz, some fresh orange juice and coffee to my office, please." He hung up.

"Questions?" Adrian probed.

"Uh..."

Kyla didn't even know where to start! She found her voice eventually.

"So, beyond what's happening to Tristan from drinking my blood, you know about what happens with my period. Is that something that's normal?"

Adrian nodded, "There is a lot of misinformation when it comes to nectar and royal pets. We guard the information carefully to protect those who have the most to lose and to manage those who would be nuisances if they knew. You were, in essence, created to feed and breed for vampires. Generations ago, this was common. Covens would keep small human populations of carefully selected people with vampire DNA for feeding purposes and breeding also happened, either to produce feeders or for turning. Nowadays, the breeding is a necessity, I'm afraid. But we are extremely cautious about it. Responsibility is important, and most vampires are careful about reproduction. We won't turn just anyone, and we don't breed with just anyone.

Female vamps rarely conceive so we have no choice but to look to suitable human females for selective breeding. Then suitable offspring can be turned at the appropriate time. This is what came about with Tristan. Both of Tristan's parents were full vampires and from highly powerful family lines. This makes him vampire royalty. Your line has powerful royal vampire blood on one side, that would be from me. And less powerful but still vamp, nonetheless, on the other side. This, with your blood type, makes you very suitable for feeding and also for breeding.

As far as the nectar goes, the fact that you didn't become pregnant after bonding is, essentially, a sign of infertility, so a vampire would innately turn on a pet who he'd bonded with as a matter of that human being unable to breed.

Before you died, he'd be fortified with nectar from the menstrual blood to sustain him until he found another suitable mate."

"Isn't it dead, though? Isn't that kind of strange that a vampire wouldn't want live blood? If that's the right term for it."

"That blood is filled with nutrients. It's what sustains a fertilized egg in the beginning stage of life. It's shed when there's no fertilized egg to benefit from it. Investigate witchcraft lore and you'll see that menstrual blood is considered very magical. It is often used in witchcraft, used ceremonially throughout history, in offerings, also used in fertilizing plants, etcetera. We would not want a witch to get their hands on *your* menstrual blood. That could be catastrophic. Iron in this blood is particularly nutrient-rich and there's significant iron in menstrual blood, enough iron to fortify a vamp who has to seek out a more suitable, fertile pet. A royal pet's blood composition is even more special than an average feeder. You're not likely infertile. I suspect you are, in fact, quite fertile based on the fact that you are beginning to ovulate now, despite birth control.

Your being on birth control skewed the results of what would be a natural test in our world. One of two things happens in an enchanted pet scenario, either the female becomes pregnant, or the male kills her when she starts menstruating and he's then fortified until he finds another. Generations ago other males in a coven would fight over an infertile enchanted pet, all wanting the advantage, the significant advantage as the fortification could be enough to change the pecking order. When that pet has got a high amount of vampire DNA, that's something that brings forth an extremely powerful vampire nectar. We try to keep things quiet regarding these matters as it can cause a bit of hysteria among vamps who aren't well-equipped to handle it. Case in point: Liam."

"So the next time I get my period?"

"We will know when it plays out. Tristan might not have killed you. We aren't certain, but it's quite possible that he'd have fed on nectar until you completed that cycle but allowed you to live."

"Are all women in danger during their period?"

"Bonded females only. When a super vamp, also known as a true vamp, one who is inherently vampire, keeps an enchanted blooded slash royal pet and feeds from her consecutively for several feedings, that's when the bonding happens and that's when it becomes an extremely symbiotic relationship. You need him as much as he needs you, probably even more."

"You've said feed and breed. Does that mean I wouldn't die if I gave birth?"

"We won't know until that plays out. *If* that plays out." He glanced at Tristan, looking contrite, then continued, "Royal pets have a better shot of survival than those who have no vampire DNA. Many pets that are chosen to breed only do so once, often because they don't survive. Occasionally we've had more than one successful birth. We've had pets breed and survive and not survive. You have a decent chance of survival considering your amount of vampire DNA. And I'm very interested in assessments based on your blood's composition should Tristan impregnate you. We've already discovered some very intriguing things from the blood sample we've tested."

Kyla looked to Tristan. He was looking at Adrian, who continued,

"Human blood types go beyond alphabetical letters. Beyond A, O, etc. Tristan, as a royal vamp, would feel dissatisfied after feedings unless being fed by a pet with at least some vamp DNA.

Royal pets have a higher survival rate for childbirth. More than 9 out of 10 women impregnated by a vampire die during childbirth and in more than 9 out of 10 of the cases where there's survival, the woman has vampire DNA. Tristan has the most royal bloodline that I've come across. You are the perfect feeder and breeder based on *your* blood type and bloodline. Tristan's bloodline and his bloodlust, together, made you a perfect mate. Innately he knew this. That's why he was attracted to you. That's why feeding from you sates him. You were bred specifically for him. It's also surprising that he didn't kill you after you being tainted by the touch of another vamp. That's also a testament to Tristan's power."

"Why am I not mesmerized by him if he's so powerful?"

"Your *not* being entranced is something I need to investigate. That was a surprise. I suspect it's due to the amount of vampire in your blood. It's extremely rare. You, Kyla, are extremely rare. I know of no other royal pet with a bloodline as unique as yours. I've come across no other royal vamp with a bloodline and strengths as powerful as Tristan's. I've been anxiously awaiting my opportunity to see the results of this union."

"If I were turned?"

"We believe you'd become an extremely powerful female vamp," Adrian answered without hesitation, "Your DNA and blood type, if you were turned, because of my bloodline, you'd be considered vampire royalty as well."

Oh
My
God.

Tristan shuffled uneasily.

"So Tristan could've been a royal pet but he was chosen to become a royal vampire by being turned?"

"Not exactly. His bloodline is full of leaders, powerful and strong vamps. Full vamp on both sides. The only way he'd be a royal pet is if we didn't know of his bloodline. Someone royal could've found out about his bloodline and fed on him and kept him in secret, never turning him, due to the potential competition his blood would bring. But that didn't happen. His grandfather was very involved in preparing for Tristan to come of age. In a royal hierarchy he's much higher than you would be, were you turned. But based on your bloodline and what I've seen so far in your lab results, you'd be a suitable queen, were you turned."

Her blood ran cold a moment. She jerked her chin at him, "Would our offspring be like me or like him?"

"Your offspring could be extremely powerful vampires. We don't know yet just how powerful."

Tristan looked to her. "But you could die in childbirth."

"Or you might survive," Adrian put in, "particularly if we took special measures."

"What measures?"

"Let us revisit that if and when it becomes an option," Adrian smiled.

Kyla looked to Tristan, "I could die if I don't get pregnant now because you could destroy me because if I start my period I'm not your perfect pet."

Tristan's expression was hard, guarded.

"Here we can do a controlled experiment." Adrian interjected, "We have options to do a variety of controlled experiments."

"How?"

"I can keep you safe," Adrian said, "I have an experimental medicine that showed promise with Samuel Jasper. We could offer you protection as well, due to another tool I've developed. Medication can be used to help keep Tristan even when you menstruate. But Tristan needs to make some decisions before any experiments can be carried out."

"What decisions?"

"Tristan?" Adrian pressed.

"Go ahead," Tristan said quietly.

Adrian leaned back in his chair and smiled, "He needs to decide whether to get you pregnant and see if you'll survive or let you go into a nectar cycle and I and my team watch his reactions under that formula and ensure we stop him before any harm comes to you. Each time he consumes your nectar he increases his abilities, so it could be advantageous to see what results come of testing him after another cycle. It could be that he opts to feed repeatedly to see how powerful he can get.

It could be that he opts to get you pregnant and if you survive, do so repeatedly so that he can populate the world with as many perfect future vampires as your body allows.

Alternately, he could opt to harvest your eggs so that we can do in-vitro with surrogates and have someone else give birth to these perfect vampire children in your absence or in an effort to protect you from the risks of childbirth as well as keep the nectar flowing. He could put you on tap for repeated nectar cycles in a controlled environment so that you're safe from him and he can opt to use that nectar in a variety of ways. He can also later turn you and attempt to conceive with you after you're turned. You could be powerful enough to do that very successfully and by my research, there's a good probability that children you have after you're turned might not even need to be turned to be at their full potential. That's something we're very interested in researching. Tristan has a lot of options to weigh out."

Kyla tilted her head at him. Regardless of biology, this man wasn't family. He didn't care a lick about Kyla, his biological grand-daughter. This was a mad scientist who was also a cold and callous vampire and Kyla was just an instrument in a bevy of possible experiments.

"These are his decisions to make. He could even order a hys-terectomy, protecting you from birth and from nectar cycles. But he's got the potential to sire powerful vampires, he has the potential to change our world for the better with your blood. Heal sick vampires. Stem cell research from embryos could also produce a great many things before and after you're turned. Many great things can come out of this. You're looking at me like you're about to suffer a death sentence but that's absolutely untrue."

Kyla looked to Tristan. He wasn't looking at her. He was looking off into space. She looked back to Adrian. She ignored the chilling in her blood at the man's words, the man's demeanour.

"This was all part of the long-term plans. Tristan's grandfather and I planned this almost twenty-seven years ago when we first planned for your parents to meet."

"Why does he smell and taste like dessert?" It was a stupid ques-tion to ask right now after all that'd been revealed but the track her brain was on, she needed to get off it. Badly. Talk about information overload!

"Endorphins. You two are a perfect match. You both appeal to one another. Are you a dessert person?"

"Uh huh."

His scent... it was of things she wanted but rarely had as an un-derprivileged foster child so the one thing she indulged in as an adult was dessert.

"That's why he smells like dessert to you. If you were a flower person, he'd probably smell like flowers. It's all chemical. A natural mating call. You're meant for him. You smell and taste the way he wants. He smells like what you want. He generates a chemical reaction in you that makes you open to mating with him, a little like being entranced but you're evidently keeping your faculties, which is astonishing."

She was quiet, reflective for a moment.

"What happened to my parents?"

"Your parents were a means to an end. This end."

"They were killed on purpose?"

Tristan answered, "They aren't dead."

Kyla's body spun to face Tristan.

"They're alive. They were brought in, underwent some testing. They were later turned. You were supposed to be brought in with them, but you vanished."

Kyla's palm flew to her chest. She could hardly breathe.

Adrian said, "They couldn't tell me what happened to you. They said you were kidnapped from your bed during the night. We were making plans to bring the three of you in due to outside dangers but we were too late. The only reason you weren't raised here in this compound until you were to be given to Tristan was because traitors sought to keep you from us. You were hidden. It took eighteen years to find you. We found you in Ottawa. For the past few years, you've been watched. Then you were given to Tristan. It was serendipitous that you moved to his city."

What on earth?

"An older lady told me on a park bench that they died in a car accident. Who abducted me? And do I have siblings?"

"There's an underground militia of sorts. They moved you from Wales, where you were born and being raised, and then hid you within the Canadian foster care system," Adrian answered, "They changed your name, birth certificate information and hid you from us. Those responsible will be caught. They will face consequences."

Early memories after losing her parents flooded her memory. She remembered thinking that after her parents were gone that people talked funny. She was a quiet and withdrawn child after losing her parents. She must've lost any accent along the way.

She looked to him, "What's my real name?"

"It *is* Kyla. Your family name was not Spencer. That was fabricated. It was Kelly. You're a Constantin. That's what makes you part royal."

"What's a Constantin?"

"Me. My name. I'm Adrian Constantin."

"And what's your ideal scenario here? What do *you* want to see happen?"

Adrian smiled and gave a look to Tristan, "There are a great number of things that I'd like to see happen. It's all Tristan's choice but I'd like to see you two breed. I'd like to see the results of that, but I'd also like to get my hands on some nectar samples as a start."

"As a start. Hmm. So, let's see here..."

"Kyla..." Tristan's voice was a warning.

She ignored it.

"You want my blood, then my period blood, and then you want me pregnant, so you can perform medical experiments ON OUR BABY!?" Kyla was suddenly fiercely protective of a baby that didn't even exist.

Adrian seemed unaffected by her anger.

Tristan hooked an arm around her waist. She hadn't realized she'd shot to her feet.

"Where are my parents?" she demanded, pulling to get away from Tristan. He wasn't having it.

"Your mother lives in Wales. I informed her that you'd be here, but she couldn't come. Your father *is* arriving today. He lives in Monaco, he works for me, but he's coming to see you."

"Siblings?" she pushed.

"That's classified information, I'm afraid." Adrian said coldly.

Kyla was taken aback.

Classified? What the fuck?

"Are you fucking serious?"

"Kyla!" Tristan scowled said right in her ear.

Kyla continued,

"So I don't get to know pertinent information to my situation?"

"That's out of scope," Adrian answered calmly.

"Um, I disagree. And what if Tristan doesn't opt for any of the things you want. What if he chooses something you *don't* want?"

She knew, then, that she had siblings. It had to be true. There was no way he wouldn't tell her the answer if the answer was No.

Adrian smiled, "Tristan is a leader. He was destined to lead and knows how important he is. He knows how important my work is. I'm confident that whatever decision he makes, it'll be the right one."

Kyla dug into her memory for the small remnants of her parents. Her mother looked kind of similar to her but with blonde hair and green eyes. Her father was tall, dark, blue-eyed, and handsome in her memory. She gulped down past a knot in her throat.

"This is too much..." she leaned back against Tristan, "My whole life is a lie. It's an experiment. This guy is my fucking grandfather? A vampire?"

A slightly maniacal laugh bubbled up, "And he wants us to have babies that he can put in experiments and then if I live, big if, though, he takes whatever of my menstrual blood you're willing to part with to..."

"Can you have someone show us to our room?" Tristan interrupted, "Kyla needs a chance to process."

Adrian smiled, "I can do that. Let me have those refreshments redirected." He reached for his phone.

Kyla felt anger rising higher and higher among the confusion. She tried to pull out of Tristan's hold.

He held her firmly and got his mouth to her ear, "Keep it together. Stop talking right now. Got me?"

She choked on a sob, thinking *what the fuck is this?* She felt emotion clog her throat and burn in her chest. She needed space. She needed clarity. She needed to fucking run.

"Stop, princess. Take a breath. Adrian? I need to settle her down. Our room; now, please."

"Follow me, I'll show you to it." He looked totally unaffected by Kyla's state of mind. And this royally pissed her off.

Tristan led her to the door, "Sunglasses. For fuck sakes, keep it together if we pass anyone."

She choked on a sob.

"Kyla," he warned, "Chill out or I'll have to get him to sedate you."

She was about to glare and retort, but common sense managed to settle in. She nodded at him and tried to clear her expression, to put on a mask of indifference. Inside, she felt like she was crumbling completely.

Adrian walked ahead of them. A man appeared pushing a cart of refreshments. Adrian told him to follow to Tristan's suite. Kyla didn't have to work hard to act like a zombie because she felt like the walking dead. They passed vampires in the hall and then as they walked through a large open lobby-type room with sofas, chairs, conversation areas, toward a staircase she was aware of a variety of things all at once.

She saw Sam, sitting at a table with another guy, drinking coffee. Sam gave Tristan a chin-jerk and then resumed listening to the man speaking to him without looking at Kyla.

Not far from Sam was a chess board and two men in lounge pants and bathrobes were playing. To the right of them there was a redheaded woman in orange pajamas whose throat was being fed on by another redheaded woman on a sofa by a big window that overlooked a garden area. Outside, in that garden, Kyla took in a man being pushed in a wheelchair by a woman wearing scrubs.

They began to climb a winding quadruple wide marble staircase in bright white with red veins with a heavy ornate marble banister. Descending the stairs was a gorgeous blonde whose eyes landed on Kyla when she said, "Tristan, you are a sight for sore eyes!"

"Faye," he replied, moving along.

"Not ill, I hope?" she looked concerned.

"Not at all. Excuse me." He ushered Kyla forward.

"Celia's here. Have you seen her?" Faye called back.

"I know," Tristan answered without looking back.

"Not thrilled with the level of exposure I'm feeling here, Adrian," Tristan muttered, "Would've been better to break everything to her in our suite."

"Not to worry," Adrian replied, "I have a cover for you. Meet me back in my office after you've settled her. We need to get those samples into temperature-controlled storage."

"Can you have a treadmill sent up? I'll wait for it."

"Yes, of course."

They walked down a hallway and Adrian handed Tristan a key card.

Tristan pushed the card into a slot and then opened the door. Kyla glanced ahead and saw their bags were already there. A man followed in and put down the tray of drinks and then left.

7

SHE DIDN'T HEAR WHAT Tristan said to Adrian as he closed the door. She was staring ahead, seeing nothing, just reeling...totally reeling as she started to feel the impact of the truth, the truth behind her blood, their connection, her whole life thus far, the danger she was in.

He spun her around by the shoulders and pulled her to him. She closed her eyes and absorbed the feel of him. Her hands slipped under his arms and around his waist. She inhaled him.

"Angel food cake," she whispered.

He caressed her head.

"Mixed with chocolate chip cookies," she started to sob.

He squeezed her tight and said, "Sunshine, mixed with laughter, fire, and silk."

She lifted her chin to look up at his face.

"You're everything I crave, too," he kissed her nose, "I smell it, I feel it, I taste it. You're my ambrosia. I love you."

"But Tristan," she whimpered, emotion burning in her chest, "Your love ... it will ... kill me."

His eyes were sorrowful. He backed her up, through the fancy old-world looking living area with lots of dark wood and fabric in colourful brocade, to the attached bedroom, and they got into a big wooden canopy bed done with blood-red linens and blood red curtains both on the windows as well as on the canopy drapes. Vamps sure did seem to like the colour of blood. He curled her against him and let out a sigh.

She nuzzled in to his shoulder. "This is fucked up."

"I know."

"You didn't know any of it?"

"Baby, I was as surprised as you. I'm not happy about a lot of things but I have no luxury of dwelling on it. My outward reaction is important. I can't appear weak or anything other than completely in control. Not even if someone seems trustworthy.

Vamps are predatory, they have innate reactions to weakness. They are opportunists. You just started your ovulation cycle yesterday and Adrian told me on the phone last night that tomorrow night will be even testier for me as you'll hit the peak by then. I've got to deal with a bunch of shit, including the fact that Sam, my right hand man, was in on this, and he fooled me. Others have been deceiving me, too. Well, keeping information from me but the same outcome. Liam's here in Arizona somewhere, fortified with your blood, and no doubt trying to figure out how to get more of it. I want to crush him into dust for putting his mouth on you, not to mention..." he tensed, then continued, "...what he did. And I've got you freaking out with all this new knowledge, and I don't trust anyone around us. I trusted Sam Jasper and I was wrong about that. There's a fuckuva lot ahead of me here."

"So, Adrian tells you that you've been played, that we're a lab experiment, we've been set up to meet, and he's got your own people working for him posing as working for you and you remained totally and completely in control? You sounded happy on the phone when you called me at the hotel. I don't get it!"

"Not even close," Tristan answered, "But I *got* myself under control quickly. I had to. Despite wanting to rip his head off he might be key to our future. I probably need him to help me *not* hurt you. He gave me hope about your next cycle. And about keeping you safe from Liam."

They were quiet a minute and he broke the loaded silence, "What are you thinking about right now?"

She covered her eyes with her hands, "So many things. I don't even know where to start."

He rubbed her back and kissed her forehead.

She took a big breath, "My parents aren't dead. And I have family, Tristan. Family who are vampires. This is crazy. I have vampire genes. I'm a fucking lab experiment. Do I have sisters or brothers? Why won't he tell me? Will he tell you the truth? And I can't believe they kept all this from you."

"I don't know the details yet about your parents, but I know your mother was pregnant when they were brought in. I don't know what came of that. When you went missing, Adrian wanted to continue the experiments. He reports to Claudio's American counterpart. Claude and I need to meet. He's likely traveling here within the next few days."

A knock on the door interrupted them. Tristan moved to go answer it. Kyla stayed in the bedroom on her back on the bed, staring at the ceiling. She could hear that the treadmill was being delivered. She then heard the door close and lock and then he was back.

She sat up in the bed and rubbed her palms over her eyes, "I don't even know what to say, where to start with my questions. My life is in your hands. What are you planning to do with it?"

He took her face in his hands and kissed her, "Rest, okay? I have to talk to Adrian, talk to Sam, deal with a few things. The treadmill is here for you, if you need to run."

"I don't want you to go."

"I won't be long..."

"I don't trust him. Adrian is a mad scientist. I don't trust him. Do *not* leave me alone here. Let's... let's get out of here."

"There's stuff we have to deal with here first. I'm not saying we're staying long, I don't know yet, but I'm assessing the situation and—-"

"Please, Tristan. I have a really bad feeling about this."

"Baby," he kissed her nose, "Try to take a nap, okay? I need to be level-headed so that'll help me if you do. I'll be back soon. The door is locked."

He started to head toward the door.

"You're going? You're just gonna leave me here? Leave me to fester in all this...this..."

He got back beside her and pulled her close.

"Go to sleep. It'll help us both. I'll hold you till you're sleeping, then I'll be as quick as I can be. I'll have my phone. You have yours."

He started to rub her back. She held tight to him.

"What are we gonna do?" she asked into his chest.

"I'm thinking we run a test to see what happens when the nectar comes. That's the only way forward."

"Tristan..."

"No. I'm not getting you pregnant and putting you at risk. If I decide next cycle that it's the way to go, that's what we do. For now, this is the only thing that makes sense."

"What if it's a trap? No one has been honest so far about any of this. What if... and if *you* decide? You? You can't unilaterally..."

"I know it could be a trap. Shh... I'm weighing it all out. I'm mulling it all over. But that's the direction I'm leaning in."

"Do *I* not have a say in what happens to me here?" She leaned back and looked at him.

"No."

"No?" she tried to break free of his embrace. He held tighter.

"No," he kissed her, "because you'll pick getting pregnant and I don't want to risk your life. And maybe I need more nectar so I'm in a better position to protect you."

"But both options risk my life. We'd have nine months to try to see... But I'd want to get the fuck away from here. If we have a baby I don't want him or her to be Adrian's guinea pig."

"Stop talking about us having a baby. You doing that makes me want to fuck you more than I already wanna fuck you. Just rest, okay. I need to go back and talk to him some more. Then when I get back, we'll eat and go for a walk and take things from there. Okay?"

She nodded robotically and buried her face in his chest. She didn't know if she had the strength to argue. Part of her niggled with worry that he wanted more nectar out of being power-hungry, but she didn't let that nag at her because she knew he loved her. She knew it in her soul.

She was suddenly acutely aware of his erection against her leg. She lifted her chin and looked at him, raising her eyebrows.

"I know," he grumbled and got out of bed, looking uncomfortable as he adjusted himself. "I'd better go."

"I'll be back as soon as possible. Sleep, if you can. Love you." He leaned over and kissed her briefly on the lips and left the room.

Kyla lay in bed for a while, but that proved fruitless so she changed her clothes and then got on the treadmill so that she could try to find *the zone*, try to find the answers, try to cope with all she'd learned. She had so many questions.

"You were created to be mine"

His words rang in her ears.

He'd said that the night in the RV park. Did he know, then, that they were an experiment?

Then the word *princess* rang in her ears. He told her he was like royalty and he called her princess almost from the start. With what Adrian had said about the fact that she could be a queen if she were turned, she wanted to hurl.

She yanked the safety key from the treadmill and it instantly halted, jerking her and making her nearly fall. She grabbed the handles and gasped for air. She hopped down and then paced the room, radiating energy that was frenetic, fully feeling everything she felt, hoping he'd feel it and get back to her. She got what she wished for.

Two minutes after she'd gotten off the treadmill, he was there, a scary look on his face.

"Did something happen? I got this spike of..."

"You knew."

"Knew?"

"You knew! You told me I was created to be yours, back in Victoria. You've been lying to me. You knew. You fucking knew that I was a lab experiment."

"No. I didn't."

"Oh, really?" she folded her arms.

"I felt it. I didn't know it. I didn't know Adrian's story. I never met the man until the day before yesterday. I knew of him. Knew a little of his work but not much. I knew nothing of you before we met. I only knew, from that first night we met, that you were *it* for me. It. End of story. Maybe it's entitlement, I don't know, but that's where my phrasing came from. It wasn't that I was in on this... this thing. I'm in turmoil here, baby. I'm wading through this shit just like you. I've just got the advantage of understanding both worlds and knowing this shit two days before you got wind."

Kyla thrust her fingers through her hair.

"I feel so...."

She couldn't finish. She couldn't articulate it. Her time on the treadmill hadn't helped with perspective. It only brought more fear, more anxiety, more shock as the things that'd been told to her sank in.

"You *do* know that the best thing you can do is trust me, don't you? Stop being so damn suspicious all the fucking time. I can't believe after everything we're still here." He poured a drink from a bar area by the window, "Want one?"

Kyla folded her arms across her chest and frowned and shook her head. Booze was the last thing she needed right now.

"How would it make you feel if every time you turned around I was throwing accusations at you, treating you with suspicion?"

"I'm sorry," she said softly. He was right. He was 100% right.

He shook his head and downed his drink.

"I'm a jerk," she admitted.

He nodded, "Yeah. So stop."

"Where were you? What's the latest?"

He sighed.

"Maybe I'll stop being so suspicious if you stop leaving me in the dark all the time. You need to give me some fucking credit."

He let out a breath and turned away from the window to face her. "You're right. You're absolutely right. I'm a jerk, too."

She sat on the sofa. He sat beside her and took her hands into his.

"I just hate the anxiety you feel, and I want it gone. Sorry if that means you get upset and feel like you're in the dark. I just don't want you to hurt. I'll stop."

She nodded, "Is the way you feel for me textbook? With royal vamps and their pets, I mean?"

He shook his head, "Doesn't seem like it. No one has said but I don't think so. Sounds like this combo, you and me? Unheard of."

He leaned over, and his lips touched hers and she relaxed into his embrace.

His kiss turned hungry and he hauled her up onto his lap, so she was straddling him. He was hard. His fingers roughly dug into her back and her shirt started to go up.

"Hey," she mumbled, "Don't start something we can't finish." But, she wanted him. Her breathing went erratic. She held tighter to him.

"I need..." he said against her lips but didn't finish. He groaned in frustration and Kyla's panties went damp. She climbed off him and grabbed the fly of his jeans and then tugged them open. She took his beautiful cock into her hands and lowered her head and then her lips parted.

He leaned back and groaned, "No, Kyla." But he didn't move away.

She ignored his protest. She licked and sucked and massaged and gave it her all, until he abruptly hauled her off and up and then put her on her back on the sofa. He was hovering over her, breathing hard. "I don't want your mouth. I want inside you and I fucking can't." He did up his pants.

"Get condoms?" Kyla breathed.

"Not safe enough." He backed up, "And I need to feel you. Not feel some fuckin' rubber."

"Umm, back, uh.. door?" she blushed. She was craving his body and closeness in a bad way.

He smiled, "Too close. If I lose it and slip an inch, we're in trouble. But let's come back to that menu item in a few days." He winked.

"Why not let me..." she reached, licking her lips, "Let me get you some relief. It'll help, no?"

"I'll wanna bury myself so deep in you that you can taste it from the wrong end. Baby, it's taking everything I have to stop myself from filling your whole body with my cum. Nothing else will help."

She stared at him, jaw dropped.

He backed off, "Yeah. It's taking every ounce of self-control and you haven't even peaked yet. God damnit. I'm getting a cold shower. We'll eat, then talk and walk."

He went into the bathroom and Kyla curled her knees up against her chest and sighed, ignoring the throbbing between her legs.

After Tristan's shower he barely got his pants on when there was a knock on the door. Food was delivered. They sat and ate soup and fancy sandwiches. Well, Kyla did. She devoured her meal, strangely enjoying every bite. Tristan barely touched his.

"You not hungry?" she asked, wiping her mouth.

"Not for this shit," he grumbled and then his expression cleared and he looked at her and shook his head.

"You're craving me?" Kyla asked.

He nodded.

"But you don't want to?"

He shook his head, "I've been urged to wait."

"I thought you wanted to feed regularly to keep us both strong. You're going to let him control how often you..."

His expression was suddenly filled with warning, "Finish and then we'll take a stroll. I'm just blood-fasting for another blood test. It's temporary."

She had to remember to guard her reactions. And with the mood he was in it probably wasn't wise to goad him right now, either.

THEY WERE WALKING DOWN the stairs and there were even more people in the bright and open lounge area. Kyla wore sunglasses and held Tristan's hand. She did her best to keep her expression even, but when they got to the bottom of the stairs they were approached by a balding pale and thin man in a gray silk dressing gown.

"Tristan?" the man asked, while approaching.

Tristan nodded, "In the flesh."

He stopped but looked like he wanted to keep moving. Kyla was at his side.

"Ruben Davidson. I was close to your grandfather. Alexander and I were good friends. We spent time together in Romania and later in the UK. I've been here a few weeks. I've had some surgery."

"Good to meet you," Tristan extended a hand. "I hope you're recovering well. Now if you'll excuse..."

The man's gaze travelled up and down Kyla.

"She smells magnificent," Ruben said. "Remarkable. And she's ripe."

"Thank you. She's mine. Excuse me," Tristan said. "I've got an appointment." He moved to walk past the man.

"Is she..." Ruben started and lowered his voice, "She is, isn't she? Of course. It's been about ten years. You know what I'm talking about..."

Tristan tensed up, halting before he finished taking a step.

"I've never smelled anything like her. I'm from a strong line so I'm attuned and she smells just so—-" The man's fangs protruded and Kyla couldn't help it; she jerked and scurried behind Tristan in response. Tristan had Ruben's throat in his hand. The room was suddenly buzzing with alertness.

Adrian's voice pierced the room.

"Ruben, a word?" Then his voice turned placating, "Tristan? I would appreciate it if you'd release Ruben and then meet me in my office in twenty minutes. Would that be alright? I assure you, Ruben will back off. Correct, Ruben?"

"Correct," Ruben choked out.

Tristan stayed where he was. Ruben's fangs retracted. Adrian cleared his throat and said low, "Tristan?"

Tristan let go of him and the man began hyperventilating and then said, "My apologies. I'm not well. That was unacceptable. If I were well it never would have happened. Please accept my apology."

Tristan swiftly moved Kyla out of the room to the outside with his arm hooked around her neck, his hand cupped around her shoulder, effectively blocking her entire throat as they left. She was aware that every eye in the place, other than those of the people in orange scrubs, was on her. The people in orange scrubs appeared to be humans, deer-in-the-headlight humans. There were at least a dozen others around, staring at them as they left. Tristan's fangs were out the whole time he stalked out the door.

Tristan walked her with a determined angry stride that invited no approach, past people in an area with patio tables, a fountain, and gardens and down a long wide staircase paved with colourful mosaic tiles toward what looked like a labyrinth-like garden bordered by many hedges but low-like, so it wasn't as if you'd get lost in a maze. It was gorgeous, painstakingly manicured. When they got beyond that garden and were in a large open field approaching forest, he continued, radiating fury. Kyla got a stitch in her side from the pace and winced and as soon as she did he hefted her up in his arms and they whooshed for a few seconds, their surroundings blurring by.

He stopped and put her on her feet. She glanced up at his face and his eyes were steely and jaw was clenched. He'd gotten them behind a large tree and let out a breath and caught her face in his palms, "Fuck, baby," he breathed.

"I'm sorry..." she whispered, "I tried not to react but then his fangs were so close to me and I—-"

"Not your fault. Fucking fuck," he bit off. "Most vamps who'd smell you but who'd see you on my arm, who'd see that collar, they would know better. He was fucking dying to taste you. Told you vamps have varied strengths? Well, he's old. Really old. And he's ill so that's obviously fucking with his deference to me. He clearly knows all about enchanted blood and royal bloodlines and royal pets because of how old he is. Adrian will do damage control but damn it...he should've ensured we had a clear coast. I'm so out of my goddamn element, here. This is no ordinary environment. There are dying vamps here, there are diseased vamps both mental and physical, and this could happen again. It can't. I've gotta do something."

Kyla was hyperventilating.

"I wouldn't put it past him. I wouldn't be surprised if he's doing it on purpose, Tristan. Something about him..."

He grabbed her shoulders,

"Listen, it's worse than I thought so I can't even talk to you properly in there. Please try not to put me on the spot with questions that I may not be able to answer in front of others and be careful with that temper. I'm already fighting to do damage control. We'll..." Tristan's cell phone interrupted him, he answered, "Adrian..." He let go of Kyla.

Kyla sat on the ground putting her back against the tree trunk listening to Tristan say, "You made assurances to me and so far you have fucking failed. This is unacceptable. If you have a series of tests planned that involve scenarios like these I'm telling you right now think again because I won't be a fuckin' lab rat, got me?"

He moved farther away but she heard him say a series of yes's and okays until he hung up, telling Adrian he'd meet him shortly.

"The cover is that you're a test subject. You're a co-operative pet who is semi-lucid based on taking a formula he's developed. He's saying it's a step between functional trance and fully lucid. That's what anyone who needs to know will be told. That'll help with reactions. Just be quiet, do your best to act as mesmerized as possible. People will think you're either in a functional trance or if anyone asks questions it'll soon become wide knowledge that you're under Adrian's care. This works in our favour as this is a research facility, so it makes things plausible. Any rumours out there can be quashed by the fact that I'm here with you, and that we're working with North America's most respected vampire doctor. This'll work."

He visibly relaxed, "People know who I am. Few know much about royal or enchanted pets, so risk is minimalized. I'm being assured Ruben was an anomaly. I don't fully trust that, but we'll be careful."

Kyla let out a breath of relief, but it wasn't deep relief. There were so many things to figure out, so many dangers.

They walked back inside and as they entered, Sam and Adrian merged with and then flanked them, Sam on Tristan's side and Adrian on Kyla's. Kyla could only assume they were serving as body-guards. They got back to their room without incident. She felt eyes on them when they got back inside but she avoided eye contact and tried to just focus on getting to their suite.

Tristan raised a finger to her as he led her into the room. He slipped back out and shut the door behind himself, Sam and Adrian standing with him in the hallway. She spent the next few hours alone, but some things occurred to her and she was anxious for him to get back.

As the room darkened. she heard voices in the living room. She strained to listen. She couldn't make out words but neither voice sounded like Tristan's. She had been on the bed, playing solitaire on a tablet PC that was in the room. She put it down and braced herself. There was a knock on the bedroom door, which was open a few inches.

She sat up straight in the bed.

"Yes?"

Adrian stepped in and he was with a man, a tall and attractive man with dark hair and blue eyes. The man wore a suit. His eyes were on Kyla. They were warm. She was about to remark that Tristan didn't want anyone with her without him present, but she wasn't sure if someone who was just semi-lucid would say such a thing. And before she could decide what to say or whether she should say anything, it occurred to her who the man with Adrian was.

He spoke up,

"Ky."

Memories flashed in her mind of zooming down a slide and directly into that man's arms.

My father.

She swallowed past a lump in her throat.

He opened his arms.

She remained rooted to the bed, gripped by uncertainty.

"Where's Tristan?" Kyla asked, not taking her eyes off her father. Because this man wasn't just her father. He was also a vampire.

"He's downstairs with Samuel," Adrian replied.

"Does he know you're up here?"

"Your father traveled all the way here to see you. He's been anxious," Adrian said, not answering her question.

Her father looked the same. He looked just the same. She had very few specific memories of her parents, but he looked identical to what she remembered. He looked like he was 25 or 30, not nearly 50. He was handsome, trim but athletic-looking. He had a nice smile.

A crash pierced the air and Tristan was there, between the foot of the bed and Kyla's father and Adrian. He had his back to Kyla, blocking them.

"What the fuck?" he bit off.

"Sir! Lyle Kelly," Kyla's father extended a hand to Tristan, "Kyla's father. I'm so glad to finally meet you. I've heard great things about you. We've been at a few events together but have never actually met."

Tristan crossed his arms and ignored Kyla's father, "Adrian, do we need to again review that no one, and I mean no one, yourself included, is to approach her without me present, without my consent prior to that approach?"

Adrian shrugged, "Her father, Tristan. He was anxious to see her. He hasn't seen her in over 20 years. For most of those years he had no clue whether or not she was alive. Some compassion wouldn't go amiss."

"Compassion?" Tristan snarled, "Since when is that a consideration for our kind?"

Adrian smirked at him and shrugged.

Wow, devious.

Kyla's father spoke up, "Again, I'm very happy to meet you, Sir. I apologize for the misstep of entering before obtaining your permission. I respectfully request some time with Kyla. Perhaps you could both join me for dinner this evening?"

"I'll let you know," Tristan folded his arms across his chest.

"I'd appreciate the opportunity to join you as well," Adrian added, "A family dinner. Won't it be lovely?"

There was definite sarcasm in his tone.

"I'll let you know." Tristan's voice was arctic.

Lyle flashed Kyla his enigmatic smile and it was painful for her to witness. It wasn't right. It wasn't genuine. Her spidey senses were going haywire.

"I look forward to getting to know you as an adult. I can't begin to tell you how happy I am to see you safe and sound. You grew up to look even more beautiful than I daydreamed about. You have my colouring but your mother's features, her eyes. I'm so very happy that things are working out according to plan. Once I knew you were alive I wanted badly to see you in the flesh but as you'd imagine, I couldn't." He gestured himself with a sweep of his hand, "It'd be a little tricky to explain..."

"How is she?" Kyla asked, without thinking, only feeling -—feeling pain pierce her chest.

According to plan?

Kyla had been stolen from her parents and their lives had been uprooted. Her birth itself had been orchestrated and he looked like it was all the same to him.

She had trouble getting a read on his expression since she didn't really know him.

"How's who?" Lyle asked.

"My mother?"

Who else? Wow.

"Oh. Right. Well...Katya and I don't see one another often."

Of Kyla's few early memories of her parents, she remembered them being very in love, their home life very fairy tale-like. Maybe that's why she expected her prince to eventually come. Her father had been *such* a gallant prince charming back then and her mother had seemed love struck, happy.

She recalled that her mother and father couldn't keep their hands off one another. Cuddling, kissing, all the time. Now though, knowing that they were hypnotized into being together? No wonder they didn't stay together after being turned. She wondered if being turned would instantly turn off mesmerisation.

She really needed time with Tristan, to talk about some suspicions she had.

She didn't know what to say to Lyle Kelly. The man felt like a stranger. The man?

Hah. The vampire, to be accurate.

She felt a chill run up her spine. Adrian was closely regarding her. The whole semi-lucid thing, was that what her father thought, too? Or did he know everything?

"Excuse me," Tristan said, motioning to the door, "I'll let you know about dinner."

Lyle smiled at Kyla with what looked like a hopeful expression, "Again, really wonderful to see you," he opened his arms," I would like to hug you. Could you come here, please? Would it be okay if I hugged you?"

"Not right now," Tristan answered before Kyla had a chance to react.

Lyle's expression dropped.

"A word, Tristan?" Adrian said.

"Not now," Tristan answered, "I'll come see you."

Adrian had the decency to look a little bit (but only a little bit) contrite as they left the room.

Tristan followed them out of the bedroom and she heard muffled voices and then heard the door slam. An instant later Tristan was

back in the bedroom with her and his expression was nearly murderous. It softened when his eyes landed on her.

"Are you okay?"

Kyla shrugged.

"How was that? Seeing your father? Adrian asked about bringing him up and I told him it should wait until I asked you and I'm
not real impressed that he did what he did."

"I... I don't know, it was weird. He hasn't aged. He seems kind
of...robotic, I think. Colder than I remember. I dunno."

Kyla felt numb.

"Thanks for getting rid of them. That was... it was a lot."

He sat on the bed and put an arm around her. She sank into him
and they laid down together.

"No way that man is getting close to you until I know what he's
about."

"You don't think he'd bite me, do you?"

Tristan shrugged, "Sorry to say but I've seen stranger things happen."

"Ew."

"Yeah. He apparently doesn't know much about you, but he does
know you were bred specifically for feeding and breeding. He knows
your blood is fit for a king. Being a vamp, curiosity might get the better of him. Not taking that chance."

"This place," she whispered into his shoulder. His grip tightened
on her and her chin slipped into the crook of his neck. "It's freaky.
It's wrong."

He sighed and softly said, "Yeah. Welcome to my world. You
haven't even seen freaky yet."

"I need to walk with you," she whispered against his throat and
then kissed it.

He squeezed, "Can't right now. It's a full house downstairs so too
much exposure for you. I've requested he move us so to one of the

cottages on the property. I'm stepping out but text me if you need me," and his chin jerked toward her purse.

She nodded.

"Be back in five," he said against her mouth, giving her a soft kiss. She rested her forehead against his chin for a second and then looked up into his beautiful eyes.

"Love you," she whispered.

"Love you, princess," he told her and then gave her a squeeze and got up.

He gave her a wink as he left the room and she reached for her purse and took out the disposable cell phone and typed a message to him,

> **"If Adrian's cover story for my reaction in front of Ruben is that I'm on an experimental drug that keeps me semi-lucid, what if he actually DID give me that kind of drug before we met? Maybe Sam gave me something before we met and that's why I can't be hypnotized."**

She hit send and then paced, waiting for his reply. She erased her message to him so that if anyone got ahold of her phone they wouldn't see it.

Fifteen minutes passed and then he was back.

"We need to be at a dinner with them," he grumbled as he entered the room with two garment bags that he dumped on the bed. "Unfortunately. Here's something to wear."

"Huh?"

Did he read my text?

"Fuck," he grumbled and rubbed his eyes with his palms, "Claudio turned up right in the midst of me ripping Adrian a new asshole for approaching you without me. Your *father* tried to crawl up my ass. Ruben tried to crawl up there with him. Sam's fuckin' groveling and he and I had an interesting chat. Too interesting. And now Claude's here and insists on a bloody dinner with all of them. And he wants you there. Bullshit. Fuck. I'm gonna talk to him. Try to get out of this."

"Did you get my text?" Kyla asked.

Tristan shook his head and reached into his pocket, "No. I got bombarded as soon as I left this room." He touched the screen on his phone. His expression hardened.

"Goin' for a shower," he mumbled, taking his phone into the bathroom.

Two minutes later she heard the water go on as her phone dinged.

She picked it up and read his text.

"I've already considered that & don't think so. He hasn't had access to you consistently so it prob would've worn off by now. Haven't completely ruled it out but unlikely. Delete these msgs after reading."

She deleted the message and opened the garment bag and saw a full-length flowy coral-coloured gown with intricate rhinestone-crusted thin straps that'd go over her shoulders and crisscross over her back. There were gold strappy sandals, too. She put the bag back down and went into the bathroom. She could see him through the mist in the shower stall, which was enclosed with glass doors. He had both palms against the wall and his head and body were bowed forward. He looked like the weight of the world was on his slumped shoulders.

She had an overwhelming urge to comfort him.

She shed her clothes and opened the door and stepped in. His chin rose, and she stepped directly into his embrace. His fangs instantly appeared and then he sighed what sounded like relief as they sank into her throat. She felt his relief. He probably felt hers. They were connected, and she was thrilled. She felt his need, his stress, his love and hunger for her.

His fingers went between her legs and her hand gripped his cock as her thumb caressed the tip. He released her throat and his mouth moved to her breasts, which he took in both hands, alternately licking the tips of each one. She sank against him again and started to stroke faster. They kissed with urgency.

"Fuck, baby," he moaned, "You shouldn't have come in here. I want inside you so fucking much."

"Do it," she pleaded, "Just do it. I don't even care."

She didn't care at all about the consequences at that moment. She was driven purely by need.

"I can't. You are pushing it and we both know it. Stop it, okay? You're gonna piss me off."

"Tristan, it's like I'm fueled by need instead of common sense; I'm sorry."

"Go down on me," he ordered.

She grinned. He gave her a disapproving look.

"I need to fuck you and if I can't fuck you properly I have to fuck that mouth. Look up at me when you do it."

She instantly complied, feeling giddy, getting to her knees. He was a sight to behold, all muscled and wet. Droplets of water trailing down his washboard abs, the gorgeous V and happy trail, his big beautiful hard cock.

She ran her hands down the ridges of his abs and then took him deep. He placed the palm of his hand against the back of her head and caressed. She looked up at him while she bobbed, twirling her tongue and rotating her fist.

He looked straight into her soul and then his head rolled back and he hissed at the ceiling and then his fangs protruded and he got a handful of her hair and his grip went tight, kind of too tight. But she didn't care. She adjusted.

She could see the veins on his arms, his wrist; her eyes traveled up his arm, his sexy muscled arm. He growled her name and hauled her back up and pierced her throat with his teeth again. She felt urgency surge through her and in her mouth she tasted sugary berries.

He backed away, grabbed his cock and started pumping it in a fist.

"No, you have to stop touching me or I'll slam right into you. Touch yourself."

She got back against the opposite wall of the shower so that there was about four feet between them. She put her hand between her legs and bit down hard on her lower lip. They stared at one another, intently, working themselves.

The passion, the heat in Tristan's eyes, it was so erotic she knew it wouldn't take long before she was shuddering out her release. Kyla hadn't touched herself in front of someone before, but this? This was *hot*.

Watching him fist his cock? That was hot, too.

Her entire life, her entire future was on the line here and yet she was completely consumed with the need to climax.

"I can't wait to fuck you again," Tristan said.

"Me, too," she said, "I can't wait to have you inside me in a way where we don't have to hold anything back. No fears, just us."

"I promise I'll do everything in my power to get that for us. Soon," he vowed.

By the look of resolve in his eyes, she totally believed him. She smiled.

"The second I know it's safe, I will fuck you non-stop for days. I love you so fucking much. Come for me," he ordered and started to stroke himself faster, his fist blurring.

Wow. I wish I could jerk him off that fast. If I were a vamp, too, I probably could.

Kneeling on the shower floor, she sat back on her calves and spread her legs wider and kept working her clit with her middle and ring fingers, separating her folds with her index and pinky fingers. She leaned forward and got her mouth over the tip of his cock while he continued to stroke. The sounds he made were so freaking sexy.

Her free hand went around him, grabbing his ass. He plunged deeper. Fuck, he had the best ass ever. Tight, round, hard, smooth. She gazed up and their eyes locked and she circled her fingers harder and harder around her clit in time with swirling and suction on him and she was so wet that she had trouble getting a grip on herself.

She kept at it until she finally hit it and fell apart, shuddering with his cock in her mouth. He came down her throat and she took what he gave. She took it all.

It took a minute for the aftershocks to stop, and when they did, he hauled her up in his arms and kissed her right on the lips,

"You're so fucking bad," he growled and thrust his tongue into her mouth. "And I love it."

She whimpered and threw her arms around his neck and they stood for a few minutes, just under the water, just recovering.

"Love you," she said against his throat.

"Mmm, love you more," he said and slapped her ass, making her gasp.

"No way," she whispered, "I love you way more."

"No," he looked in her eyes, "I had no capacity for love for years and the amount of love I feel for you? It exceeds anything I've ever felt."

"Ditto," she said.

He gave her a dazzling dimpled smile and then reached for shampoo and squirted a glug into his hair. He passed her the bottle. She followed suit.

When he was done and out of the shower, she asked him to bring in her toiletries bag so she could shave. She was extra cautious with the razor, despite the fact that she knew he wasn't about to blow a gasket over the scent of her blood. She didn't know if anyone else would swoop in at the scent of it, so she was slow and concise with the razor.

When she was back in the bedroom ,he was on the bed, on his back, towel around his waist and his eyes were trained on the ceiling. He was in deep thought.

She crawled in and put her cheek to his shoulder, "Hey."

"Hey."

"Prep me for this dinner?"

He shuffled uneasily, "Get dressed. In the bathroom. Nothin' but towels between us is too tempting."

"But we just..."

"Doesn't matter. You're getting closer to that peak. I can feel it. It's making me crazy. It better not have this kind of effect on anyone else. You need to be good, okay? Don't push."

She got up and picked up the garment bag and nodded at him.

"I'm serious, princess."

"I'm trying," she said contritely.

"Try harder."

Mm, harder.

He gave his head a shake and waggled his finger at her.

She couldn't help it. It was as if she'd been fed an aphrodisiac. She chewed her bottom lip and nodded as she headed toward the bathroom.

"Take your phone," he said softly.

She walked a few steps backwards and lifted it from the nightstand, carrying it into the bathroom with the garment bag and her purse.

As soon as she got into her undies there was a text from him,

"I'm pretty sure tonight is one of Adrian's experiments. Test us to see how I handle you being at almost peak cycle with others around. Do your best to be as on-guard as possible."

"Gotcha," was Kyla's reply.

Yeah, based on the long list of possible outcomes for Kyla listed by him, Grandfather Dearest seemed the type to run continuous experiments.

8

The dress fit her like it was designed for her. She loved it; it was gorgeous. She felt beautiful. She wished she had this dress for some other event in some other place, though. If only they lived in a world where she could wear beautiful little black glittery dresses or long coral dresses without it being when her life was at stake!

She'd put her hair up in a twist with a claw clip at the back, but Tristan walked into the bathroom as she was just about finished with her mascara and he immediately yanked it out.

"Hey! It took me like fifteen tries to get that just right!"

"Yeah, well your bare throat isn't something I want on display," he grumbled, tossing the clip aside, "Bad enough your body'll be on display."

"Oh," she said softly and picked it up, deciding to use it to pull back the sides of her hair, since she didn't have nearly enough product or styling tools with her to do anything fancier. The dress was too fancy for her hair to just hang limply after air drying, "If that's your way of saying I look hot in this dress, thank you."

He raised his eyebrows at her.

"Levity?" she suggested.

He rolled his eyes.

She shrugged and went back to working on her mascara.

Tristan was gorgeous in his dark suit, dark shirt, and black tie. Of course he was; he was always gorgeous.

She called out, "Wait," as he finished running his fingers through his still wet hair and gooped up her hands with a little styling gel and started to run it through his hair.

"I really don't give a fuck what I look like tonight," he mumbled, backing away from her.

Yikes.

THEY LEFT THEIR SUITE hand in hand and there were five men stationed outside the room when they entered the hall. Tristan had told her that Adrian promised security going forward.

One guard (they were all dressed in black suits, looking like secret service agents) walked ahead of them, leading the way: two walked on either side, and two walked behind them, effectively surrounding them. Kyla tried to ignore them.

They walked down the stairs to the first floor and through the open lounge area, which was still littered with "people" (she felt eyes on her but didn't make eye contact with anyone), through doors to a hallway with several sets of doors and to the end, where French doors were opened for them into a dining room that was breathtakingly beautiful, designed like an ancient palace.

The room had a long table set and seated were Adrian, at the head, Sam at one side, Kyla's father at his other side, and a tall dark-haired goateed man beside Sam. Tristan sat her at the foot of the table and he sat beside Lyle, swapping Kyla's water glass with an empty goblet. Clearly, changing the planned seating arrangement, not wanting Kyla beside Lyle.

"Kyla, meet Claudio," Tristan introduced with a sweep of his hand gesturing toward the man with the goatee.

Kyla looked to the man and he was watching her, an assessing gaze, a glass of red wine in his hand.

No, wait, not red wine. Blood.

She gave him a nod as she sat down. He didn't return it, but watched her.

A server moved to Tristan and was about to fill that goblet with blood, but Tristan waved his hand in refusal.

"Nothing for you, Tristan?" Adrian queried, his brow notched, and his eyes darting to Kyla.

"Wine. White."

"Good to meet you, Kyla," Claudio belatedly said, and Kyla's eyes moved to him.

At once Kyla was struck with the fact that he appeared arrogant, cunning, predatory. It was written all over him. He was a handsome man, looked to be about ten to fifteen years older than Tristan. His hair was short; his eyes were grey but fairly luminescent. He had a goatee and a squared jaw. He was sitting down, but based on his posture and the lines of his expensive-looking grey suit, Kyla suspected he was a built like a bodybuilder.

"Tristan?" Adrian interjected, "Have you fed?"

"I have," Tristan didn't look at Adrian.

"But we agreed..."

Tristan waved his hand, "We'll discuss it later."

A server moved around to top up water glasses and then two more male servers moved in and began delivering an orange soup to everyone.

Tristan immediately leaned over and inhaled deeply over Kyla's bowl. Then he lifted her spoon and tasted it.

"Honestly, Tristan." Adrian said, amused.

Tristan glared at him and his fangs shot out.

Kyla steeled herself and clutched the edge of her chair.

"Gentleman, I realize emotions are high at the moment with all the revelations that have come to light. Let's enjoy a nice meal, some conversation, and move forward, shall we?" That was Claudio.

Tristan continued glaring Adrian's way for a beat and then his fangs retracted.

Kyla reached over under the table and put her hand on his knee and gave him a small reassuring squeeze. His face gave nothing away to anyone else at the table, but he put his hand on top of hers and his thumb skated across the back of her hand.

"Bon Appetit," Adrian said and raised his glass. All others but Tristan raised their glasses. Kyla raised her water glass.

A server moved over and offered her wine. She nodded, asking for white as well, and he poured her a glass.

Tristan leaned over and lifted Kyla's wine glass and put it to his lips and drank some and then passed it to her with a nod.

Kyla glanced at Adrian, who was watching Tristan.

"Royal taster?" Lyle mused, "I'm impressed."

No one replied.

The soup was cream of carrot. It was delicious. Kyla decided to focus on the soup.

Does he really think they'd poison me? Or maybe slip me one of Adrian's so-called concoctions?

"There are a few things that need to be settled," Claudio started. "Tristan and I have spoken briefly but I wanted us to enjoy this meal together so that we can put everything on the table. Move forward. As discussed, this was planned 27 years ago when the last Kovac mating experiment failed. We need to move forward. We all want the same thing. Prosperity for our kind."

Kyla couldn't hide her jolt of surprise.

He continued, "Alexander, along with other counterparts around the world, and Adrian, along with Adrian's medical council counterparts, have worked together closely to solve problems of a medical nature as well as ensure our population continues at healthy levels, despite the challenges we've faced in that area. There are regular ongoing clinical trials as well as contingency plans in addition to this plan for Tristan. Tristan, you have the allegiance of myself, of Sam, of the entire leadership team. You have the ability to do amazing things for our kind. You've already done impressive things for Kovac Capital as well as on the councils you've participated in. Breeding is the next step, a royal responsibility. You have already demonstrated the skills and you have the lineage to lead. Your offspring are essential to our future. Your bloodline with hers? *This* blended bloodline, it will ensure strength. We can only imagine what kinds of results we'll get with a blend of Kovac and Constantin blood. I know Adrian has outlined a variety of options for you. I want you to know that myself, Sam, and Adrian are here to help. All our resources are at your disposal to ensure success here." Claudio kept looking at her during this little speech.

"I'm still reviewing options, Claude. I'm not jumping the gun."

"Kyla's too important, Tristan," Claudio said, still looking at Kyla, "I know this. And we will take every precaution we can. As mentioned, there are alternatives if you want her taken out of the equation, but you need to make some decisions and I hope that logic and the usual foresight you display will prevail over emotions."

Tristan looked like he was carefully controlling his anger. "Well, given the course of events I'm sure you'll understand if I'm not immediately jumping on board. I've been deceived. For a decade I've been deceived. And after finding out what Alexander went through..."

"We've learned," Adrian said," We've learned from those errors and we need to move forward."

What the hell was he talking about? Failed experiments? Errors?
That didn't sound like it boded well for Kyla.

"Tristan?" she asked before she could stop herself.

His eyes moved to her and he jerked his head in a "No."

She moistened her lips with her tongue and gazed around the room in a quick sweep but then her gaze doubled back to Sam.

Sam was staring at her and his chest was rising and falling rapidly.

Kyla's eyes met his and his widened. She felt an incredibly sharp sense of impending doom. Sam was struggling with knowledge of her blood. She knew it. She *felt* it.

Tristan went wired, "Kyla?"

"Stop him! He's gonna..." Kyla shrieked at Tristan at the very same instant Sam's fangs shot out and Sam sprang from his seat, looking like he was heading toward Kyla.

Tristan jumped up. Sam wasn't heading to Kyla, though; he was heading for the door. He was a blur and he was gone.

"Excuse me," Adrian said and zoomed out behind Sam.

"Clearly," Tristan motioned toward the door Sam and Adrian had left from, "the science isn't refined enough. I'm not taking chances with her."

"Sam's bloodline is what makes him a wildcard. Believe me, he's loyal to you. I've been working closely with him for 25 years and he is the most trustworthy friend you'll ever have. There will be safeguards in place for you."

"Regardless..." Tristan shook his head and sipped Kyla's wine again.

Servers moved in and began clearing the soup bowls.

"Tristan," Claudio said in an attempted placating tone.

"Why not you?" Kyla spoke up.

Claudio's eyed darted to her.

"Why haven't you been mated with an enchanted pet?"

"I have two," Claudio answered, "Mating attempts have not been successful. We've had repeated miscarriages and stillborn births."

Tristan's body locked tight in response. Claudio continued.

"All true vamps, often referred to as super vamps, those who are vamps with vamp DNA rather than just being turned vamps, are given enchanted pets at their ten-year anniversary. Vamps aren't in-formed of this until they receive their pet and demonstrate to us their common sense by the acts that follow. We do not want news of this to travel. Tristan's case was handled differently because of what was at stake with your blood as well as due to who he is. Your lucidity was also an unexpected twist. I expected a phone call when he tast-ed you. I expected my protégé to confide in me. He didn't. So, we watched him to see how things would progress. It has all been very enlightening." Claudio's expression was sour, "If Tristan were any ordinary vamp it would not have been looked on favourably. But based on who he is, I've overlooked a few missteps."

"So, you haven't killed any pet by accident?" Kyla asked, not sure how to respond to Claudio's comments.

"I have not. Being a true vamp, I have the control necessary."

"Are they mesmerized, entranced, whatever?"

"*They are.*"

Kyla took a big breath, "But Liam..."

"Liam is neither royal, nor a true vamp. He's turned. The problem with enchanted pets occurs when turned vamps stumble across them. They do not have near the control or power that we do. The older a turned vamp gets the more strong and powerful he becomes. The better he lives, the more powerful he becomes. Turned vampires are very accountable for their actions. It affects their longevity, their power, their health. Super vampires, true vamps with vampire DNA are better equipped than that. Tristan here, he could eat garbage and not exercise for a decade and he wouldn't be depleted. That's because his blood is not only true but also royal. Tristan, being who he is, wouldn't do that to his body. Tristan, being who he has been... I expected a different outcome from him after you were delivered. I did not get what I expected. You are not what we expected."

Kyla didn't know what to make of that last comment. Tristan watched Claudio, expressionless. Kyla looked over at Lyle. He sat there quietly. He didn't look reflective, bothered, anything like that.

Tristan's phone made a text noise. He lifted it and then began thumbing away at it.

"And what about you?" Kyla asked, "What do you think about all of this?"

"All of this?" Lyle asked.

Kyla nodded, "Yeah. Your life plans are railroaded and that results in a whole lot of things happening. They orchestrate a bunch of
things, including your marriage, me, and then turn you and your wife
into vampires. I'm taken away from you and then you find out I was
created to become a gift for a royal vampire. How did that make you
feel?"

Lyle gave her a smile, "Proud."

Kyla raised her eyebrows and her mouth dropped open.

Adrian was back. Adrian guided Sam the long way around so
that he walked by Kyla instead of directly to their seats. Clearly a test.
Tristan rose and stood behind Kyla. Sam looked at Kyla and gave her
what she took to be an apologetic look. Sam then made it to his seat.

Kyla resumed asking her father, "Proud that you lost me for all
this time? That you didn't know if I was alive or dead? That now I
could die because the list of lab experiments could go wrong?"

The room hushed as salad was served.

After the servers were done, Lyle answered. "Proud that I can
help our kind. By fathering you I've contributed. I know that I was
beside myself with worry when you went missing. I remember those
emotions. But then I found out who I was. And when I got word that
they found you I knew everything was going to be as it was supposed
to be."

"Whether you wanted it or not."

"Sometimes things are bigger than the individual, Ky. I have
vampire DNA; I'm true. My being turned was fate. Had it not happened, that would've been unfair to me. It's your fate to be turned as
well. You have contributions to make first, just like I did. And you are
going to love life as a vamp. It's absolutely amazing!"

Hearing him call her Ky again, like he'd done when she was
small, it tore at the hole in her heart. She didn't think she'd remembered much about him but right now, these conversations, seeing

him, hearing him talk, it was digging in and churning up more memories, more feelings.

Bedtime stories, walks in the park, horsey rides on his back. With all of those memories she saw her mother in the background, green-eyed and smiling with happiness. She heard herself squealing in delight, calling him "Horsey-Daddy" and riding on his back.

The more she saw him, the more she really wanted to see her mother. But this wasn't the typical craving for a long lost loved one. This was different. This was strange.

"Perhaps you and Lyle could spend some time together tomorrow. Talk some more," Claudio suggested, interrupting her reverie and signaling to his empty goblet of blood. The one server that had stayed stationed in the room moved back over and refilled it.

In other words, he was asking them to save their heart to heart long lost father-daughter chat for another time. Clearly the arrogant prick thought his time was too valuable.

The door opened. It was the dark-haired woman they'd seen when they first arrived.

"Good evening gentlemen," she said, stepping in as if everyone had been awaiting her arrival.

"Celia!" answered Adrian brightly.

"God damn it Adrian..." Tristan muttered in what sounded like a warning and Kyla felt something coming off him that tweaked her anxiety levels.

"Claudio!" she beamed, flipping her glossy straight long jet-black curtain of hair, "A lovely surprise. Good to see you. Forgive the intrusion. Tristan, could I trouble you for a quiet word?"

"It isn't a good time, Celia," Tristan replied and then he said, "Could you be any more obvious?" to Adrian.

Adrian shook his head innocently as if to say, 'I don't know what you're talking about.'

"It'll be only a moment," Celia batted her eyelashes at Tristan.

"*Not* a good time," he repeated.

She pouted.

He didn't react.

Her eyes went cold, "I *neeeed* to speak with you."

"Celia, seriously."

"It's very important."

"So is what I'm in the middle of."

She stomped a designer shoe-clad food hard, glaring at Tristan. Actually stomped.

Wow.

Kyla was flabbergasted at the gall.

Claudio spoke, "Celia, this was a closed-door dinner meeting. How are you even present?"

Celia threw her head back and laughed hard.

"Oh puh-lease..."

"Have you done something to the guards?" Claudio asked.

She snickered.

Sam rose, "Let's take a walk, CC. Tristan will call you later, when he's got time. Yeah?"

Sam tried to lead her by the elbow. Her face went ugly and she shoved and Sam went flying onto his ass, landing about twenty feet away, which was about three feet from Kyla's feet.

"Tristan!" she demanded, "Now!"

What the fuck?

Tristan stood and glared at her, "Get the fuck outta here, Celia."

Sam moved back to his seat.

"Why?" she looked affronted. She put her arms across her chest.

"This meeting is closed door. That's why there were guards stationed outside. You know better. I'll find you in a little while."

She stomped her foot again, "I need to talk to you now!"

The way she was acting reminded Kyla of the little rich *"I want it NOW!"* girl from the Charlie and the Chocolate Factory movie.

Kyla knew Tristan didn't want to leave her unattended.

Tristan's mouth was in a tight line, "Fuck off, Celia."

Kyla saw Lyle blanch and Sam wince.

"I'll come see you when I'm good and ready. Now, get the fuck out."

Celia headed toward their table. Tristan got up and quickly moved so that he was between Celia and Kyla.

"I'm serious," he told her.

"What's the big deal?" she batted eyelashes at him again, "You can't take one eensy weensy little minute to talk to me?"

She used her thumb and index finger to make an inch sign.

"Right now, no."

"If you'd talked to me when I first asked, this would be over by now. Just step into the hall with me."

"No. Out. Now you won't even get my time."

"But why?"

"Because I fuckin' said so. Now are you gonna leave or should I remove you myself?"

She patted him on the cheek, "Aren't you cute? Now, come before I put you over my knee for insubordination."

Insubordination?

Kyla felt a spike of possessive anger at the woman's touching his face, even.

"Why won't you come into the hall with me?" Celia asked, reverting to another pout but then she glanced over Tristan's shoulder and frowned. Her eyes landed on Lyle, who was directly in her line of vision. Lyle was looking at Kyla. Celia's eyes then moved to Kyla. Kyla had been watching but trying as hard as she could to be not-too-obvious about it. She didn't know if word had traveled about her so-called 'semi-lucid' state or not.

"Her?" Celia said, "You're not willing to come into the hall to talk to me because you don't want to leave your pet alone with the big bad vampires? Tristan, so unlike you." she started to laugh, "Then, by all means, bring her to the hall."

"Celia," Tristan warned, "Say what you need to say and then go. I'm done playing this game."

"Fine," she placed her hands on Tristan's chest, leaned forward, and said, "I'm summoning you. I want you in my suite later. I want your cock."

Tristan recoiled, but before he got more than a few inches away Kyla did something completely utterly stupid and completely and utterly out of her control. She felt that cold whoosh start at her toes and rapidly climb up her body and before she knew it she had Celia's glossy curtain of jet back hair and she used it to give Celia a shove that surpassed the shove Celia had given to Sam. By about double.

The female vamp went right into a wall and the force of her body caved the drywall in.

"His cock is fucking taken," Kyla screeched, "And so is the rest of him!"

Kyla vaguely heard an, "Oh shit," and she thought, but couldn't be sure that it was Sam who said it.

Then Kyla was behind Tristan, who'd zoomed them back against a wall so that Kyla's back was against the wall, his body shielding her from the female vamp who'd instantly gotten to her feet and whooshed into their space.

Tristan held his right hand out to stop the she-vamp. His left hand was curled behind himself, around Kyla's waist, keeping her plastered between his back and the wall.

"What in the fuck was that?" Celia thundered, and her voice sounded demonic. Kyla got a very unpleasant cold shiver from her toes straight up her spine but despite that shiver, Kyla was breathing hard and she was fucking pissed. She clenched the back of Tristan's suit jacket.

"Move!" Celia hissed, "I will kill it!"

Suddenly, Lyle, Sam, and Adrian were all in the space, too, as if they were providing back-up to Tristan. Celia's throat was in Tristan's grasp. Celia started to turn blue and reached for Tristan's wrist. Kyla could see that Tristan was using considerable strength.

"You won't get my cock, Celia. Those days are done."

"What is she?" Celia choked out, "She's not vampire. What the fuck is she? Let me at her!"

Claudio's voice rang through, "Celia, I order you to back off. You touch Tristan's pet and you'll answer to me."

"Tristan's pet?" Celia was astounded, "What is she? How did she? No...I don't give a damn. I'm gonna kill her. You know I have every right with Tristan. I'll program these minions so they're all rocking in the corner and sucking their thumbs in about three seconds if you don't move right now."

"Let her at me!" Kyla shouted, stupidly, feeling that cold rush bursting again.

"Baby, stop," Tristan said over his shoulder, still holding Celia's throat.

Kyla held her tongue and the cold fizzled out.

"Clear this fuckin' room!" Tristan demanded, "Lock her down and get me and Kyla escorts back to our suite. Now."

Adrian opened the door and then grumbled, "She's already played with our door guards. Give me five minutes."

He disappeared from the room.

Kyla didn't have a clue what that had meant.

"Is she an un-turned royal, Tristan?" Celia demanded but her voice had gone funny.

"Back off, Celia."

"Tristan! You need to answer me. Now! I'm warning you..."

"You don't boss me around, Celia. You know your shit doesn't work on me."

"What is her deal?"

"Fuck, Claude... get her locked down." Tristan bit off.

Claudio stepped up to the group casually, like it was all the same to him.

"Celia, darling. Come." He put his hand on her shoulder.

She let out a little breath and her features relaxed. She was staring over Tristan's shoulder at Kyla now. Staring right into Kyla's eyes. Kyla stared back, and her eyes narrowed on Celia.

"I want you to slit your own throat," Celia demanded, staring deep into Kyla's eyes, "You will not to allow yourself to see morning."

Kyla felt a little spark biting behind her eyes, but she still had her faculties.

"Do you hear me you little, bitch? Answer!"

Kyla laughed, "Fuck. You."

"Kyla, shut your mouth," Tristan demanded, his hand tightening on her waist.

"Is she blocking my orders? Bark like a dog, you little bitch!" Celia was in shock.

Kyla laughed, "Uh, meow," she said instead, "Now why don't *you* moo. You cow!"

"Enough!" Tristan snapped.

"Yes, enough. Tristan, release her throat," Claudio said.

Tristan didn't move, "Dagger."

"What? No. Not necessary," Celia said, alarmed, "I'm done."

"I don't believe you," Tristan said.

Adrian was back.

"Dagger her, Adrian," Tristan ordered.

"It's not necessary, Tristan," Celia pleaded.

"Adrian, do it or Kyla and I are leaving."

"If you leave then I can't help you through the next few trying weeks," Adrian reasoned.

"Dagger. Her. Now."

"Just release me. I'm over it. I'll behave."

"You won't," Tristan replied.

She snickered.

Tristan had obviously read her right.

"You're getting so strong," she said with a smile, "You shouldn't be able to read my mind for another fifty years. What's happened, Ade? Have you developed some sort of accelerant?"

The room was silent. Kyla suspected that if a pin dropped it'd pierce the silence in the room like a bomb.

Celia glanced at Kyla, "*She's* the accelerant? Un-turned royal *and* an accelerant?"

Adrian stepped up, producing a small jewel-handled dagger that looked like the one Sam had in the hotel room that day.

"Don't. I'll behave," Celia stated, "I get it now..." but Adrian leaned over and thrust the dagger into her lower back and she looked confused for a split second but then went limp. Tristan released her and she sagged to the floor.

Was she unconscious? Dead? Kyla didn't know.

"Get her out," Tristan ordered, and Sam got to Celia's shoulders and Lyle got to her feet and they hefted her up and carried her out. Adrian followed.

Only Kyla, Tristan, Claudio, and a server remained in the dining room.

"This has been an absolute cluster fuck," Tristan snapped at Claudio, still holding Kyla behind him with his left arm that had her plastered to his back.

"I'd say," Claudio looked pissed.

"Adrian is outta control. I have no doubt that Celia being invited to the compound was a test. He's coming."

"It *was* a test. And look at the results," Adrian walked in, pointing out he'd heard them, "The strength that came from her, that was a surprise! A very pleasant one." Adrian gestured to Kyla, "She'll be strong. She already is. I've never seen that before turning. I heard a rumour of it happening once, in my own family in fact, but that was well before my time. I'll need to dig into the Constantin family history."

Tristan still hadn't released her. She was still clutching his jacket, feeling crushed against the wall. He spun around and held her in his arms. His hold was tender, protective, but the look in his eyes? *Yikes.*

He looked absolutely pissed at her. She paled under his glare.

"Escorts. To our suite, Adrian."

"Coming any minute. I'll have the rest of dinner sent up as well."

Two dark-suited men stepped into the room.

"Two?" Tristan asked.

"That's all I have right now. She played with the others."

Tristan sighed.

"I'll help," Sam was coming in.

"No," Tristan snapped, "back up."

"No need. I've cleared the way, citing early curfew due to a security issue. We'll move you to a private cottage tomorrow," Adrian said.

Tristan took Kyla's hand and Sam side-stepped several paces away from the door, so they could pass. He walked fast, holding her hand. They were flanked by the two guards and Adrian wasn't lying, there was no one around. A few moments later they were back in their suite, alone.

"DO YOU HAVE ANY IDEA how fuckin' stupid that was?" he roared as the door was slammed and locked.

She backed away from him. The vibe coming off him was frightening.

"I don't know how..." Kyla started. She had no idea where that strength came from. It was stronger than when Liam had attacked her, even. She hadn't calculated, only reacted.

"Celia is the second most manipulative, strong, most vicious female vamp I know and you fuckin' shove her, challenge her, insult her?"

He let out a laugh, not an amused one, either, it was the sound of exasperation and disbelief. It wasn't a good thing. Kyla swallowed hard.

"Adrian was fucking with us, testing me. Testing you. But what you did?" Tristan moved to the bar area, poured a whiskey and thrust his hand through his hair and then downed it.

"Can I have one?" Kyla softly asked.

He poured her a drink and passed it to her, giving her a death glare.

"What you did played right into his hand. He wanted to see what you were made of, test my control...what a goddamn mess! And with Claude there? He thinks I've got no control over this situation and that is not fucking good." He poured more whisky and downed it.

Kyla drank the shot that he'd poured her, but it didn't help. *It never did.* She put the glass down and let out a sigh.

"I didn't know that'd happen. When she said she wanted your cock, I just...I flew into a rage. I lost it."

"No shit!"

"Who is she? Why does she think she has a claim over you?"

"She's the vamp who turned me. In the past, all she had to do was snap her fingers and I'd play her game. I enjoyed her game. But the last few times I saw her it started to get old. I still played for the fuck of it and she expected that to continue. She isn't accustomed to being told *No* and when that rare occasion happens she does what she needs to in order to see that she gets what she wants. She mesmerizes vamps and she's got the gift of programming, so she programs people *and* vamps into functional trances. Good thing she has no control over you or you'd have offed yourself."

Kyla felt her rage rise.

"But she can't program you?"

"Clearly not. Another benefit of my bloodline. She can only turn unturned people and turned vamps as well as low-level true vamps. No elders, no royals."

"What's the difference between entrancing or mesmerizing and programming?"

"Programming continues after a vamp has left. Mesmerizing has a lifespan."

"Why is she here?"

"Adrian said she was here to help him with a project unrelated to us. Clearly bullshit."

Kyla massaged her temples.

"You don't know how dangerous that was. Don't you ever fuckin' do something like that again."

"Uh, I told you, it just happened. I had no control over it."

"Some good that excuse'd do if it ended differently, huh? You need to get a lock on it."

"Maybe just don't put me in that position again, how 'bout that? Every time you have me around other vamps it goes wrong so how about you learn from *that*? I'm going for a shower. You aren't going anywhere, are you?"

"No."

She headed for the washroom. He caught her by her bicep, "No. I mean, no, you're not going for a shower."

He pulled her closer and then his lips were on her lips and then his tongue was in her mouth, forcefully, hungry, dominating. He cupped her cheek.

She whimpered into his mouth.

"Fuck, I want you so fuckin' bad. That was stupid, but it was also hot as fuck watching you get all possessive over me with her. When you threw her across the room? God. I wanted to fuck you on the spot. I wanted to fuck you in that room in front of all of them, so they'd know you're mine. Only mine."

Kyla was surprised at that reaction. She had a feeling it was more about her body chemistry right now than anything, though. Just smelling him felt like foreplay. He smelled like sex. Sugary sweet sex.

"She's really beautiful. She's also a screaming bitch."

"She's got nothin' on you, princess."

"Am I a screaming bitch, too?"

"No. Fuck no. You're the most beautiful thing I've ever touched." *God, make a baby with me.*

"Stop it."

"Stop what?"

"Stop thinking those thoughts or I won't be able to control myself."

"Say things like that and how can I? What did you just read from me?"

He stared at her, "That you want me to fuck you hard. That you want me. That you want me forever."

"Not exactly, but close enough. And I do."

"Me, too." He ran his nose along her collar bone. Then he backed up, "What was it you were thinking if I missed the mark?"

"Never mind. Let's play. Like earlier?" She moved toward him.

He grunted, "No. Too dangerous. And besides, I'm mad at you."

"M-A-D mad or really mad?" She touched his face.

"Pissed, Kyla. Fuck."

"But I couldn't help it! You're crazy possessive on a good day, never mind at *my* ovulating. Clearly, I'm having a similar effect. I'm like... in heat... and it's doing some seriously messed up things to me. I'm challenging vampires, for heaven sakes. And every time I get pissed at *you*, we fool around, so fair is fair..."

He growled into her mouth and pinned her against the wall and then ran his nose up her throat, "*In heat.* Fuck."

She reached down and grabbed for his crotch and felt that he was hard. Rock fucking hard.

Yum.

"I can't wait for you to be inside me. When can we?"

"Mmm. Three or four days, maybe."

"Goddddd!" She didn't think she could take it.

His nose was in her hair and then his teeth clamped down on her throat.

"Ahh!" She felt it and the sensation extended to her clit.

She rubbed her palm up and down his crotch while he drank and then she felt his hand rise up her leg under her dress to her hip and he dug his fingers in.

"Touch me, babe. I need you," she whispered.

His hand skated upward until his index finger hooked the rhinestone-crusted spaghetti strap of her gown and pulled it down. He reached for her now-exposed breast and then his teeth released her throat and he bit into the side of her breast while doing a swipe across her hardening nipple with his thumb.

She squealed and hooked her leg around him and started to grind her crotch against his leg. He walked her back towards the bed, threw her down roughly on it, and while she was still in mid-bounce he grabbed her ankles and pulled her down a few feet until her bottom was right at the edge, making the dress ride up.

He got to his knees and hooked her panties with both thumbs and slid them off her legs and tossed them. He grabbed the heels of her stilettos and then hooked her legs over his shoulders and his head descended with a fuck hot look on his face. And then his mouth was on her. His tongue dipped in and he made a sexy humming sound that vibrated through his upper lip, which was right on her clit. The roof of her mouth as well as her toes tingled.

She squirmed. He sucked. Hard. Kyla arched right up and then rested on her elbows so she could watch.

"God, you're sexy," she told him and he smiled, winked, and then he dipped his tongue again and he crooked it and hit her g-spot, which made her arms give out and then she was flat on her back.

God his tongue was strong!

He rubbed his palms up her thighs to her hips and then let go with one hand and she heard him unzip his suit pants.

"Are you, are you touching yourself?" she asked.

"Mm, yeah," he said.

"I wanna see!" She tried to scamper back. He released her legs.

He rose up and put a knee to the bed and climbed in as she moved back, suit jacket falling off, tie coming off, shirt being ripped off, buttons flying, and then the pants coming down further, showing his sexy V, and showing that his cock was out and way way *way* awake.

"You have the most beautiful cock I've ever seen," she said and reached for it. "I need it."

"You can't have it." He smiled, teasingly, fisting it.

She pouted.

"Can my mouth have it?"

He crawled up and lay on his back, flipping her by the hips so she was on top.

She rubbed her very wet pussy along his shaft, coating him in her juices and he growled in frustration and then quickly flipped her, super fast, like it was a magic trick, and she was facing the other way and her bottom was against his chin. He grabbed her thighs and lifted so that he got access to her pussy and she leaned over and greedily slurped the tip of his cock into her mouth. She grabbed his hips and hungrily sucked. She tasted herself. She didn't care.

"Fuck, Kyla. You're the best fuck, the sweetest blood, the most delicious pussy I've ever...mmmm." He was devouring her pussy with his mouth, his hands on her ass, opening her wider.

She started to hit the peak. She cried out his name, bucking wildly against his tongue, and when she hit it, he bit her right on her ass cheek. She squealed and tasted him as he sent a hot gush down her throat, moaning out her name.

She rolled and collapsed.

Whoa, wow, wow, wow.

He crawled down to the bottom of the bed and pulled her close, flicking the covers over them.

"It *is* mine, isn't it?"

"Hm? What?"

"Your beautiful cock."

"Yeah, princess. All yours," he kissed her.

A FEW MINUTES HAD PASSED, and they were cuddling, talking about what'd happened.

"I need to keep you segregated. No way can we put you at risk like that again."

"What'll happen to her? What's with that dagger? Why didn't he stake her in the chest?" she nuzzled in to his shoulder and kissed it.

"He wasn't trying to kill her. And she didn't know that, probably why she went down looking confused at where he jabbed her. That dagger contains a rare metal that temporarily paralyzes a vampire. Adrian's recently discovered it. He's having one made for me. That was what I was excited about when I called you at the hotel. We can use that to keep you safe. It should've been ready today. I'm told now it'll be done by tomorrow."

"Sam used one of those on Liam?"

"No. Unfortunately. If he had, Liam wouldn't be a problem any longer. Sam went after him with it and they struggled, but Liam got away. That was Adrian's dagger. There's only the one so far but Claudio, myself, and a few other leaders are getting them."

"So, Celia was paralyzed with it. Now what?"

"She's been locked down. Adrian and I need to talk about what'll be done. She's a huge danger to you. Not just because you pissed her off, but because she knows now that you're a threat. She likes being what she thinks of as Queen Bee. I don't want her uttering a thing about you to anyone. Female vamps would want you eliminated before there was a chance you'd be turned. The super she-vamps hate competition."

Kyla winced.

"Tomorrow and the next day we have to be careful. You're hitting that peak. I don't think I can take much more of your antics. You'll trap me in your web and then we'll have no choices left."

She nodded. He was right. Again, he was right.

"I hate the idea of you being away from me, though."

He caressed her face.

"I know. I hate the idea of not being there to protect you, so I have to find a way to keep you safe from me but yet safe from others, too. If anyone got near you? Fuck. I'm meeting with Adrian and Claudio in the morning to strategize."

"Can I be there?"

"No. I don't think that's a good idea. You shouldn't have been there tonight. Obviously, it was one of Adrian's games. I'm not letting him get his hands on you and he can't wait to find out more about you so he's running these stupid experiments. I have to make decisions and I need you to trust that I'll make the right ones."

"I can't sit idle and let you make all the decisions for me. Besides, you don't exactly have a great track record with that."

He cocked a brow at her. "What?"

"Uh, dog cage, elephant tranquilizer guns, hello?"

He got a defeated look on his face.

She climbed to the top of the bed where all the pillows were, pulling him along.

"Put some clothes on," he mumbled and got out of bed, grabbed jogging shorts for himself and threw yoga pants and a t-shirt in her direction. "No way I'm sleeping beside you naked."

"I'm not naked," she gestured to the dress, which she'd pulled the strap up on.

"You stay in that dress much longer and you *will* be..."

SHE WAS DRIFTING OFF, feeling really sleepy, but then she heard him on the phone.

"Claudio...

Fine, yeah...

Listen, can you arrange to fly my mother here tomorrow in the private jet? She needs to program Celia to forget Kyla exists."

Whoa.

8

KYLA SLEPT SURPRISINGLY sound. She didn't dream, didn't remember any tossing and turning, and she woke up without having slit her own throat, so thankfully hadn't been 'programmed' by Celia. On that thought, she recalled Tristan's phone call.

He'd said his mother was in Montreal. He'd said he didn't see her very often and that their relationship was complicated. And then he'd asked Claudio to bring her to Arizona, so she could program Celia to forget Kyla existed.

She heard him in her mind,

"Celia is the *second* most manipulative, strong, most vicious female vamp I know..."

Did that mean that since Tristan's mother could program that powerful vamp to forget Kyla existed that Tristan's Mom was *the* most manipulative, strong, vicious female vamp he knew?

Yikes.

If so, no wonder he had qualms about turning her. And it wasn't like Kyla wanted to be a vampire and drink blood to survive and it also wasn't like Kyla felt like, at this juncture of her life, that she was ready to be a mother or especially ready to count down nine months until death, either, but she'd been grasping for solutions to their problems, looking for a way out, a way out that didn't include her and Tristan being apart.

Clearly Tristan's mother was a powerful she-vamp. What about his father? Vampire royalty, too, reportedly, but Tristan hadn't said a word about his father.

"I smell smoke," she heard Tristan sleepily say.

She sat up fast, "Oh no!" She inhaled the air but couldn't smell anything.

He'd been asleep beside her and was now pulling her close, "No, silly girl, those wheels are turning mighty fast." He poked at her temple.

She snickered, "Oh. Yeah, they're going at about a million RPM. Definitely smoking."

He ran his nose along her throat, kissed her on the jaw, and then released her and got out of bed.

"Getting a shower and then moving you. I feel that peak comin', princess, and it's coming on strong. I'm putting you in a cottage, there are several on the grounds, and I'm putting you behind a locked door the rest of the day. I wish I had someone I could trust here. I'd put Adrian's dagger in my gut until this was over."

"Maybe we should go home. Fly home. Get me in the panic room for a day or two, then come back?"

"I considered that. But more movement equals exposure to Liam. We'd probably be better to stay put. I don't want to leave here without a dagger. Let's head down. I know it's early but I want us out of this building. Earlier means less chance of traffic in those common areas."

He took a shower and Kyla purposely waited until he was done to get hers and when she was out of the bathroom, Tristan had their bags in hand and motioned for the door.

"I need coffee," she gave him a pout.

"Five minutes," he said, jaw tight, seeming impatient, "Game face on."

She straightened her posture, put her sunglasses on, and followed him out.

ADRIAN AND SEVERAL guards showed them to a cottage on the edge of woods that were on the property. She was surprised at how woodsy it was, considering they were in a state that she thought would be mostly desert. It was a pretty stone house that looked like it was on the set of a fairy tale or a Lord of the Rings movie and there were mountains lining the horizon off in the distance. It was romantic. There were pretty gardens planted around winding stone walkways and a rounded wooden door. Inside the front door was a big but cozy room with heavy-looking old furniture and a huge fireplace that separated the living area and kitchen. The kitchen had a door that opened to a back patio area.

At the back of the house was a dining room, large office, and a bathroom. Upstairs were two bedrooms and another bathroom and the long upstairs hallway overlooked the main living area with a heavy wooden banister. The place was filled with well-loved rustic antique furniture and Kyla hated to admit it but she absolutely loved the place. It had character. It'd be a great place for a getaway... if they weren't in the predicament they were in.

Tristan said the plan was for Kyla to spend the day in the bedroom, for Tristan to spend his time downstairs. Separated, but still in the same building, as he didn't trust anyone with her. He said Adrian had offered to put her on guard there while Tristan stayed back at the main house, but he had zero plans to go along with that idea. He didn't trust Adrian at all, it seemed.

After they were alone in the cottage, breakfast had just been delivered, she tried to talk to him. He was in a supremely shitty mood.

"This omelette sucks," she grumbled.

"It's alright," he shrugged, taking another bite.

"You make much better omelettes," she said.

In truth, it was fine, but it was nothing like the one he'd made back at his Tuscan villa, shirtless and singing Led Zeppelin in his jean shorts.

Here he was in a suit, looking handsome, but looking angry. And they had a battle in front of them. A big one.

He gave her a half-hearted smile, but it didn't reach his eyes.

"Talk to me," she said.

"It's gonna be a rough few days," he mumbled, taking a sip of his coffee. "I'm just getting my head ready for it. As soon as you're done there, we need to separate. I can't take it."

She reached across the table for his hand. He squeezed it briefly and then let go and snatched his hand back, "I can't even touch you."

She winced.

He pushed his plate back. "I am using every ounce of control I have to pretend that throwing you on this table and fucking your brains out isn't all I'm thinking about. Well, not all I'm thinking about but the thing I'm thinking about the most. The other shit in my brain includes Liam, the shit Adrian pulled last night, the fact that Celia is locked down and we've got to get her head straight, so we can release her, and a pile of other shit."

He threw his fork down and got up and looked out the window.

"Like your mother coming?"

He shook his head, "You heard me on the phone. I suspected as much. Your smoking wheelhouse brain kept me up half the night."

"Tell me."

"Tell you what?"

"About her. About why bringing her here is upsetting to you."

He shook his head, looking deep in thought.

"When did your mother become a vampire?"

"A year after I was turned."

"And she's not a nice one, I take it."

"Hah. That's funny. She makes Celia look like Mother Teresa."

Kyla winced.

"Yeah. I don't want her anywhere near you. But that's not likely because she'll get wind and then you'll see."

"Talk to me, Tristan."

"Kyla, things are fucked. I'm just trying to get through the next few days before I have to face the next set of hurdles, okay? Please. Gimme a fuckin' break with the questions. Haven't you had enough enlightenment in the last 24 hours?"

She swallowed hard and felt her heart sink.

"We," she whispered.

"What?" he snapped.

"*We* have to face these hurdles. Not just you."

He thrust his hand through his hair, "We. Yeah, just eat up and get upstairs so you can give me a wide berth and give me some space so I can take care of the problems *we* have. Okay?"

She dropped her fork and pushed away from the table. She went upstairs to the room she was told she needed to stay in and threw herself on the big sleigh bed. Then she tried to shut down her feelings. She tried real hard to shut down her ability to give a shit. She failed miserably.

A few hours later there was a knock on her door. She got out of the bed, where she'd been reading on the tablet computer, and stood against the door. "Yeah?"

"Miss Kelly? I have your lunch."

Kyla opened the door cautiously. A server had a covered tray for her.

"Spencer, not Kelly."

"Apologies, Miss Spencer."

As it got dark the same woman showed up with another tray for her. Dinner.

Later, she was tossing and turning in bed. She got up to go to the washroom but she heard voices, so she peeked over the banister, where she could see that below, Tristan was sitting on the sofa, working on his laptop.

Sam and a blond curly-haired guy, someone whose face she couldn't see from her vantage point, was sitting with him. They were talking but she couldn't hear them. Tristan looked agitated. Then she saw Tristan drop his laptop on the table, hard, and then grab the unknown guy and physically throw him across the room. The guy landed on his back on the floor about ten feet away from Tristan and Kyla felt her body tighten.

Tristan's eyes darted up to her. He pointed at her in and mouthed "go" with a scowl on his face. She ducked back into the bedroom and shut and then re-locked the door.

A few hours later, she needed the restroom again so she quietly ducked into the hall and down it into the bathroom. When she came out she heard a woman's voice.

"I'll just say *Hello* and be on my way."

"Not tonight," she heard Tristan reply.

"Awe, sweetie... don't make me wait to meet the love of your life. I want to know that she's good enough. I won't rest until I see for myself. Celia said she's a hellcat."

"Celia better have nothing to say about her after tonight."

"Don't fret, darling. I'll take care of that."

"Why didn't you just deal with it when you were with her?"

"I wanted to speak with you first."

"Well, it's getting late. Deal with it, please? I'm ready to go to bed."

Kyla quietly ducked back into the room. She looked out the window as she heard a door close and saw a woman in a black full-length evening gown with cocktail gloves and a wide brimmed hat walking down the stone walk. She looked straight out of an old black & white movie. Her beauty looked sort of timeless. She didn't look old enough to be Tristan's mother. Glamorous. Dark hair. She looked up and right at Kyla and smiled and gave her a little wave. Even from there and even in the dark she could plainly see where Tristan's eyes came from. Kyla gave a hesitant wave back.

The woman turned on her heel and headed down the path. Kyla backed away from the window and sat on the bed. She heard noise outside her door.

She turned the knob to open it, it opened inward, but as she turned the knob she heard, "Don't." That was Tristan. "Leave it shut," he ordered.

"What are you doing?" she called out.

"Leaning against the door."

"Why?"

"Need to be close to you. As close as I can be without being in the same room."

Her chest burned with emotion.

"We're almost over this first hurdle, babe," she told him.

"I know," he replied. But he sounded exhausted already.

And how many hurdles were there? First ovulation, then waiting with a sense of impending doom for her period. There was Liam Donavan to deal with, and who knew what hurdle would be next?

She wanted so badly to be in his arms. She wanted to smell him, to taste him, to feel his strong arms around her. She wanted to feed him, feel him inside.

"Go to sleep, okay?" he called out. "Sooner you do, the sooner this day is over. Need anything to eat or drink?"

"Nope."

"Goodnight."

"Love you. 'Night."

"Love you," he replied, sounding exhausted.

She heard noise and she suspected he was gone. She got ready for bed. As she worked in her moisturizer she decided that this day hadn't been great, but it seemed a little *too* easy to get through.

She'd later change her mind about that. And the night following that one would be the longest night of her life so far.

SHE WOKE UP IN PITCH black darkness, freezing cold, so she tried to nuzzle deeper into the blankets and in her semi-conscious state, reached for Tristan's warmth, but then she remembered he wasn't in bed.

As she realized this she was acutely aware of fuzzy sensations, like her body was covered in static, so she leaned over to switch the lamp on the bedside table on and that's when she saw him. Tristan was standing over her, at the edge of the bed.

She held her hand over her eyes to shield against the sudden brightness of the lamplight and when they adjusted enough that she could see him she saw through a squint that he didn't look so good. He was grey, and he was breathing cold fog into the room.

Oh shit. Am I bleeding?

He grabbed his temples and closed his eyes, looking like he was having an internal struggle. Then his fangs shot out.

Oh God.

He was suddenly on her and his skin was suddenly normal, his eyes were normal. He wasn't cold.

"Baby?" he asked, looking confused, like he didn't know how he'd gotten there. He gave his head a quick shake and then took a deep breath and then scrambled back off her.

"What the hell?" he asked.

Kyla was about to speak, but then she saw the blue in his eyes fade to black again and the grey rushed over his skin like a shadow. His fangs shot back out.

"Oh my God!" she breathed and tried to scamper backwards, but he rushed her again and was on her, his hands pinning her shoulders.

The black gave way to blue and the grey faded. Fangs retracted. Tristan was breathing hard, struggling, his mouth contorted. "What the fuck?"

Kyla shook her head frantically, "You have to go! Go!"

He let go of her and ran out of the room, slamming the door.

She got up and ran to the door and twisted the lock but decided instantly that it was an absolutely idiotic thing to do. She lifted her nightie, a short one, light pink, sort of like a very long tank top that hit just above her knees and quickly snapped the elastic of the waistband of her pale blue bikini briefs to see if there was blood in her underwear. There wasn't. Why was he like this, then? The ovulation peak?

What do I do?

The lock turned back unlocked and the door flew open. Hard. The door bounced off the wall and there he was, in front of her, only about a foot away, billowing cold out of his mouth. His eyes and skin were wrong again.

And then he was on her, his nose on her throat and he advanced, backing her up until she fell on the bed as his teeth sank in. Her fists clenched the sheets and she felt so much fear that she was afraid it'd kill her. His palm went to her shoulder to pin her and it was freezing.

She heard him swallow and felt a foreign sensation inside her, but then the heat returned. Her eyes opened, and she couldn't see his face but could feel him. Not rust or emptiness or cold, but warmth flooding her instead, *Tristan* flooding her instead.

"What the fuck, baby?" he muttered and looked at her.

"You have to go," she whispered, feeling him get erect against her.

"Yeah, I know, okay," he kissed her throat and backed off the bed and zoomed out of the room.

She felt throbbing in between her legs. She was suddenly drenched and completely throbbing with need.

He was back. He was back, and his skin looked normal and his eyes looked normal, but he looked like he'd just come in from a marathon the way his chest was moving up and down rapidly. He was at the end of the bed.

He looked so fucking sexy she wanted to jump him.

"I have to fuck you," he told her and the way he said it, it was as if he was trying to preach to the choir that the sky was blue.

"Yeah," she scampered up and launched herself at him.

"You have to stop me from fucking you," he said as he caught her.

His hands were on her ass and her legs were around him, her short nightgown hiked up around her waist, her arms around his neck, and she had his earlobe in her mouth.

"Stop," she said feebly but then ran her hands up his chest and tangled her fingers into his hair and then her tongue was in his mouth.

He rounded the bed and put her on her back horizontally across it and then her hands were in his track pants, pulling his cock out.

"I have to stop," he said against her lips, but his hands were hiking her legs up and then ripping her panties to shreds, and then his cock was right against her entrance.

"You have to stop," she mumbled.

"You smell so fucking good," he said, with anger, "You are so fucking wet right now."

"So fucking wet," Kyla agreed on a whimper and then jerked her hips forward and then he thrust inside her, hard, to the max and they both moaned. Kyla's ankles locked against his back and she dug her nails in and he let out a very masculine sound of pleasure.

"Harder!" she demanded, goosebumps everywhere.

"No, got to get outta here," he said but he *was* definitely going harder. He was also going faster. She was thrusting her pelvis at him, digging her nails into his back, and then tears were streaming down her face because she knew that they were in over their heads. She knew this but couldn't do a thing to stop it.

"Go, Tristan. You have to stop this right now before ... before you come inside me...Oh God...bite me. Bite me, bite me, bite me. Fucking bite me."

He complied, biting her throat and swallowing twice, kissing it, then circling his hips, plunging hard into her, and then suddenly, he flew back, leaving her empty and his hands were in his own hair and he was shaking his head. "I can't..." He vanished out of the room and Kyla went after him.

When she got to the bottom of the stairs he was standing there, his back to her, his head in his hands.

"Tristan..." she breathed.

He spun around and his eyes were coal black.

"Get the fuck back upstairs!" he demanded.

"Ohhhh...kay," She spun around to do as he'd told her but then after she got up just one step he grabbed her arm, spun her back around and his mouth caught hers and they tumbled onto the stairs. Him on top, her on her back, her legs automatically wrapping around his waist. He hiked the nightie back up; she heard the fabric stretch in protest. He grabbed her by both hips, and slammed inside.

"Fuck!" he growled and then his eyes were blue and glowing bright, brighter than she'd never seen them glow before.

"Fuck, Kyla! Holy fuck!"

"What?" She threw her head back and moaned because he was still pushing in over and over while this was happening.

"Your eyes..." he said, "they're glowing!"

Her fingers went to her clit and she started moaning loud, rotating her hips with him inside her. He grabbed her hand and sucked her fingers into his mouth and put his own fingers to her clit instead.

The stairs dug into her back and the back of her neck, but she didn't give a shit. She was drunk with desire and Tristan was fucking her harder, faster, kind of supersonic-like. She felt buzzing on her clit, felt her g-spot like it'd grown ten sizes, and her inner walls started to spasm. She started to come. She started to come hard.

"Tristan! I love you so much. Please don't stop." His free hand skimmed her torso and then held her jaw.

"I can't stop. Fuck, but I tried. Kiss me." His head descended, and his tongue plunged in and she let him. He kissed her so deeply and so hard, tasting like ambrosia fruit salad, that the thought flitted through her mind that she could die right now and know no greater bliss. Being fucked on the stairs by her vampire prince right smack dab in the middle of ovulating.

Ovulating.

Fuck.

Her faculties returned as Tristan came inside of her. She felt it like a hot jet and when that hot whoosh hit, she felt something else. She felt the area inside her pelvis start to tremble, heat up, like it was 900 degrees inside, and then everything faded to black.

EVERYTHING HURT. HER back felt bruised. *The stairs.*

Her mouth felt swollen. *All the kissing.*

Her vajayjay felt raw. *The sex.*

The sex.

THE SEX.

Shit. Shit, shit shit.

She opened her eyes and looked around. She was in the sleigh bed. She sat up slowly, feeling achy all over.

She looked under the covers and lifted the nightgown. Nope, no underwear on. They were definitely gone. And she was definitely raw and sore down there. She had no doubt that it hadn't been a dream.

She got up and went to the bathroom. Then she looked in the mirror and washed.

Am I pregnant now?

Am I nine months away from giving birth to a baby? Tristan's baby? Our baby?

And am I gonna die?

She put her hand to her belly.

A baby...

Her other hand covered her mouth and she stared at herself in the mirror, her eyes filling up.

She shook the trance off, went back to the bedroom, put a robe and underwear on and then quietly opened the door and listened. She didn't hear anyone downstairs, so she tiptoed down there.

She found Tristan, sitting in a chair facing the front door, a glass of whiskey in his hand and he looked like shit. The sun was up but he obviously hadn't slept.

His eyes were bloodshot, his hair was a mess, like he'd spent hours just raking his fingers through it in frustration. He had changed from his track pants into a suit. No tie, top few shirt buttons undone, and scruff on his face.

He looked at her and she saw a flash of pain in his eyes. Then he threw the contents of the glass back gulping he rest down. Then he whipped the glass against the fireplace and it smashed.

Kyla took a big gulp of air, of nothing. She tightened the sash on her robe and then her palms were on her face.

"I..." she didn't know what to say.

He shook his head and his mouth contorted sourly.

She rushed the rest of the way to him, climbed onto his lap, pulling her knees up against herself, and then she put her arms around his shoulders, burying her face into his neck.

He sat, stone still. Not putting his arms around her, not touching her at all. He was just stiff.

"You're not coming down from it," he finally said.

She lifted her head up and looked him in the face, not understanding.

"You peaked last night and today would've still been a danger zone because you would've been descending. You're not descending."

She knew what that meant. That meant the egg had been fertilized.

She put her arms around herself and her forehead back into his throat and felt a swirl of crazy scary emotions.

Fear, sadness, more fear. More sadness. Foreboding.

She looked up at his face.

His eyes looked dead. Dead cold.

There was a knock at the door. Tristan didn't move. Kyla didn't move, either. A moment later, there was another knock. Tristan continued to ignore it. He was staring off into space with dead eyes and Kyla went to get up, but his arms whipped around and caged her in. His palm was on her back. He tightened his grip. She buried her face into him again and closed her eyes. His other hand tangled into her hair.

She heard a key and then the doorknob turned, and the door creaked open.

"Good morning," she heard Adrian call out.

They must've been a sight. Her in his lap, both of them looking like they'd been through a war. They had.

She didn't look up.

Adrian spoke again, his voice far less cheerful, "I was...I was going to invite you both to breakfast, but it looks like this is a bad time. I'll have food sent here for you both. Tristan, call me when you're ready to talk."

"Just Kyla," Tristan said.

"Pardon?" Adrian asked.

"Just send food for Kyla."

"Annnnd......should I..."

Dead silence.

"Tristan?" Adrian pushed, "Should I—-"

"No."

"No?"

"No."

"I see."

There was silence. Adrian didn't move.

"We'll talk later," Tristan's voice was as dead as his eyes.

"The window is short, Tristan. If we—-"

"No!" he barked. His grip on her tightened to the point of pain, but she kept her face buried.

Kyla didn't allow herself to think about what they were talking about. But she knew.

"I'll have food sent," Adrian said, and she heard the door close and then heard the key as Adrian re-locked it from the outside.

Tristan rose, lifting her up into his arms from his lap, and carried her upstairs and put her in bed. He covered her with the blanket, kissed her on the forehead, and she put her fingertips to his chin cleft. They stared at one another for a beat. Tristan's eyes warmed and looked like they were filling up with wet. Her chin started to tremble. He kissed her lips softly and then he left, leaving the door open.

Kyla stayed in bed for a long time, just listening to birds singing outside, just lying there in what felt like a trance. She couldn't dig in and think about this. She couldn't. There was no way to run from it, but she just couldn't process it right now so instead she just stayed there, staring into space, listening to birds chirp and tweet sometimes happily, sometimes sounding annoyed, and then she heard the front door and a few minutes later Tristan stepped back in, put a tray on the nightstand and said, "Eat."

She shook her head, "I don't think I can."

"You have to," he said softly, not looking her in the eye, and then he left.

She got up and lifted the lid and saw scrambled eggs and ham steak and a dish of blueberries with yogurt plus coffee and orange juice.

She robotically shoveled in every bite, drank every last drop of both, and then she slept like the dead. But then she woke up, looked at the clock, and saw that she'd slept 11 hours, then felt carbonated bile and a sour taste rise in her throat.

She dashed to the bathroom and violently threw up and then on the way back to bedroom she got crippling cramps in her stomach and ended up doubled over, on the floor, unable to move, gripping a spindle on the upstairs railing.

Tristan was there. He was lifting her up.

"Hey?"

"Hurts so bad, Tristan," she cried, "I ate and then I slept all day and now I feel so sick. My stomach hurts. I puked." She dissolved into whimpers as pain gripped her whole midsection and squeezed it in an invisible vice. This was like the time after that banquet when she was about to get her period, but this pain was about ten times fiercer.

He got into bed with her and held her close, but she was in so much pain she couldn't get into a tight enough ball.

She cried out, "I'm f-f-freezing. More blankets?"

Tristan got out of bed and left and returned with another blanket. He got in and pulled her over to him but then looked down at the bed, "What the fuck?"

He pulled the blankets back. She was about to ask why he'd take the blankets away when she was so damn cold but then she looked down and saw what he saw. The sheets were covered in blood.

He lifted her nightie a little. Between her legs was coated in blood.

She choked on a sob, "Oh my God..."

Tristan roared out this horrible gut-wrenching sound and her eyes darted from the blood up toward his face and that's when she saw the look of absolute anguish fade and the shadow moved across until his face was grey. His eyes went black. His fangs snapped out and they were fucking huge.

Tristan's freezing cold hand came to her chest and pushed her back onto the bed and his head descended toward the blood and Kyla heard a crash and a bunch of shouting. And then everything went dark. She passed out.

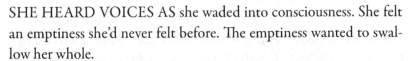

9

SHE HEARD VOICES AS she waded into consciousness. She felt an emptiness she'd never felt before. The emptiness wanted to swallow her whole.

She saw Adrian's face, Lyle's face, and then she saw black because she let the emptiness have her.

"KYLA?" IT WAS HER FATHER.

"Daddy?" She felt like she was little again. She opened her eyes and realized she wasn't little. She realized where she was. She was in that cottage, in that bedroom, and she was in a fresh nightgown and in the sleigh bed.

Blood. So much blood.

Tristan!

She bolted upright. But Tristan wasn't there. Her father was there. Claudio was there. Adrian was there. Adrian sat on the edge of the bed, Claudio stood by the door. Her father was in a chair sitting beside the bed.

"Tristan!" she yelled.

"Tristan's locked down," Adrian said.

"Locked down? Like... like Celia?"

"For your protection initially, and now ours as well. We'll be releasing him as soon as is feasible. We're still trying to talk him down."

"Down from what?"

"In his words? From turning this place into a bloodbath," Adrian replied and didn't crack a smile.

Kyla rubbed her eyes. Her stomach cramped up. She winced.

Lyle passed her a glass of water. She took a sip.

"You're dehydrated, drink all of it," Adrian said and put a thermometer in her ear and took a reading while Kyla drank. He looked at it, looked at Claudio, and gave a nod and then Claudio opened the door. Two women in orange scrubs rushed in. Adrian and Lyle rose.

Lyle kissed her on the forehead, "I'll come see you tomorrow."

"Wait, where *is* Tristan. What's going on?'

Adrian stopped at the door. Lyle and Claudio left.

"You're going to have a rough night, so these are nurses who will help you through it as the rest of that medication runs its course. Tomorrow we'll talk You'll likely still be bleeding so he won't be released until you stop."

"Huh?"

Adrian said, "Claudio is medicated so that he won't attack you. I'm glad to see it's working. Myself and Lyle are unaffected because we're your father and grandfather. It's helpful that mother nature protected you that way."

"What's going on? What medication?"

"You're in the midst of a medication-induced abortion. Couldn't be helped. We weren't ready, but Tristan didn't listen to reason. As it's a supernatural pregnancy it'll be rough for you. I'm sorry about that. But you'll survive it."

And then he left.

Her stomached spasmed and as she doubled over in pain the two nurses moved in and one said, "Let's get you to the bathroom."

Kyla was sure she felt her heart shatter into about a million pieces.

THE NEXT MORNING, ONE of the nurses tipped a medicine cup toward her mouth with clear liquid, telling her that it was the last of the medication and that she needed to take it. She feebly tried to fight her off but two more women in orange scrubs came in and held her down while one forced the medication into her and then they continued to hold her down while the first nurse did a pelvic exam that felt a little too much like rape, during which she took samples on swabs. Kyla wished for the cold gusts of strength to fight them off, but they never came.

The women finally left, and she fell asleep again.

It had been a horrible night with pain in her belly, with so much blood she thought she'd die, and with so much pain in her soul she didn't think she'd ever feel the warmth of daylight again even if she was a foot away from the sun itself. It was a night that took years to end.

Tristan had fertilized her egg and obviously, during that short and vague conversation with Adrian about Kyla's food demanded that they not abort it and then *Granddaddy* had done it anyway by drugging her. And then when she started to bleed out, Tristan had gone crazy grey hulk on her and they'd locked him down.

Adrian came in with a breakfast tray.

She glared at him.

"Good morning. Feeling okay?"

She narrowed her eyes, "What do you think?"

He sat on the edge of the bed and put the tray on the nightstand.

"I think you'll feel better soon."

"Where's Tristan? What's happening?"

"He's still locked down."

"Tell me. Tell me everything that happened."

"Well, he lost it and then we had him daggered. We almost lost you. Thankfully, that was avoided. I think you'll be glad things worked as they did once you look back on this."

She said nothing in response.

"You should eat."

"Need to feed me more drugs?"

"No. Not today." He smirked.

"Go fuck yourself!" she spat.

He got to his feet, "When you stop bleeding, let me know. If you haven't said anything in three days, we'll have another exam done so don't waste your efforts hiding it."

"When can I see him?" Kyla asked.

"When you've stopped bleeding."

"But..."

"And don't think about lying about the fact that you've stopped bleeding when you haven't. You'll put yourself at risk if you do, so we'll have a pelvic exam done to confirm it."

"So, what do I do in the meantime?"

"You don't need to stay in your room. You can even enjoy the meadow around the cottage. You're a good distance from the other buildings so you're safe here. We have several nurses and orderlies here to watch you." He winked. "I need to go."

"How are you locking Tristan down?"

"It hasn't been easy. He was very unruly. He's particularly unruly due to that nectar infusion. It's astounding how strong he is and he broke through several locks until we found a solution. I've lost a lot of men, actually. I think he'd benefit from at least a full regular cycle before getting you pregnant again, maybe two. Maybe next ovulation he'll actually listen to reason. I need to go see to some things. If you need anything, ask one of your nurses for me and I'll come straight away. Your father is here to see you."

Before getting me pregnant again echoed in her mind.

"I don't wanna see anyone. You do know you've murdered your great grandchild, don't you?" Kyla spat acidly, regretting the words as soon as they came out of her mouth because saying them aloud would mean she had to face what'd happened.

Adrian looked like he was choosing his words carefully. "That wasn't done lightly, believe me. But there is much to be done before we go down that road. Tristan wouldn't listen to my recommendations for keeping you safe while you were fertile, and this was the consequence. It had to be this way. Your father is leaving for Monaco today. He's in the hall so I'll let him in now so you can say goodbye." He flashed her a big smile and excitedly left.

"Asshole," she mumbled and heard him laugh from the other side of the door and say, "She definitely *is* a spitfire. Gets it from my side."

The door opened, and Lyle was standing there.

"May I come in?"

She shrugged, suspecting he was asking as a courtesy but had every intention of coming in regardless of her response.

"I just wanted to say goodbye. For now. I need to get home. Are you feeling alright?"

"No. Not at all. But what does that matter to you? Adrian drugged me and killed my unborn child, your grandchild, but I'm good. Yeah, whatever."

"I *am* sorry, Ky."

"All for the cause, right?" She snickered and shifted so that her back was to him.

He rounded the bed and sat on the side she was facing, "I hope that in time you'll come to understand how important you are, that you and I can build a friendship."

She snickered again.

He leaned over and kissed her forehead, "I'm not who I was. I can't relate to those human emotions, but I have recollections that tell me that as far as human relationships go, you meant an awful lot to me. I feel affection for you. I'm proud to be your father, to have helped bring you into this world. For what that's worth. Be well, Kyla. See you on the other side."

The other side? What, when she was forced to be a vampire? When they were done all their pre-turning experiments on her?

"Wait. Do I have brothers or sisters?" she asked.

He gave her a sad smile and shook his head and then the door closed. He was gone. She shook her head. She didn't know if that head shake of his was sympathy or a 'no'.

The emptiness didn't feel bigger for the loss of Lyle Spencer, rather Lyle Kelly. All she felt the loss of right now was the loss of Tristan. She couldn't let herself feel the other loss she was suffering from. She didn't know how she'd *ever* let herself feel that loss. It'd only been a few hours from conception to death for a tiny bundle of cells, but that bundle of cells would've been a product of their love. Would've become a person. She pushed those thoughts away.

She reached out to Tristan in her head, in her heart, and she didn't know what she wanted him to feel but she hoped he would feel her, that he'd know that she was thinking about him.

She didn't think much time had passed when she heard the door open again. She turned over and was face to face with Tristan's mother.

Holy shit.

The woman stood at her beside.

"Up. Get dressed. We're taking a walk." She clapped her hands in a "chop chop" manner. Her face then went sour and she muttered, "Smells like despair in here," with disgust. She left.

Kyla didn't feel like she had a whole lot of choice in the matter, so she got up and saw that all their dirty clothes had been laundered and folded and were in a pile on top of the dresser beside the Puma duffle bag. She went to the bathroom with a pair of yoga pants, underwear, socks, and her thin cotton hoodie. It covered below her butt, thankfully, and would hopefully camouflage the ginormous overnight pad she was wearing.

Her stomach felt raw. She was bleeding pretty heavily when she went to the bathroom. She changed the pad, put in a tampon as well, and then washed up and put her hair up in a half ponytail, half bun and brushed her teeth. She could barely handle looking in the mirror, though. At a quick glance of herself all she could think about was him. Where did they have him? Was he himself?

She found Tristan's mother near the front door. The woman was tall, taller than Kyla and beautiful. Her face was unlined, although she looked to be in her early to mid forties, and she was elegant and graceful. Clearly Tristan got his movie-star looks honestly. She was wearing riding clothes and riding boots.

"Kyla," she held out a gloved hand and removed it and then reached for Kyla's hand. Kyla shook it.

"Taryn Walker. Shall we?" She opened the front door and gestured for Kyla to go ahead.

The sun felt hot on her skin, but inside she felt cold and empty.

"Are we going to see Tristan?" Kyla asked, finally, as it looked like they were heading toward the main house.

"No. Just a stroll."

"Have you seen him? How is he?"

"I haven't today yet, but I saw him yesterday. He's...agitated."

"Is he himself?"

"Yes. More himself than ever," she got an evil gleam in her eye.

Kyla didn't know what that meant, but she shuddered inwardly.

"Does Tristan speak of me?" Taryn asked.

"No. I've asked but he doesn't say much."

"Our relationship is complex."

They were passing a corner on the stone path that led from the front of the cottage to where it forked. The path Taryn chose headed in the opposite direction of the main house and went back towards the back of cottage.

"Why is it that you wanted to talk to me?" Kyla asked.

"I'm very intrigued by you. I suspect you're a lot like I was, before I was turned."

"Really?"

"Tristan wants to do the right thing for you, but he also needs to do the right thing for everyone," she said.

Kyla wasn't sure what she was getting at.

"My relationship with my son has been strained since I was turned. We were very close before that. Tristan's father was murdered while I was pregnant with him and I gave him all the nurturing and love I had. We were one another's world, my son and I. Things changed after I became vampire. He and I have diverging opinions on a lot of issues including where *you* are concerned and that has already made a tense situation even worse."

"Oh?"

Taryn stopped and faced Kyla.

"Tristan needs to follow the path that has been planned. I hope you'll do whatever you can to help with that. He's being unreasonable. You need to work on Tristan. He needs to follow the path. He needs to be very wary of Claudio. Claudio isn't ready to give up the throne, so he needs to be watched. Tristan needs to sire as many children as possible and get as strong as possible as quick as possible, so that he can claim that throne. When he turns you, you'll have a lot of responsibility and I can help you with that, so I want you to be very open to my instruction. He'll be extremely receptive to your recommendations; you'll be extremely receptive to mine. Do you understand? And get over your anger at Adrian. You and Tristan need him right now."

Taryn was looking at her in such a way that Kyla was fairly certain the she-vamp was trying to mesmerize her. As Taryn spoke, Kyla had been feeling that electric spark-like sensation behind her eyes that she'd felt with Celia, only this time it was stronger, more painful.

Kyla guessed Tristan's mother figured she was strong enough to do it, despite the fact that Celia had failed.

Her blood chilled at the woman's stare. And then she felt a chill coming up from her toes, that coldness that had come over her with Celia, with Liam. She tried to hold it back but not send it away so that she could summon it if she needed it. She had a feeling she was doing this successful, but of course wouldn't know unless she actually tried to unleash it. She had to decide at that instant whether or not to make Tristan's mother think she'd successfully programmed Kyla. She decided that it'd be the best course of action. If Taryn thought Kyla was under her influence, maybe Kyla could use that to her advantage. Or, at the very least, not anger the woman without having the protection of Tristan right now.

She nodded slowly.

Taryn smiled and then pointed off in the distance, "Oh look, a moon flower is blooming."

It was indeed dusk and the instant Kyla glanced in the direction Taryn had pointed in, she saw a riot of yellow flowers bloom quickly. Behind them was a clearing in the meadow and there was a rope swing swinging from a big tree in the breeze.

What the...what?

Kyla's stomach plummeted, because she'd dreamt of this place. She'd dreamt of being in a meadow watching flowers bloom at rapid speed. In the dream they hadn't been moonflowers, which she knew bloomed at dusk; one of her foster parents had some in their garden and the whole clan would wait around them at night during the summer to watch for them to bloom, but in Kyla's dream there'd been loads of flowers blooming. In that dream, Tristan had been pushing her on a swing and then he'd bitten her throat. And then she'd seen her ex, Jackson.

Suddenly, Taryn's teeth clamped down on Kyla's throat. Kyla screamed and shoved her back with considerable strength. The woman went back on one foot, didn't fall over, though, and she smiled big, her fangs and other visible teeth covered in Kyla's blood.

"You are delicious. And strong. My goodness. You won't remember that I did this, though."

Kyla was astounded. She forced herself to nod robotically.

"I just had to know what you tasted like." Her fangs retracted, and she removed a hankie from her riding jacket pocket and wiped her mouth daintily. She stepped over and reached for Kyla.

Kyla avoided the urge to flinch, to punch, to run, to do something, anything. She miraculously managed to remain still.

"Let me just close that wound for you." Taryn leaned over and gave Kyla's throat a quick peck with her lips and then she dabbed at it with her hankie. She sniffed the hankie and smiled.

"All better now." She smiled and turned on her heel. "Let's go!"

Kyla shivered and followed. Kyla's brain was travelling at Mach 25, but she tried her best to hide it. Evidently her poker face was getting better because Taryn seemed to buy it. Taryn stopped at the front door.

"When you and Tristan are back home I'll visit, and we'll have to have a girls' day. Get you some decent clothes. Not sure if you'll be home before or after you've been turned. Now go inside and rest."

What the fuck?

Taryn gave a little wave and was about to head back toward the main house but suddenly Adrian was there, in front of Taryn, his fangs showing and his face blood-red. He was pretty damn scary-looking. Kyla was surprised at his demeanour. He'd been so normal-looking thus far.

"Did you kill my fucking stallion?" he screamed in Taryn's face.

She giggled school girlishly.

"And what are you doing here with her?" Adrian added.

"I wanted access to my future daughter-in-law and you wouldn't grant it. So, I took it. And that horse was delicious. Very memorable."

Adrian scowled a scowl so big and menacing that it was hard not to quake in her boots.

"Where are the security guards? Have you bitten her?" Adrian was pointing at Kyla's throat.

Taryn giggled again and shrugged. Then she zoomed out of Kyla's sight.

Adrian ran a hand through his hair and sighed and then looked at Kyla.

"Are you alright?"

Kyla raised her brows. "Like you care."

"What did she want? What did she say?"

"Like I'll tell you..." Kyla walked back into the house and slammed the door.

Adrian was inside a split second later, "Stay here. I need to figure out what she's done with your guards and nurses."

He walked toward the back of the house and then she heard a sigh and then heard beeping and then he was on the phone, "I need a clean-up crew down at Cottage 2. Six casualties. I need replacements. Code red." He beeped off and then sat on the sofa, "I'll stay until security replacements arrive. She did, didn't she? She fed."

Kyla massaged her throat and Adrian's expression dropped, "Damn her."

"Just a taste. I shoved her off. She thinks she convinced me to forget about it. Well, you'll forgive me if I can't be bothered to keep you company." She headed for the upstairs, thinking about how Tristan warned about female vamps being cold and calculating.

Killing six people in order to get alone with Kyla? Killing a horse, clearly to piss him off or punish him? Yeah, obviously Tristan wasn't just blowing smoke about his mother.

"Don't trust Taryn," Adrian advised.

"But trust you?" she asked, stopping mid ascent.

"Don't trust anyone, Kyla," he said, "Except Tristan. You can trust that he will do anything in his considerable power to keep you safe."

What an odd thing to say. And it seemed sincere. It was unexpected. His face was unguarded and for a split second he looked different, not cold, not callous. But then it was like shutters came down and the arrogance was back.

She turned on her heel and ascended the rest of the way up the stairs.

She went into the bathroom and took a long shower. The bleeding was still happening, so she took care of business in the bathroom, got dressed, and then went to the bedroom and found that there was a meal there for her. She ate a little bit of roasted chicken, mashed potatoes, and mixed vegetables and then got into bed and closed her eyes for a while, trying to mull things over, get her head straight.

Okay, so first she'd dreamt of being in a stone tunnel with blood and after Liam had found her and violated her she found herself against a wall made of stone with blood on her hands.

She had also dreamt about being on a swing in a meadow with rapid blooming flowers and then found herself in that meadow watching moon flowers bloom. In the dream he'd bitten her and that day his mother had bitten her.

There was also the fact that she'd dreamt of her dead parents after a lifetime of not dreaming of them and then getting the news that they weren't dead at all.

She drifted off to sleep after a lot of tossing and turning.

She had a dream about a sweet chubby-cheeked blue-eyed baby boy, smiling and cooing at her. She woke up drenched in sweat and tears and her arms were itchy.

Withdrawals.

Already?

And grief. She let herself cry it out for a while, a long while. She cried into the pillow in the dark, fully feeling the immense loss, fully feeling her frustrations. And she let the fear engulf her. She acknowledged everything she was afraid of, including the fear that she'd never have Tristan's baby because she'd die first.

The itchiness got worse as the night wore on. It kept waking her. By pre-dawn, her teeth started to chatter, and she was getting alternating hot and cold sweats.

"Are you bleeding? Let's get you to the bathroom to check." It was a nurse in her room, waking her up like ten seconds after she'd finally fallen back to sleep. Adrian was in the doorway.

"You're in withdrawal." Adrian said as the nurse helped Kyla past him.

"No shit, Sherlock. You get your PhD in a crackerjack box?" she snapped.

He laughed and ruffled her hair as she passed him. "Taryn feeding from you didn't stop the withdrawals from coming. Good to know."

She shuddered at the memory of Taryn and stopped the nurse outside the bathroom door, "I can handle this myself."

The nurse was a big sturdy woman, the one who seemed to be in charge the last few days. Kyla suspected her name was something like Inga, Olga, or Helga or something that. Right or wrong, those names were attached to a stereotype that conjured images up of six-feet-tall Russian female basketball players for her. Sure, there were probably gorgeous and petite women by those names, many of them, but Kyla's brain named all big scary sturdy women those names until she knew different.

"I'll help you."

"No!" Kyla hissed, "I'll be fine."

Then she got into the bathroom and shut the door and sat on the toilet, feeling really weak. Maybe she should've let her in.

Her legs started to tingle and pinch inside.

She peed and examined things, seeing that the pad was clear, the toilet tissue was blood-free, and the tampon had just one tiny dark red streak along it. Maybe the bleeding was over?

She put a fresh pad on, since the existing one was damp from all the sweating, and then yanked up her panties and pj pants and washed her hands.

She looked sickly pale.

She stepped into the hall and the nurse was gone but Adrian was there.

"Well?"

"Well, what?"

"Bleeding?"

"There was some. Not a lot. It looked like it was old or the end but..." she shrugged.

"Try to rest; we'll check in the morning. I'm staying here for the night if you need anything. Do you want a mild sedative?"

She shook her head, "No. A major one. I want to sleep until I can be with him."

He gave her a sad smile. It looked like it was sympathetic.

"How is he?" She didn't think he'd tell her the truth but had to ask anyway.

"He's climbing the walls. He knows he needs to stay put until you're safe. He's much calmer than he was, however. He understands that we needed to make that call."

"He does?"

"Yes. It's all going to be fine, Kyla. Try to sleep. If the withdrawals become too much, let Ingrid know and we'll administer a sedative."

"Ingrid?"

"The tall redheaded nurse."

Wow, she'd been pretty darn close.

She went to the bed, climbed in, and wondered how Tristan was really doing.

She wished she could feel him the way he felt her. But if he felt half the pain and frustration she felt, it wouldn't be fun to feel that in addition to her own pain.

Twenty minutes later when the teeth chattering, sweats, and itchiness was back she wished she could turn off her feelings, so he wouldn't have to feel them because she was sure it was far from pleasant to have a bird's eye view into her thoughts right now. In addition to the withdrawals and the worry about him, she couldn't stop thinking about her dream, about the baby with the blue eyes. She was thinking about the fact that Adrian had poisoned her, in essence, in order to kill her pregnancy, and then that caused bleeding that made Tristan turn into the monster, the monster who fed on *that* blood.

Tristan fed on blood that might've contained that fertilized egg. Against his will. Against both of their wills. And that hurt so fucking bad. She wanted to make this place a bloodbath, too.

And something supernatural had obviously happened when they were having sex during her ovulation because Tristan's eyes had glowed so bright, *the* most beautiful she'd ever seen them and he'd told her that her eyes were glowing.

And she had something supernatural in her now, being non-vampire, because she was able to fight against Liam, fight off Celia, and avoid Taryn's royal vampire programming skills. She wished she knew how to leverage whatever that cold surging power was so that she could break Tristan free and get them both out of here.

She was having a hard time falling asleep when something occurred to her and she jumped up and went to that duffle bag and pulled out one of Tristan's hoodies. They'd bought it at Walmart in Oregon. It had only been worn a few hours so was still in with their clean clothes. She put it to her nose. It smelled like him. Cotton candy and s'mores and musk.

She put it on backwards so that she could bury her nose in the hood and then she cried herself to sleep, pretending that he was holding her close, comforting her.

SHE WOKE UP IN THE morning to a bed soaked in blood. She'd leaked straight through.

She saw no one but Adrian and that nurse that day and because there was blood, she knew she wouldn't see Tristan and that put her deeper into the pit of despair. Adrian had been back and forth to the cottage a few times, ensuring she ate, getting a new mattress brought in, and offering her medication to help with the withdrawals, which she'd refused.

Apparently, Taryn had flown back home so she wasn't a threat at the moment.

The following day, the blood tapered to nearly nothing. But the day after that it was back with a vengeance and Kyla was ready to pull her hair out with withdrawals and worry. She was pretty much bedridden with them.

The next day, there wasn't blood and she hoped that was the end. The day after that, there wasn't blood, either. There also wasn't much to Kyla. She was pale and sickly-looking. Adrian had hooked her up to an IV for hydration and a cocktail he'd said he'd whipped up to help numb the effects of the withdrawals, which she hated but was far too weak to argue about. And they did seem to help, but made her sleep a whole lot, which was fine, too.

Nurse Ingrid had helped her in and out of the bathroom and the shower and got a bit of food into her each day as well.

At two days full blood-free, she got good news.

"Forty-eight hours with no bleeding. I think it might be safe for you two to be reunited. Interesting timing, too. Happy twenty fifth birthday," Adrian was all smiles. She wanted to punch him in his stupid James Franco face.

"What day is it?"

Pretty bad that she had no idea when her actual birthday was.

"July 29th. I'll be back shortly."

"With Tristan?"

"With Tristan."

Her heartrate picked up.

Ingrid got her to drink some orange juice and eat half a banana and half a piece of toast with peanut butter and then Kyla asked her to help her with her hair. The woman efficiently French braided it.

But then it was hours of being alone, waiting. Hours. What was happening?

Sam was there, in her doorway.

Sam?

"Hi, love. How are you keeping?"

She frowned, "What are you doing here?"

"Tristan sent me to get you."

"He sent you?"

"He did. He's at the main house, still laid up, until he feeds. He's not strong enough to come down here without feeding first. We attempted bagged blood but that wouldn't do. He probably would've been okay, but he depleted the balance of his strength laying out Adrian the minute he was un-daggered. He beat the daylights out of him and then daggered him with Adrian's own dagger." Sam chuckled.

"What?"

"Adrian'll live. He's just in a world of hurt right now. Tristan needs you. Looks like you need him, too. Shall I carry you or can you walk?"

Kyla didn't trust Sam. No way, no how. Even though she wasn't bleeding.

"I'm not going anywhere with you!"

"Trust me, you'll both feel a whole lot better when you're in the same room. I'll have you there in a jiffy."

She heard Tristan's voice loud and clear in her mind.

"Besides me a lone vampire will never be alone with you. Ever. Not even Sam. If you find yourself alone with any vampire for any reason, any reason whatsoever, it's a problem, and against my wishes."

"No, Sam."

"Sorry, darling. You haven't much choice. He needs you."

He went to lean over and lift her, but she screeched and tried to struggle.

He sighed and put her down and backed up. He put his hand over his forehead a second and then lifted his phone from his jeans pocket and tapped the screen, then put it to his ear, "Tristan. She's resisting. Yeah. Alright. Okay."

He glanced at her, "Word of advice. Not a good idea to struggle against a vampire who is already fighting his predatory urges. Okay? You're teaching an old dog patience; you know that?" And then he left.

She was alone. She took a few slow calming breaths and another sip of the orange juice on the bedside table.

Not long later, she was still wondering what the heck was going on and wishing she had the strength to run, but then Sam was back.

She felt strong enough to stand. She put a hand up to block him,

"Stay back. I'm not going anywhere with you!"

"Sweetheart, save your strength. Here. Take this dagger. I ran to fetch it. If I get out of line, shove it in me and then carry it with you. Any vamp gets near you, poke him or her and they'll be out like a light. Okay?" He passed it to her.

She held it up and inspected it. It felt heavy, old, and like power emanated from it, which was an odd sensation.

"For how long?"

"Stick it in, just a quick jab, yank it out and they'll go down long enough for you to run away if you're quick about it. A few minutes. Stick it in and keep it in and they'll stay down until it's removed. I'll carry you. Faster that way and less exposure for you to others."

She was hesitant, "Why don't you carry Tristan here?"

"He's a vampire but he's still a guy. The only way a guy'd let another guy carry him is if he were unconscious."

She chewed her lip. She didn't have a good feeling about this.

"Alright, I hate to do this to myself but jab me quick and then wait so you can see it works and know you've got the upper hand. Just not the heart, please. That would be the end of me. And don't think about going it alone without me. You need me. If you want, call Tristan to confirm—-" before he finished she jerked forward and jabbed him with the dagger quick, poking him in the ribs with it. Barely any force at all and it jabbed him as if she'd plunged it with all her strength. He grunted and went to the floor and was out.

She leaned forward and got into his jeans pocket and pulled out his phone and went to the last number dialed and hit it.

"What now? Fuck, just grab her and hurry!" was how he answered but his voice sounded weak, exhausted.

"Tristan?" she gasped.

"Baby?" His voice was a song in her heart.

She let out a big breath.

"What's happening? Why are you calling me?"

"I jabbed Sam with the dagger and he's out."

"Shit. Where?"

"In the bedroom at the cottage."

"No, where on Sam?"

"His ribs."

"Okay. You need him. Take the dagger out."

"It's already out. I just poked."

"Okay, then you have to wait. Wait for him to wake up and he'll bring you to me."

"Tristan you said never ever trust any vamp alone, even Sam."

"I know, princess, but I have no choice right now. I'm depleted. Sam's medicated. Medicated to lethal levels to get you to me without hurting you. And he and I are good. Some things have come to light. We don't have a whole lot of time before it wears off. When he comes to, get to me."

"Should I come alone now? Try to..."

"Wait for Sam."

"Okay."

"Fuck, baby..."

He let that hang.

"Yeah," she choked out, in agreement.

They were both just holding the phone then.

And then Sam started to stir.

"He's moving."

"Watch him when he wakes in case the medication has worn off. It shouldn't, but..."

"He's awake. He isn't trying to attack."

Sam gave her a sour look and got to his feet slowly grunting, "Damn, that smarts."

He lifted the hem of his t-shirt and rubbed the spot, which had a puncture that wasn't bleeding, strangely, and then it faded before her eyes to a bruise. He dropped the hem of the shirt and held his palm out at her.

"Your chariot, mademoiselle." Kyla held tight to the dagger and said to Tristan, "I'm on my way."

"Okay," he said softly and then she handed Sam back the phone and took his hand.

He jerked her forward and hefted her up into his arms and then zoomed out of the room, down the stairs, and out the wide open front door. He wasn't as fast a whoosher as Tristan but they were to the main house quickly.

He set her on her feet as he opened the door.

"Slip that dagger into your sleeve and be casual. No eye contact," he said. "You're strong enough to walk?"

She nodded.

They walked through the front foyer, which was empty and instead of walking down the hall toward Adrian's office or that big lounge area that led to the staircase, they walked in the opposite direction down an identical hallway jutting out in the opposite way.

There were several doors along that hallway and thankfully they hadn't seen anyone so far. They got to the end of the hall and Sam reached into his pocket and pulled out a key card and pressed it against the reader. It clicked, and the light flashed green. He opened and held a glass door. She went ahead.

They were in a tiny alcove that had two more glass doors: one to the left and one to the right. He put the key card against the reader on the right and it clicked, turned green, and he opened it for Kyla. She stepped in.

She glanced back, feeling something prickle on the back of her neck and saw a man standing there behind the glass door that was on the left. He put his palm against the glass and leaned forward, his forehead against the glass and it hit her like a ton of bricks that he looked exactly like Jackson. EXACTLY like him. Blond curly hair, big brown eyes, big shoulders.

Jackson who had jumped off a bridge, been put on life support, and was to have the plug pulled causing her to flee Ottawa to Toronto, to head toward what would eventually lead her right here.

He sucked on his lower lip and looked at her longingly and her heart seized for a split second.

"Sam?" she looked ahead at the back of Sam's head for a quick second.

"Hm?" He was a good ten paces ahead of her in a long door-lined hallway that had a set of double doors at the end.

She looked back over her shoulder and whoever had been at the other door was now gone.

"Sam?"

He turned around and looked at her.

"What's wrong?"

"Who was that?"

"That who? Who was who?"

"At that other door," she pointed, "That door back there? It looked like..." She shook her head.

It couldn't be. Could it? The lip sucking was even characteristic of Jax.

She said it out loud, starting to walk again, "No, it couldn't have been." It was like Jackson but cleaned up, healthier-looking. Not strung out. Not hooked up to tubes and machines and...

Sam blew out a long breath and Kyla's heart skipped a beat.

"It was," he said. "That conversation'll have to wait for later."

Oh...My ...Fucking...

What?

She didn't have time to process that thought, though, because he pressed his thumbprint and the key card against panels on the next door and opened it and a light flashed red on the panel so he grabbed her hand, put her thumb against the panel, and then it turned green and he motioned for her to go ahead. She gave him a quizzical look.

"It sensed two bodies. I have to identify the second body for the database or it'll trip the alarm."

She nodded and moved ahead into a big room that looked like a lab. There was a long counter littered with microscopes, cabinets along one wall filled with bottles, and a long desk with several computer monitors. There was a glass wall with a glass door beyond the desk and Sam opened it and she walked in to an area that what was set up like a bedroom.

Adrian was on the floor, unconscious, his face beaten to a bloody pulp. Behind him was a double bed and Tristan was in it. Her heart seized at the sight of him.

He was sitting up against a red suede headboard, dark blankets around his waist. He was bare chested, unshaven, looked a little pale, and his eyes were bloodshot. But he looked, essentially, like himself. Sam leaned down and hefted Adrian up over his shoulder in a fireman's hold.

"We'll give you two some privacy," Sam left the room with him, saying, "call when you're ready and I'll let you out."

Kyla's eyes met Tristan's. The world stood still as he stared at her.

"Get over here," he said hoarsely, almost in a whisper. His voice sounded pained.

She moved in what felt like slow motion and then collapsed on top of him. His arms wound around her, and he pulled her close.

She closed her eyes, let out a breath, and absorbed the feel of him, the smell of him, the strength of him. Weak or not, he still felt so solid, so real.

God, he felt so good.

She could feel him inside. His teeth weren't even connected yet, but she could FEEL him and what she felt made a sob tear out of her as her arms went around him.

The room started to spin. Her blood started to heat up. Her body started to tremble, and then his nose swept up the length of her throat, his teeth elongated into the curve of her throat, and as the skin was pierced, BAM! Fireworks.

An explosion and an overwhelming sense of peace at the exact same time flooded. Like this is where she needed to be. In his arms, nourishing him. Him nourishing her. She felt like she was getting healthier and healthier by the millisecond. So was he.

He drank just a bit and released her throat. He sighed loud. She looked at his face. The colour was returning.

But then emotions started to rise in her and they were hers and they were his, too and there was so much of it that she didn't know if she could handle it all. Her brain was a jumbled kaleidoscope of emotion. And then evidently, she couldn't handle it at all because everything faded to dark as she got dizzier and then passed out in his arms.

10

KYLA WOKE UP. SHE WAS back in that cottage, back in that sleigh bed she'd been in for the last week without him. Again, she was without him.

She sat up straight, hearing a commotion of glass shattering and yelling. She dashed out of the room and got half way down the stairs and saw Tristan, Adrian, and Claudio all standing close and, it appeared that they were all in one another's faces. No. Tristan was in both of *their* faces and both men appeared to be trying to reason with him.

Kyla felt fear straight down to the marrow at the vibe coming off Tristan. His eyes darted up to her.

"Back upstairs, Kyla," he demanded and then he grabbed Adrian's shirt with both hands and hollered, "Out!" and threw Adrian toward the door.

Claudio headed toward the door as Adrian rose to his feet.

"We'll talk tomorrow."

"We won't. I'm done," Tristan said. "As soon as that dagger he promised me is ready I'm taking it and I am gone. Have it to me early, Constantin. I fuckin' mean it!"

"Sleep on this and let's talk in the morning. Don't be hasty," Claudio said.

"Hasty? Are you kidding me, Claude? After what you've both done? I've been fed a trough of shit about how I'm the one to lead, to be a change agent for us. To help us move forward. But you've both manipulated things from the start. I'm sure you get why I'm ready to call this whole thing quits after what you've done. You've stolen from me. You've stolen something from me that I can't ever get back..."

Kyla's heart hurt so bad. *So bad.* She choked on a sob.

"Kyla, get the FUCK upstairs!" he shouted. There was a chair sitting beside him with a side table sitting beside it and they both moved, like they had gotten caught up in a gust of wind and landed at the bottom of the stairs, blocking her ability to get to him. Or maybe blocking Claudio and Adrian from her. She wasn't sure. Adrian stared, wide-eyed at the furniture and then looked up at Kyla. Tristan moved in front of the furniture, his back to the staircase, to her, blocking them.

Kyla ran for the bedroom and slammed the door. The lock turned on its own. She stared at it, hyperventilating. His rage was inside of her, worse than snaking spiders, worse than the arctic chill of his angry eyes when she'd tried to leave. She was bawling so hard it was as if the tears couldn't come fast enough, couldn't pound down hard enough. The emotion that tore out of her acid-filled stomach was gut-wrenching.

Tristan was downstairs, and he was horrifying. The look on his face, the hate in his eyes. The energy coming off him. The feelings inside of him. She still felt them.

She heard a slam. And then she heard a series of bangs, crashes, and more slams.

She tried to catch her breath. She braced, waiting for him to come in. But he didn't. She got her breathing under control and spying a bottle of water on the dresser top that was unopened, she guzzled it down.

She opened the door and quietly made her way downstairs. He wasn't there. She moved the chair and table away from the staircase. The couch was tipped over on its face, the coffee table against the front door. Framed art pieces that'd been on the walls were on the floor. The place looked like it had been in the eye of a twister.

She wandered the main floor checking the other rooms. He wasn't there.

Where was he? She carefully opened the front door. No one.

She closed it and walked back to the kitchen and opened the door that was there and looked outside. She saw him. He was walking. She ran back upstairs and got her shoes on and then ran back down and out and tried to catch up. She couldn't see him. She followed the path and it led to that meadow with the swing. He was against the tree that held the swing and he was staring out at the pond. He looked over his shoulder and saw her.

"Go back to the house."

She froze in her tracks. He wasn't looking at her.

"I need a minute," he said, still looking the other way.

Excruciating pain tore straight through her. She ran back to the house and up the stairs and threw herself on the bed. Her already broken heart wasn't being glued back together by him. Instead, it shattered further.

Feelings. Fucking feelings. Fucking her over. As usual.

SHE WOKE UP COCOONED by his arms. It was dark, and he'd just gotten into the bed. She tried to pull away, anger gripping her. His arms tightened.

"Don't," he whispered and held tighter.

She stayed still there for a minute, quick and shallow angry breaths coming out fast, but he held tight, saying nothing.

"I'm sorry," he finally whispered and that unleashed absolute agony inside of her. Her agony and his braided tightly together and they both felt it. All of it. She let him hold her and stroke her hair and rain kisses on her face. They said nothing. They didn't need words because they were in some sort of mind meld.

Her pain and his pain, two mirrors facing one another, showing one another an infinite spiral of hurt.

Eventually she fell back to sleep, their hearts beating in perfect time together.

SUNLIGHT STREAMED INTO the room. She was alone. She was alone physically but she felt like she was also alone in every way possible. She couldn't feel him. After having felt him and not feeling him now, she felt like part of her was missing.

Panic gripped her. Was he okay? Was this what he'd felt for all this time whenever they were apart?

She got up and saw that the bag and folded tall pile of clothing were gone but there was a clean outfit sitting there for her. She took it to the bathroom and took a shower. When she got out she dressed in the black walking shorts and purple t-shirt and then she put on her black t-strap sandals. She headed down the stairs. She smelled coffee.

He met her at the bottom of the stairs, dressed in jeans and that cyan blue tee he'd worn the night he found her in Victoria. He had shaved, too.

He handed her a coffee cup, "Grab the rest of your things from up there and put them in our bag." He motioned to the sofa where their things were stacked.

She took the cup and nodded and turned back around on her heel.

He hadn't tried to kiss her, hadn't smiled, hadn't really made eye contact. Her heart twinged with pain.

She heard voices as she came back down the stairs with her bathroom things and what she'd worn the day before. Adrian was just inside the door and Tristan didn't sound happy. She felt his anger, like hot bubbling liquid inside her brain.

"Don't try to keep us here another day with your stall tactics. You told me it'd be ready today so get it to me, so I can fucking go."

"It would have been ready, Tristan, if you hadn't repeatedly injured me, putting me at very limited capacity. It should be ready tomorrow."

"Give me yours then."

"I will not." Adrian's voice got louder. "Just one more day. I'll do my best to have it finished."

Kyla took a sip of her coffee and walked by them toward the kitchen, feeling them both watch her go.

She drank her coffee staring out the back door. Sam was standing there smoking a cigarette and sipping from a coffee mug. He gave her a little smile.

She opened the door half way but didn't step out.

"Are you safe for me to talk to?" she asked.

He nodded, "Adrian developed a slow-release patch." He patted the back of his shoulder, "Seems to be working so far. Though I'd feel better you talking to me if you had one of those daggers in your hand."

She gave him a half-hearted smile, "It's nice that you seem to really not want to hurt me."

He returned the smile, "I really don't."

"Thanks for the help yesterday," she said.

He gave her a nod.

"That was Jackson? In that doorway?"

Sam blew out a slow breath, "You should talk to Tris about that."

"He knows about that?"

He nodded, "He does now."

"Okay, um... he hasn't been exactly approachable for conversation, so what if you tell me?"

"Yeah, not exactly approachable," Sam scoffed, "Understatement."

"But you don't wanna tell me about Jackson?"

"It's not my place." Sam glanced over her shoulder and his eyes changed. She could feel Tristan's presence behind her.

"Okay. See ya later."

He saluted her.

She turned around. Tristan was standing there, arms folded, looking past her to Sam.

She froze.

His eyes darted down and met hers. His jaw was twitching, teeth clenched, "Don't approach a vamp for conversation. Ever. Any vamp," he said.

She gave a little nod, eyes darting away, and put her coffee mug on the counter and then moved to get by him so she could go back upstairs. He caught her wrist. She stared at her feet.

They stood still, quiet, for a long time. She flinched, wanting him to let go but not quite struggling, just sort of tense. He kept hold of her.

"Why won't you look at me?" he finally asked.

"Because right now it hurts too much," she whispered, not looking up.

Suddenly he pulled her tight into his arms. She resisted about half a second but then melted into his chest and put her arms around his waist, her cheek against his peck.

Sensation crested again, and she could feel him as if he were feeding from her. She could feel immense frustration and anger coming from inside of him. She could feel something else, too, but she didn't know quite what it was. Grieving, maybe?

"I can feel you and you're not feeding..." she sobbed into his shirt and his grip on her tightened almost to the point of pain.

There was a knock at the door. He looked her in the eye for a second before moving away to answer the door and for a millisecond she could also see everything she felt inside of him. Pain, anger, grief, fear.

He came back to the counter removing a lid from a tray and examining the two meals of pancakes, bacon, and fruit. He smelled and then tasted them and then moved them to the table, seeming satisfied. "You should eat."

"Not hungry."

"I need to feed. Please eat."

She let out a huff and nabbed her half empty coffee mug and rinsed topped it up from the coffee maker.

"Coffee?" she mumbled.

"No thanks." He started to eat.

She prepped her coffee and stirred it and then reached to grab her plate and made to leave with it when his hand hooked around her and caught her hip. "Sit with me?"

She shook her head, "No, I..." she shook it again and didn't finish. She went back upstairs. Feeling his emotions on top of her own? It was just way *too* much.

She sat on the edge of the bed and wheeled over the hospital style cart that Nurse Ingrid had used with her and Kyla started eating the food. She got through only about half. She finished her coffee and pushed the wheeled cart back with her feet and then laid down in the bed staring at the ceiling, still feeling things so intensely and now not knowing if the feelings were her own, his, or both.

The door opened. It was him. He approached her cautiously.

He sat on the side of the bed and reached out and brushed her hair away, tucking it behind her ear with his fingertips,

"Hey," he said.

"If you need to feed, you can go ahead." She turned her head sideways so that her neck was exposed and stared off in the opposite direction.

He took her cheek and moved her face back so that her gaze was back on him.

"Please don't," he said.

Pain burned in her chest, radiating to her shoulders.

"I'm sorry," he said, "I'm hurting you. I don't want to hurt you. It's the last thing I want..."

She swallowed and closed her eyes.

"Kyla. I don't know how to do this."

"How to do what?" she asked angrily, feeling totally pissed.

"How to feel all of this. It's my job to protect you and I keep fucking failing. And now I'm hurting you because I don't know how to make it better."

Her anger crested, and she sighed. He looked so sad, so lost.

"How can I be the one destined to lead? I can't protect the most important thing in the world to me and yet I'm supposed to be some protector and leader of my race?"

"Maybe all this is what'll help you learn to lead."

"But what if I lose you in the process? I'm scared to death, Kyla. So goddamn scared." He flopped on the bed beside her and stared at the ceiling, covering his eyes with his palms.

She leaned over and lifted one of his hands and kissed his eyelid. He let out a heavy sigh and grabbed her and pulled her on top of him and squeezed and then flipped so he was on top. He held her head and buried his face into her hair, kissing behind her earlobe and squeezing.

"I'm not scared anymore," she told him, feeling new emotion well up inside of her. She ran her palms up the length of his back.

"No?" He went up on an elbow and looked her in the eye and it was as if a cloud lifted and hope floated high up above them.

"Nope."

"Then you really *are* crazy, baby, because you're right, my track record fucking sucks. Dog cages, elephant tranquilizers, scaring you thousands of miles away, fucked up road trips where I almost drain you, leaving you alone and you get attacked by the Toronto Mangler. Then bringing you to Adrian's compound of fucked up medical experiments..."

"But it's gonna be okay," she touched his chin cleft.

"Okay?" he looked at her like she'd grown another head.

"*We're* gonna be okay."

"How do you know that? Because I wanna believe that but..."

"'Cuz you're what I've been waiting my whole life for. My prince who'll swim through the molten lava moat and slay the dragons and free me. I know this in my soul. In. My. Soul. I keep having all these dreams that sort of come true and when I was a little girl I dreamt about a prince with blue eyes rescuing me so I know that's what you'll do. You'll rescue me and you'll cook me beautiful breakfasts and chocolate brownies and we'll go skinny dipping and you'll give me beautiful blue-eyed babies some day and we will raise them together. Both of us."

"I'm the luckiest kidnapping, bloodsucking monster on the planet, you know that?" He put his arms around her.

"I love you," she said.

"I'm sorry. I'm so sorry that all this happened. That they took something so precious from us. I'm just fucked right now. You need me and I'm lost. What they took... I didn't know how much it meant until I felt it. I sensed it almost right away and..."

"Shhh. Don't. I can't go there."

He swallowed.

"I felt your pain, Kyla. I was in a pit. They had to put me in a concrete pit in the ground because I kept breaking the locks they tried to use to contain me and in that pit your pain almost killed me. While I was daggered I wasn't out, I was paralyzed but feeling everything. Every. Fucking. Thing. *God*!"

"Oh baby," she said but then there was a frantic-sounding knock on the bedroom door.

"Come," Tristan answered.

The door burst open and it was Sam, he was breathless, "Liam, Tris. He's been spotted. Just outside the perimeter of the property."

"Be down in a minute."

Sam nodded and backed out, shutting the door.

"I want this dagger so you've got it to keep you safe from me whenever you bleed or when you're fertile you can use it against anyone else who's a threat and I want to get us outta here and home, but if he's close I'm thinking maybe we wait and I eliminate that threat. But that leaves Adrian, too, and I want you away from that maniac. What do you think we should do?"

"I don't know," she said, "I wish I knew."

"I'm gonna go talk to Sam. Stay here. I'll be back," he kissed her. She put her fingers into his hair and sank into the kiss.

He caressed her face, moved off the bed, and then left the room.

IT WAS THE FOLLOWING day. He hadn't come to bed the night before but had slipped in around dawn and pulled her close and passed out for just a few hours. In the late afternoon, Tristan and Kyla were in bed together, again. He'd come in, interrupting her from her boredom, put a small laptop-sized box on the dresser, said "Hey," and then moved in and his teeth were on her throat, piercing. Her eyes rolled back, and her hands were in his soft hair.

She'd been craving this. She'd been staring out the window, tired of being in this room. She'd spent so much time waiting behind closed doors for him. She wanted that part of her life to be over with. She wanted them to have a life together.

Who knew, at this point, what it'd look like, but she couldn't wait to move forward.

"I have the dagger," he whispered against her chin, kissing her after his fangs had retracted, and his chin jerked to the box on the dresser. He lifted her up and got into bed with her, then spooned her.

"Yeah?" she asked.

"Adrian just dropped it off. He's offering to make a second one if we stay for a month. That'd mean you carry one and I'd have one, too." He kissed behind her ear and ran his fingers through her hair.

Kyla both sighed and winced. She sighed at his touch but winced at the idea of another month.

Another ovulation? Another period?

"He wants to talk to me about options for your next cycles. He wants to run tests. I don't trust him, baby, but I think we need him while we get this figured out. If he hadn't been here when you bled..."

"I hate him, Tristan. I hate what he did."

"I know, princess. But if he hadn't been here maybe I wouldn't have stopped. Maybe I'd have drained you."

"Or maybe you would've stopped."

"Historically speaking, the woman typically gets drained. Anyway, here's what I'm thinkin'..."

"Maybe I wouldn't have been bleeding. Maybe our baby would've been growing inside me like it was supposed to do."

His expression dropped.

They stared at one another for a beat.

She folded her arms across her chest, "Anyway, you were thinking?"

He sighed, rolled onto his back, and pulled her close, her head rested on his shoulder.

"You carry the dagger..."

"Does it work? He didn't give us a dud, did he?"

Tristan smirked, "No. It works. I tested it on him. He's flat out downstairs."

"Good," Kyla snapped. "Asshole."

He gave her a squeeze, "He'll be up and about any time now. Anyway, we're thinking we should stage a vulnerability so Liam gets in. But we'll be ready."

"Okay..."

"So, you need to stay in here, stay armed with that dagger. They think I should carry it, but I want you to hold it. We'll have the building guarded by programmed vamps who will be medicated, too. They shouldn't have a reaction to you even if you start bleeding."

"Right."

"We're allowing vulnerabilities with a delivery later tonight and then again first thing in the morning. If he gets in during either of those two times he'll be apprehended and then daggered."

"How many daggers are there?"

"Two. Yours and Adrian's. He's promised to make more. He's low on the metal he needs but he's getting more."

"Okay. Who programmed the guards?"

"My mother's back and working on them right now. Celia isn't on site and we don't want her in the know, either."

She nodded, "Your mother is something..."

Tristan looked at her funny.

"I met her. While they had you."

His face contorted, "What?"

"She came to see me."

He jumped out of the bed to his feet, "And Adrian allowed it?"

"No. Well, he tried to stop her but apparently when his back was turned she killed the six people he had here, some nurses, some guards. She killed one of Adrian's horses, too, I guess to punish him."

"I need to know what happened in that conversation."

Kyla snickered, "She's something..."

Tristan rolled his eyes, "I hate that she was anywhere near you. What happened?"

"We took a walk. We walked to that meadow with the tree swing and I recognized it. I've dreamt about that place. About my ex being there. What's up with that, anyway? He's here. The ex, Jackson, that I thought was dead."

"First things first. Taryn? Tell me."

"Moonflowers were blooming and she was trying to program me to work on you for the 'the cause', convince you to make lots of babies and drink a lot of... you know... and she told me you shouldn't trust Claudio but we should let Adrian help us 'cuz we need him. I let her think she was getting her way."

"She tried to program you?"

"She failed. And then she bit me, and..."

"She bit you? She bit you?" His face was scary.

"Yeah, but she told me to forget it happened. She—-"

"SHE BIT YOU?!" He bolted out of the room.

Kyla's mouth was still open in shock, but he was long gone.

She went into the hallway, glanced over the railing and didn't see him. But, Adrian was there. She went down the stairs and Adrian was sitting on the sofa with his head in his hands.

"What are you doing here?"

"Recovering. Tristan daggered me. He just ordered me to keep you safe and then left."

"Is his mother on the property still?"

"She's in the main house. Did you tell him that she toyed with you?"

"Yeah, when I said she bit me he..."

"Fuck!" Adrian snapped. It was rare, so far, to see him lose his composure but both times had been to do with Taryn.

He got up, about to head to the door, but the door flew open and standing there was Liam Donavan who was instantly twisting Adrian's throat with both hands. Adrian went down, looking like he'd suffered a broken neck.

Oh my good God.

Kyla's thoughts immediately went to the dagger that was upstairs in the box on the dresser and she made a run for it.

She slammed the door to the bedroom, locked it, and fumbled, getting to the box, but before she got it opened, she heard a crash. Liam had broken the door down and then he had her.

He spun her around and had her by the shoulders, "Long time no taste..." He had a big smile.

"No!" Kyla screamed and scrambled for the dagger, but the box went flying in the struggle and landed on the floor. Kyla landed on the floor. Liam flipped her and was hovering over her on his knees. He had her pinned, her wrists over her head.

"I spent years craving her taste but after tasting you I can't even remember what she tasted like. But you... I'm going to fucking feast on you!"

Where was the cold? Where was that power she needed to throw him off?

"Tristan is—-" she started.

"Busy. He's arguing with Mommie Dearest."

He gave her that wide toothpaste commercial smile. And then his fangs were out. And then finally, FINALLY, that cold feeling burst out of her with a huge amount of force, so much that she feared she was about to explode, and she flung him and he crashed into the wall.

Thank GOD Tristan had just fed.

She scrambled to get to her feet, but he was coming back at her. She shoved at his gut and he went flying back and glass smashed as he went right through the bedroom window.

Kyla crawled quickly over to the box on the floor and pulled the dagger out. It was the same as the other one but this one was a little bit smaller, a bit lighter in weight.

Liam was back, through the bedroom door, and he looked very surprised.

"That was fun. Joseph was right. You *are* a feisty little thing."

She pointed the dagger at him and he stopped in his tracks.

"What *is* that? Jasper had one too." He jerked his chin up.

"Come here so I can show you," she sneered, "I'll show you and then Tristan will fucking END YOU!"

She lunged for him, but he backed up into the hall saying, "I'll be back. I'll be back, and I'll feast on you and then I'll crush Walker into dust." He zoomed down the stairs and out the door.

She rushed down the stairs. Adrian was sitting up, his head bowed,

"Adrian!" she yelled.

He looked up, looking dazed, oblivious to what'd just happened and then he saw the dagger in her hand and his eyes went wide.

"Liam was here!" she shouted, "He's here!"

Adrian rushed to his feet and said, "Come with me."

"He's outside somewhere; I threw him out the window. He was back and now he's gone—-" She ended that sentence with a squeak because without warning Adrian grabbed her and zoomed away with her in his arms and a moment later Kyla found herself in Adrian's office. He wasn't as fast as Tristan but was faster than Sam.

She could instantly feel Tristan; he must be close by. She could feel his fury. Arctic chill. It was cold and angry and scary. She shivered in response.

Adrian set her down on a chair and went right to the phone on his desk and pressed a button.

"Lock down," she heard him say, both from right in front of her and she also heard it through an intercom, "Code black. Lock down. Code black."

An alarm sounded, and it was so loud that her hands automatically covered her ears. She still had the dagger in her right hand. She examined it. Adrian's eyes were on her. He reached into a drawer in his desk and his body went solid.

The alarm sound halted in time to hear him say "No."

He yanked the desk drawer out all the way and threw it, "Fuck!"

"What?" Kyla breathed.

"*My* dagger. My dagger is gone."

He flipped a laptop on his desk open and was furiously clicking for a minute and then his face went enraged.

His phone was ringing from his pocket.

He hit a button, "Tristan. I have her. No, she's fine. She has it. But there's a problem. Liam Donavan has my dagger."

Kyla wanted to barf.

"My office," he said into the phone and then hit a few buttons on the computer, "No, you're clear to move. The system is open for all basic doors. Get here."

She heard a bleep over the loudspeaker.

He looked at her and shook his head.

"How did Liam get in? I thought ..."

"I don't know yet." He hit some buttons on his computer and was studying the screen so Kyla rounded the desk to see what he was doing and saw a series of camera views around the property. As he scanned through frame after frame she saw rooms in the cottages, hallways, corridors, and rooms in the guest suites.

Tristan had been absolutely right; there were cameras everywhere. She felt sick for a second, thinking about the sex they'd had since arriving. That thought took her to the staircase in the cottage and she didn't let her brain stay there. She must've made a sound of disgust because Adrian glanced up for a second and gave her a warning look. She guessed it was something to the effect of a "not now" type of look. He knew she was connecting the dots.

"Security is important. Just because there are cameras doesn't mean someone is always looking."

She made a harrumph sound. The door was being banged on, making her freeze in fear and look up.

"That's it!" he said and then rushed to open the door and then Tristan burst in. Tristan went right to her and enveloped her in his arms.

"He parachuted into the woods," Adrian said to Tristan while keying something into his cell phone, "I spotted the parachute. I believe he found her first and then came here and got the dagger. The ID used belonged to cleaning staff. Functional staff members. He followed one in, using his print, and I have zero movement reports for his print since then. I have his print and have now disabled it from any level two or higher security zones. We should put you both in the lab. That's level 3, top security. Keep you there until he's found. He's taken the dagger and probably went to lay low until he could find another opportunity to use it."

"He doesn't know what it is," Kyla said.

The both looked at her with quizzical expressions.

"Tristan, he got into the cottage. He almost got me, but we struggled, I got that cold gust through me, shoved him, he crashed out the window, and by the time he got back I had the dagger and threatened him. He asked what it was because he said Sam came at him with one. I told him to let me show him, so you could kill him or something like that and he took off."

"He had to have been watching me to know it was in the desk. He's got to have had surveillance in here or hacked into my feeds somehow," Adrian said, "And if he has, that is really not a good thing."

THEY WERE IN THAT ROOM off the lab, in the bed, curled up together.

"Don't leave me alone in here. You do that, he finds me, and this goes badly. *For sure* it goes badly!"

"Kyla, I can't just leave this to them. I do not fuckin' trust a single one of them. Did you see how freaked Adrian was? There's something he hasn't said. I don't know where the fuck Claudio is. Sam's missing, too."

When they'd gotten into the lab Adrian had a bit of a meltdown because he said that something was missing. He was frantically searching through the plethora of bottles in his cabinets, searching through his computer, looking at security footage. They'd gone into the room with the bed in it and were watching him through the glass wall. He was in a state, alright!

Adrian burst back into the room they were in, "He's hacked into my files," Adrian told Tristan, "He's got something and the something he has... it could be very bad."

"What is it?"

Adrian closed his eyes and shook his head, "If he injects her with it, it'll force her to go into a nectar cycle."

"What?" Tristan's hands went into his hair.

"I haven't used it yet. I have it, but I haven't used it. It's a hormone cocktail that will force menstruation. He's been watching. He's hacked my files. He has cameras in my lab and in my office. And one of Kyla's blood vials is gone."

Tristan had Adrian by the throat, "You fucking moron!"

Claude was there with Sam, in the lab. They could see them through the glass wall that separated the room they were in from that lab.

"Stay here," Tristan told Kyla.

"No!" She screeched, "Do not fucking leave me alone. That's how it'll go bad...if we separate..."

"Not leaving, princess. Going into the lab to talk to them. Not leaving." He kissed her forehead and he and Adrian stepped into the lab and Kyla watched as the four of them talked.

She was shaking like a leaf, sitting on that bed, holding the dagger. She started to say a prayer. This did *not* feel good.

God, please keep us safe. Don't let me lose him. Please don't let me lose him.

Sam, Claudio, and Adrian rushed out of the lab. Kyla couldn't see them any longer. Tristan was back.

"We'll stay here and wait. I wanna track him down myself but you're right; no way I can leave you alone." He caressed her cheek and snuggled up with her in the bed.

She put her arms around his middle and snuggled in. "Please don't leave me. I have a horrible sinking feeling about this. Don't let him hurt you, Tristan. Please don't let him hurt you." She tucked the dagger under the pillow and put both arms around him.

"I won't. I'll never leave you."

"Promise?"

"Promise. Never. No matter what."

She shuddered. The feeling of impending doom was real and tangible. It was as if she were in a movie theatre watching the heroine walking down a dark corridor, the ax murderer right behind her with the ax held up high.

"Kyla, c'mon..." he said, "This guy has nothing compared to me in terms of strength. I can protect you. Have faith in me."

"Tristan, I know you're stronger than him. I feel that. Honest, I do. I just can't shake this awful feeling..."

It was worse than fear. It was all-consuming.

Suddenly, there was a loud click. A light above the door to the room they were in turned on and it was red.

"What?" she breathed.

Tristan jumped from the bed and pushed on the door. It was locked. He glanced over his shoulder at Kyla.

Claudio was in the lab, alone. He was at a computer.

"Claude, what the fuck?" Tristan shouted. Claudio ignored him and kept typing away at the computer. And then she heard a swish sound and the room started to fill with mist.

She saw Claudio reach down and then put a mask with goggles on.

"Tristan!" she shouted, "What's going on?"

Tristan made the lock click open, but the room was filling with steam and the steam was getting thicker. She couldn't see Tristan. She started to choke on the steam. She tried to move in the direction she thought the door was in, but she wasn't sure if she was going the right way. It wasn't hot, not smoky, but sweet tasting. Like burnt marsh-mallows but it kept making her cough and choke. She heard glass smashing but couldn't see anything with the fog around herself.

Suddenly she was aware of hands on her shoulders and then teeth extending against her throat and just as everything went black she knew that it wasn't Tristan who had her.

11

SHE WOKE UP IN STRONG arms. She felt woozy. Her throat was bleeding.

That room they were in off the lab was no longer separated from the lab because the glass wall was mostly gone. The hiss of whatever had sent the steam into the room was still hissing but there wasn't steam.

She looked up and the face hovering over her zoomed into focus. She wasn't in Tristan's arms. She was in Liam's arms.

He smiled his stupid toothpaste commercial smile and said, "Now, the real fun begins. Let's see how much I can get before he notices," and his head descended to the side of her throat that wasn't already ripped.

Across the room she saw Tristan rip Claudio's head off. Literally. Claudio's hair, attached to his detached head was in Tristan's hand and Tristan threw the head. The head had goggles on its eyes and fangs out and those fangs were blood-coated. The head bounced off the wall and landed on the floor and then Tristan spun around and saw that she was in Liam's clutches.

She pushed, but she was weak. No cold rose up in her. Nothing rose up in her. All she could feel was her body was failing. That, and Tristan's pure unadulterated rage.

The gash that was already on her throat must've really weakened her. Blood trickled out steadily.

Tristan was there, hands on Liam while Liam's teeth were still on the other side of Kyla's throat.

"Let her fucking go!"

She knew he couldn't yank Liam off while those fangs were attached to her or he'd rip her throat apart.

She was panic-stricken, feeling weaker by the second.

Liam's wrist came up and she saw the green glint of the jewels on the dagger and then the dagger came down in the air and sank into Tristan's shoulder.

Liam pulled it out and released Kyla's throat to watch Tristan fall to the floor.

Oh God. No.

Liam licked his lips, "Fuck, you're delicious!" He looked at the dagger in his hand. "That's handy. I was wondering what this'd do."

Adrian rushed into the room and froze in his tracks when he took in the scene. Liam let go of Kyla and darted to him, jabbed the dagger in him, and then Adrian went down, too.

Kyla sobbed as she saw Tristan on the floor, out like a light, but not looking all that injured. And Liam obviously didn't know that the dagger had to stay in for Tristan to stay down. The dagger was bigger than hers. It was Adrian's! Was the other one still under the pillow? It must be!

Liam's teeth sank into her throat again and he moaned, gulped a few times, and Kyla's eyes darted to the bed. If only they were in the bed she could reach under the pillow. Was it still there? She felt so weak. Her throat was bleeding out on both sides. One side onto her chest, the other side into Liam's mouth.

He lifted her up off the floor and put her on the bed and she thought *"YES!"*

Her hands were laying limply above her head.

"I'd better close that wound," he muttered and put his mouth to it, "That's a bad one. Fucking D'Alonzo. I watched footage of him stealing that vial of your blood from the lab. When he drank it? I knew I had to hurry or he'd drain you before I got here."

Please God, let that dagger still be under this pillow.

Her hand reached under and she felt it. She gripped it.

Her body felt so weak that lifting her arm with the light dagger felt like lifting a fifty-pound barbell, but she got it up and then summoned every ounce of fight she had left, felt a tiny cold burst through that arm and she drove it down, into his back. She left it there.

Liam went limp on top of her.

She couldn't move. She had no strength. The throat wound she had was still gushing.

She looked down at Tristan, who was still laying on the floor, and prayed that he'd somehow wake up before she was empty.

Her eyelids started to flutter closed and everything started to go fuzzy.

"KYLA!" TRISTAN SAID, his voice sounding panicked.

Tristan?

Was she dreaming? Was she dead? Was she in heaven?

"Oh fuck, Kyla. Oh fuck, no, baby..." Her eyes opened just enough to see him and feel as he removed the weight of Liam from on top of her.

"She's not gonna make it unless you turn her. She's lost too much blood." That was Adrian. He was behind Tristan.

"I love you," she said.

"I love you, baby. No no no, don't close your eyes. Stay with me, princess."

He went fuzzy and then it was dark.

12

Tristan

HE FELT SICK. SICK to his stomach, sick at heart, sick in whatever small amount of soul there was left.

She was gone.

He'd turned her. He'd opened up his wrist and fed her his blood and she still had a pulse; she was still breathing. Barely.

She'd wake up soon. But she'd wake up and be someone else. She'd have green eyes and peaches & cream skin, and luscious lips, long curly eyelashes and a smokin' hot toned body, but she wouldn't be his princess. Not even close.

She'd be powerful. She'd undoubtedly be more powerful than Taryn, but because of that she would also be a cunning, calculating, cunt.

He'd be doomed to live with someone who looked like the love of his life, the reason he felt anything resembling human emotion. But that's where the similarities would end.

He wouldn't desert her. He couldn't. He'd promised.

He'd never leave her, no matter what.

And he wouldn't.

So he'd suffer.

He'd suffer like Andre, but worse. Worse because as sweet as Becky used to be, and as much as Andre had cared for that girl, no one could love *any* girl the way Tristan loved Kyla.

It would hurt, it would kill, watching a vamp with Kyla's body, Kyla's eyes, Kyla's voice. A nasty, hateful, spiteful creature, and he'd spend whatever life he had left, which could be an eternity, as her servant.

She'd lie, steal, cheat, murder, manipulate, and she'd laugh in his face if he dared show her a shred of emotion. It would be an eternity of constant reminders of what he'd lost, and he could already feel his heart turning to stone.

He took a swig straight from the bottle of Jack Daniels. He'd need it. She'd be conscious soon and that was when his nightmare would come true. She'd wake ravenous and then it would be hell on earth watching her desecrate everything and everyone around her for her own primal urges.

She's awake.

Relief moved through him, despite that train of thought because she'd almost been dead when he'd bled life into her, and now she was stirring. He couldn't bring himself to let her die. He deserved the punishment of watching her as a she-vamp for all his many, *many* sins.

And now her eyes were open. Those gorgeous green cat's eyes that said so much... that sparkled with her jokes, that lit up with mischief, that went liquid with arousal, that went like lasers with anger, shiny with excitement, or that shone with love once she'd admitted that their connection was real. He cradled her and rubbed his thumb across the apple of her cheek, "Baby?"

He ached as soon as he said that. Immense loss rushed through his heart, his veins.

He had a thermal pitcher and glass with body temperature blood ready. He had a feeder in the next room, on standby, in case the pitcher wasn't what she wanted or in case it wasn't enough.

She blinked at him.

"You're okay," he said, looking into her eyes, searching, "You feel okay? Your throat should heal shortly."

"Hm?" She looked dazed.

"Hungry? You should feed now."

She'd feel better after her first feed.

He'd been parched when he'd woken up after being turned. He'd been absolutely ravenous. He'd drained two feeders completely as soon as he'd woken.

She nodded a little.

He lifted her a little and tipped the glass to her lips. She took a mouthful and winced and then started to cough, spitting it all out.

"Kyla? Drink, baby. You need this." He held it to her lips again. She swallowed and then she started to get the dry heaves, so he lifted her and got her into the bathroom, over the sink. She threw up the blood.

He helped her by wiping her face with a cool cloth and then he carried her back to the bed. She seemed really weak. She should be the exact opposite right now. She should be clawing her way to satiety.

Her teeth started to chatter. He got under the blankets and held her close.

Why wasn't she feeding?

On the verge of death, after being close to the brink from Claudio's bloodlust and then half-dead from Liam Donavan, he'd fed her his blood. She was now awake. But she wasn't feeding.

He'd waved them away, Sam and Adrian both. They'd both offered to stay and help him once she was awake, Adrian had said that with her bloodline, the signs of strength she'd shown before turning, and Tristan's blood being what had sired her that she'd be a real handful.

Maybe he should've kept them there to help with this, but he'd dreaded this moment and didn't want an audience to see it as it happened... that moment when he'd know, when he'd see and feel that she was truly gone...

He'd chosen to endure that pain alone, with at least some dignity, but right now he was absolutely stumped.

He remembered vividly how he'd been when he'd turned. He remembered, too, how it was with Becky when she'd been turned, how it was with Taryn, when he'd turned her. He was also around numerous times when other vamps woke after being turned and this was *not* how it went. *Ever.* Whether royal or turned vamp: they all woke the same way.

He tipped her chin back and she blinked at him.

"Kyla?"

"Hmm?"

"Do you feel okay?"

"Yes," she answered softly. Blinking at him. Just looking at him, looking ... vacant.

"Open your mouth, princess."

She opened her mouth immediately.

Blinking at him.

He hesitantly touched above her incisor, put a bit of pressure on the gum. Any vamp, even a new vamp's fangs...they would've dropped with that pressure. They dropped as soon as they woke as vamp for the first time. Every single time.

Nothing happened.

She didn't have fangs.

He let her go and she dropped to the pillow. She just looked off, vacantly.

He leaned over, dropped his own fangs, saw that her throat was still in need of time to heal, so moved down to her inner thigh and bit. Warm blood started to flow into his mouth. It tasted like his own blood. It didn't taste of sunlight, of warmth, of Kyla. He retracted his fangs and looked up at her face.

"Princess?"

"Yeah?"

"What's my name?"

"Tristan."

"Yeah, baby. Tell me what you're feeling."

It hit him then like a tonne of bricks that he couldn't feel a fucking thing from her. Not a thing.

"Hmm?" she blinked some more.

She'd been turned. She should be a vampire. A cunning, selfish, hateful, hungry she-monster with fangs. But she wasn't.

She was like an empty vessel, a deer in the headlights, filled only with his blood.

She was mesmerized.

The End

Book 3, Essence is available. Read it for the conclusion of this trilogy.

Amazon: bit.ly/nectar3essence

Other e-book retailers – books2read.com/nectar3essence

Acknowledgements:

Thanks for reading my books and for making my writing dreams come true. I hope I've entertained you ☺

Thanks to Melissa, Pauline, Kass, Joy, Kirstie, Molly, and Susan, and Kat.

Thank you to my Facebook & Goodreads & Twitter friends. I LOVE YOU GUYS!

Big thanks to the members of my Nectar Spoiler group on Facebook who cheered me on through writer's block!

Thank you, dear reader, for helping me live my dream! I write not for fans or for praise nearly as much as writing because I need to.

My fans make living this dream even better than I ever dreamed it could be!

Thanks *so* much for supporting indie authors! If you enjoy this book, please consider leaving a review on Goodreads wherever you bought this book to help me get found by readers like yourself who like these sorts of stories.

Want to connect with me on social media? Links are below!

More Books by DD Prince

Dark, paranormal, contemporary, and mind fuck romances.

This list may have been updated since publishing, so check http://bit.ly/ddprinceonamazon for a full list of DD Prince & Scarlett Starkleigh books.

As of the date of publishing, the Nectar Trilogy is available from a number of retailers. Other DD Prince books are currently available from Amazon & Kindle Unlimited. Some books are available in paperback. See DD Prince's website for further information and links.

MC Romance: Romantic suspense with comedy, angst, steamy scenes, and a little bit of gritty darkness.

Detour (Beautiful Biker 1) Deacon & Ella

This alpha-male is not an alpha-hole. You're going to FLOVE Deacon Valentine.

Joyride (Beautiful Biker 2) Rider & Jenna

Rider starts out as a little bit of an alpha-hole. Jenna resists, but resistance is futile when a Valentine brother has you in his sights.

*A total of 8 books for the Beautiful Biker series are expected.

Dark Mafia Romance: dark romance with a debt flesh payment plot.

This one DD's most popular book, but it *is* dark. Non-consensual / rough sex. An anti-hero you may love to hate and hate to love.

The Dominator

The Dominator II; Truth or Dare

Sex slave rescue romance with dark themes.

The Dominator III: Unbound

More Tommy, More Dare; More Domination!

Spin off Dark Romance (maybe DD's darkest book yet):

Saved (Alessandro & Holly's story)

Dark Paranormal Romance: Vampire dark romance / kidnapping

Nectar Trilogy (Includes Nectar, Ambrosia, and Essence)

Amazon links at http://bit.ly/ddprinceonamazon.
https://www.books2read.com/tristanandkyla (book 1)
https://www.books2read.com/nectar2ambrosia (book 2)
https://www.books2read.com/nectar3essence (book 3)
https://www.books2read.com/nectartrilogy (box set)
Dirty / fun / instalove alien romance
Hot Alpha Alien Husbands: Book 1 – Daxx and Jetta
Sign up for DD Prince's free newsletter to get notified of new releases, sales, and contests - http://ddprince.com/neswletter-signup/.